Ethan Tennant Series

THE MORE THINGS
CHANGE

sands press
Brockville, Ontario

Ethan Tennant Series

THE MORE THINGS CHANGE

Perry Prete

sands press
Brockville, Ontario

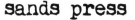

sands press

A division of 3244601 Canada Inc.
300 Central Avenue West
Brockville, Ontario
K6V 5V2

Toll Free 1-800-563-0911 or 613-345-2687
http://www.sandspress.com

ISBN 978-1-988281-05-6

Cover concept and artwork by Kristine Barker and Wendy Treverton
Original cover concept and artwork by John Tkachuk
Formatting by Kevin Davidson & Renee Hare
Publisher Sands Press

Publisher's Note

1st Printing June 2014 2nd Printing July 2014 3rd Printing November 2014

To book an author for your live event, please call: 1-800-563-0911

Submissions

ands Press is a literary publisher interested in new and established authors wishing to develop and market their product. For more information please visit our website at www.sandspress.com.

Disclaimer

I've been very lucky to have had an EMS career that started in 1982, serving the sick and injured and still work on the road today.

During that time, I've come to know some great police officers and firefighters. Quite often, at the crime scene, a police officer will ask our opinion of what happened or what we think might have happened, not unlike asking a firefighter what he/she may think caused the fire.

As paramedics, we offer a unique perspective on the human body that a uniformed officer or detective may not immediately see.

In my Ethan Tennant books, I've taken those times when I've been asked for my unique perspective at the scene of an accident or crime scene and turned it into a work of fiction where the police and paramedics work as a team. Does this happen in real life? Yes, it does. Does it happen to the extent in does in my books? Well, my books are a work of fiction after all.

As I write this, the funeral for three slain RCMP officers is taking place in Moncton, NB. Const. David Ross, Const. Fabrice Georges Gevaudan and Const. Douglas James Larche were killed and two other officers were wounded in a shooting spree. I will not name the gunman. I hope that those who helped me write this book understand that I felt it necessary to mark the passing of these officers and recognize those wounded by the gunman. I have not forgotten those who were there for me and helped me complete this project.

As a Paramedic, I joke that our job is to delay death, not save lives. I love my job and know what medics around the world have to endure. I get frustrated by the public and their view of "Ambulance Drivers" but this is nothing compared to the outright disdain of police officers.

As hard as our job is, it pales in comparison to being in law enforcement.

To the fallen, the injured and their families, my heart goes out to you.

CHAPTER 1

The baby was limp and lifeless in the crib, lying on her back, head turned to the left side, arms and legs resting outward, looking peaceful, as if she were simply sleeping. The room was illuminated with a single night light. I reached in to find a brachial pulse in the right arm and found her cold to the touch. Her tiny arms and legs already showed signs of stiffness; rigor mortis had already started to set in. The child had been dead for at least two to three hours. I noted the time: it was quarter after four. She'd died sometime after midnight.

I continued to stare at the little girl, chubby cheeks, full head of thick, jet-black hair, muddled the way you look after a long night's sleep. She had a slight overbite. Her lips pink and warm at one time, were now cyanotic and cool. Her tiny fingers curled up around her thumbs, making her hands look like half-formed fists.

You had to resist the temptation to scoop her up in your arms and hold her while you had a good cry. All this for a child I had seen for the first time only moments earlier.

Rigor mortis is an excellent indicator of death, and there was little I, or anyone, could do for her. Just to be certain, I auscultated her chest for any heart sounds or breath sounds. Nothing. The night light cast a soft glow, bathing the infant in cool light. Appropriate, I thought.

I could hear my partner attempting to calm the parents in the living room, the mother crying uncontrollably, the father speaking in a calm, reassuring voice to his distraught wife. It's the same scenario played out time and time again when we attend calls like this. Sudden Infant Death calls are arguably one of the worst calls a paramedic can respond to. No trauma, no blood, no immediate reason for death: simply a body in a crib, an innocent life taken far too early, having never had a chance to become what it could have been.

I walked around to the other side of the crib to look at her face from a different angle. My position blocked the glow from the night light, but as I moved a little further, her face became visible again. From this angle, her little face didn't look symmetrical. I tilted my head, squinted my eyes to force them to refocus in the dim light, and looked more closely. I retrieved my flashlight, thumbed the switch, and shone the beam on her face. "Geez!" Startled, I dropped my flashlight and stepped back. With a metallic thud, the aluminum flashlight hit the hardwood floor, sending it rolling, creating a twisted, rolling beam along the far wall.

I located my flashlight on the floor and turned on the overhead light. This time, I was prepared for what I would see. My steps were precise and slow, in case my mind was playing tricks, light casting shadows, morphing the innocent into something horrific. I wanted to be prepared.

The left side of her face had an asymmetrical mass that almost covered her eye similar to the swelling seen from a right cross. The mass engulfed the left cheek and nostril. With a gloved hand, I lifted her head slightly, the body moving as one from the rigour. No bruising, no sign she had been hit, if this was indeed swelling from an impact. Maybe this was a birth defect that had blocked off the airway and the parents were aware of this?

Instead of using the radio to contact dispatch indicating we would not transport the patient, fearing the parents would overhear the transmission from the radio on my partner's belt, I used my cell to call.

The parents were sitting in the living room. The husband had his arm around his wife, the mother quietly sobbing into a tissue. My new partner, Bradley, standing over them, looked uncomfortable and out of place. A police officer was also standing to the side, remaining silent, taking notes. I removed my gloves and sat down across from the mother. She appeared young, late twenties, maybe; the father was possibly in his mid-thirties.

"My name is Ethan. I'm terribly sorry, but there is nothing we can do. I'm sorry for your loss." I touched the mother's hand. She looked up at me and smiled acknowledging my cliché condolence. It was obvious they already knew that their daughter was dead.

"Can you tell me anything about--?" I stopped, realizing I did not know the baby's name.

"Clara," the father said.

"Clara. How did you find Clara?"

The mother wiped her eyes then her nose. "I don't know. I just didn't hear anything on the baby monitor, so I went in to check on her. Instinct, I suppose. I felt something wasn't right. Clara was cold and stiff, so I ran to get Brian."

The husband held his head low, almost in shame that he had not been capable of helping his daughter.

"Did you notice anything out of the ordinary with Clara when you went in to see her?" He looked at me strangely.

"Anything? A bump on her head, a cut, anything? Nothing is too small."

He shook his head from side to side. "She was so cold and stiff, and her skin was white--cold and white. When I touched her, she felt like ice. When I tried to lift her, she was stiff, and I couldn't, I wouldn't . . ." His voice trailed off. He swallowed to prevent himself from shedding any tears. His eyes were red, but no tears. He looked like a guilty man caught in some horrific crime.

"Did Clara have any medical problems that you were aware of?"

Brian continued to speak, "None that we knew of. The adoption agency said Clara was given a physical and everything came back fine before we brought her home. She had an ear infection about two months ago. Saw the doctor for that, but that's it."

"Clara was adopted." I looked up at Bradley. He was still unaware of what I was doing. "Did the adoption agency give you any details of the birth mother?"

"Only that she was a single teenager from Ottawa and opted for adoption rather than an abortion. Why? Is there something wrong?"

Even the police officer was starting to look concerned. He let me lead the questioning. I ignored Brian's questions.

"Do you have any recent pictures of Clara I could see?"

"I took some pictures last night right after dinner before we put her to bed. They're on my phone." He left the room.

"How old was Clara?"

The mother wiped her tears and looked at me, "She was three months old when we brought her home. That was four months ago."

"Five months," Brian interjected as he returned. "Remember, we brought Clara to your brother's birthday party." The mother started to cry again. Brian touched the phone screen a few times, brought up the pictures and handed the device to me. Bradley and the uniformed officer moved to view the photos over my shoulder.

"These were taken right after dinner. We gave her a bath and put her to bed about an hour after this last picture." I used my finger to slide the photos from right to left. Mom was holding Clara, smiling like a proud parent does with an innocent child in her arms. Clara was smiling, giggling without a sign of any mass on her left cheek. Clara was a beautiful child, happy, and appeared to be perfect in every way.

"Wait, I have a video I made while Clara was in the sink having a bath." Brian found the video and the three of us watched as the infant played in the kitchen sink, splashing water while her mom laughed loudly. The sound from the video only made the mother cry even louder.

"She was a beautiful baby," I offered. I handed the phone back to Brian. "Excuse me. I'll be right back."

I stood and went back to Clara's room to make sure I hadn't imagined what I had seen. Back in the bedroom, Clara still appeared to be sleeping. I gloved up and lifted her head off the mattress. The mass was still present, the left side of her face deformed. A mass that had grown overnight that might possibly be responsible for her death. If this mass had grown in such a short time, I was worried about a possible hazardous situation or some type of infection.

I closed the bedroom door to secure the scene.

I walked back to the living room, pulled the officer aside and briefed him on the findings. We walked back to the baby's room, both parents curiously watching us. A short time later, I emerged and spoke to Bradley.

"Do you have everything we need?" I asked.

Bradley nodded his head that we did indeed have everything we needed on this call.

"Would you like us to stay for a while?" Bradley offered.

Brian extended his hand to both Bradley and me. "Thank you for your help. We appreciate all that you've done." He placed a comforting hand on his wife's shoulder.

Once we were back in the rig, we called the shift supervisor and updated her on the situation at the scene. She indicated that she would head to the scene and we were to head back to HQ, clean up, change uniforms, write an incident report, and change rigs so that the techs could take it out of service for a thorough decontamination.

CHAPTER 2

As I look back on my youth, I realize how the passage of time becomes altered and skewed in my memory. Summer vacations used to last forever. We would ride our bikes everywhere, no destination too far, no challenge too great. We had no fear of strangers. The sun was hotter, it seldom rained, and friends were always there for you, everything was better. Now time passes quickly. The list of things to do grows longer; time to do it is shorter, time is no longer infinite. Friends have families of their own, priorities change, and you're always looking for the better things in life. In essence, we have become our parents. A horrible thought.

Tom Lister, my regular paramedic partner and friend, is at home now recovering from his injuries sustained in a motorcycle accident a few months ago. Tom and I had been paramedic partners and friends since we were at Algonquin College for the two-year Primary Care Paramedic program, started working in Ottawa, and we both took the Advanced Care Paramedic course. We later paired up again as an ALS team, but after his near-fatal accident and rehab, we have, unfortunately, drifted apart. I pray he will return to work soon. The one fortunate thing about Tom being out of commission is people started calling me Ethan again instead of "Nash." I hate, with a passion, actually despise, that nickname. Tom started calling me Nash because we argued all the time over hockey. My team is the Nashville Predators and Tom, like any true fan from Ottawa, cheers for the Senators.

As a way to annoy me, he started calling me Nash. And annoy me it did. Once the name caught on, everyone in the service starting calling me by my new moniker. Since he left, it has fallen out of favour. I was happy about that.

I was assigned a new partner while Tom was recovering. Becky was a new medic with almost no road experience, and after she was kidnapped, I never heard from her again. From the moment we met, I felt an instant connection. For a few days a while back, I could actually see myself with another woman in my life. Having been married to Maddy, I seemed to have forgotten a lot of the skills honed as a single male in the dating scene. Becky and I spent just a few days getting to know each other; everything felt natural, a friendship with a girl without effort. It could have been the kind of relationship you look for, cultivate, and nurture; the kind of relationship you keep. Of course, having a crazed killer stalk you can make any relationship difficult. That episode is behind me now.

Work no longer holds the joy for me it once did. My new partner is...well, new...too new for me. I do my job. I do my job well, but once the shift is over, I leave and go home to an empty house. The cats, Molly and Snickers, greet me when I come home, but are seldom around when I leave. The house has been renovated, glass repaired, smoke damage cleaned, carpets replaced with hardwood floors from the smoke bomb set by the killer I helped catch. Well, actually, I wouldn't say helped, more fumbled my way to assisting the police. Memories of Maddy living in the house with me, times we shared, things we did, seem as if they happened yesterday. Those memories haven't yet faded with time or been blurred with new memories attempting to fill their space. It's as if those memories of my wife, those few years, have been burnt in some part of my brain that can never be dulled by the passage of time. Images and memories today are as sharp as the day they were created.

I placed the SD card recording of Maddy's voice in a safety deposit box after it was downloaded to my PC, laptop, and my new phone. I wasn't taking any chances. I seldom play the recording any more, but it is comforting to know I have it ready if I need it. Maddy's cell contract has been cancelled and her number reassigned to some young girl, I suppose, who uses the number as her texting lifeline without any clue as to its past. She probably receives texts and emails, giggles, replies with BFF, LOL, and icons to show her mood. The keys on her phone snap away as her thumbs press each character, never caring about spelling or grammar or if any of those texts hurt another person never intended to read or see that message. Maddy's cell phone number is still locked in my mind, but now belongs to someone new.

So I sit at home, alone, watching TV; I didn't spend as much time with Tom as I should've but I still drove him to and from rehab when time permitted; and play poker with Galen Hoese and my new poker pals. That's my life. Life is not good. Life is boring. Life is stale, mundane, day to day. If I could describe my life with any more zeal I would, but realistically, I can't. Even when Tom tried to set me up with his sister, I refused. Deep down, I guess I am holding out for Becky to call.

After the investigation was completed, the Ottawa Police refused to provide me with any new details of the case, thanked me for my help for putting myself in harm's way, wrecking my car, and peeing my pants just before I thought I was about to get shot in the head! The insurance company refused to cover the loss on my car, claiming the car was damaged outside the coverage parameters. Apparently, being chased down the highway by a serial killer who pushed me off the road into a large sign, almost killing me, falls outside normal automotive insurance coverage. At least the police arrived in time to save my life. The killer wasn't so lucky.

Now I drive a Neon! It is a fall from car heaven to sheer automotive hell. Things I want the car to have aren't there; things I don't want, I have in abundance. Rust eating away at each fender over the wheels and the bottoms of the doors; even the hood has rust where it meets the plastic grill. The radio is just that--a plain AM/FM radio; no CD, no tape player. I half expected an eight-track player.

So now my life consists of work, helping out an old friend to get better, the monthly poker night with my new friends, and spending time with my cats. I feel old...very, very old.

Looking around, I see my neighbours getting ready for fall. Winter is not too far off. The gutters are being readied for the fall leaf attacks. Winter tires are being pulled from the basement or the garage to be installed before the first snow. The last vestiges of summer are being put away for another year.

The real estate "For Sale" sign on my front yard was leaning. I righted it. It took a lot of soul-searching for me to decide to put the house up for sale, but it is time I moved on. This house is big enough for a family, a real family, not a single man with two cats. The first open house is this weekend. I will be working this weekend. Tom said he would love to have Molly and Snickers over for the day. Truth is, the cats would probably be better physiotherapy for Tom than rolling a large rubber ball.

For the past few weeks, days have blended into one another. Time is definitely not what it used to be. I long for the days of my youth when things were simple, friends didn't get hurt or die or leave. Tom says I need to talk to someone. I think he is right.

*****

The wind was picking up. I opened the door and the two cats entered the house on command. Neighbours must look at me and wonder if I will become an old cat man and a hoarder and be featured on a reality television episode in the near future.

Molly and Snickers were fed, I made a PB and J and sat in front of the TV with a can of Diet Coke. Another quiet day in the Tennant household! I have to work nights again tonight.

Time didn't change, I did.

CHAPTER 3

He picked up the soft, black nylon laptop briefcase from the desk, and it slapped against his leg. He is amazed that the project resting inside the case could be so powerful when it is so small and weighs so little. The other printed files in the case cannot be read without it, and he decides it would be safer if the two were not together. He reaches in, retrieves the jump drive, and lets it mix with the coins in his pocket. Perfect! No one would ever suspect.

He feels a little unsettled that he carries the two halves together, but it is only for a short time until he meets with his superior later.

The office is located on the third floor of the Centre Block at the back of the building overlooking the Ottawa River with Gatineau on the north shore. Not a very prestigious office, but it is in the Centre Block of Parliament Hill. Centre Block houses the House of Commons and the Senate. He looks out over the Ottawa River from his office every day and seldom sees pleasure boats or fishermen and wonders why. That is a question for another day. Tonight, more important matters must be attended to.

The office lights are turned off, the door is closed and locked, and he walks down the hallway toward the stairwell leading to the parking lot. It's late. Few lights illuminate the corridor, and the marble floors reflect the overhead light and echo his solitary walk. The two-tone black and beige marble floors have a sheen so clear what little light remaining in the halls reflects strange shadows in all directions. The walls are a mix of solid oak and cedar, stained and old, but retain a classic look crafted years ago by artisans who possessed a skill no longer seen today. The wood is perfectly preserved, cared for, polished to retain its original luster.

His hand grips the faux leather handle of the cheap, foreign-made bag. Ironic, he thinks, a project studied in this very building meant to stop the foreign onslaught onto our shores was being delivered in a bag made from a foreign country, purchased from a store that sells foreign products almost exclusively.

He is proud that he was bestowed with the honour to be, not only the bearer, but the one also to deliver it. The laptop case was chosen as a point of irony. It was his suggestion to put it in that particular case. The style of the case downplays the importance of its fragile, yet priceless, contents. The person he is to meet tonight will surely be impressed, and, if all goes well, his future in the group will be assured.

There are few offices still occupied. He walks past the occasional closed door with light emanating from beneath it. Fools, he thinks to himself. If they only knew how little the work they did really mattered. They should be at home with their families, friends, anywhere but here. Just down the hall, men of real power, men from all over the world have gathered to discuss issues of real importance to the world. Canada was chosen for a reason. No one would suspect that Canada, the peace-loving country, would aid or be involved in such a scheme, let alone house the men that helped devise the plan. Surely, anyone with any sense of international politics would assume the United States, Russia, Germany, or some other foreign power would coordinate such a plan.

Down the hall, the yellow cleaning cart that he has come to know and recognize as being in that same spot every night at this exact time is parked where it should be. The door to the left is open, and the light within brightens the section of the hall. He had never met nor seen the cleaning staff, the two of them keeping to a strict time schedule; each night as he leaves, he walks past this very office, and the cleaner is always inside, invisible to him. Odd they had never met. He passes the cart, looks into the office without slowing his pace, sees nothing, and keeps moving.

These halls are like a library at night. Everyone keeps to him/herself, attempting to do his/her job quietly so as not to attract attention or cause a distraction to others. He will miss this place and wonders if they will ever discover why he did what he did.

Mid-thought, the bullet enters the back of his occiput, travelling through the brain, destroying the man, his mind, his being, blowing the frontal section of his skull forward. With it, all that he was is now lost forever, wiped clean by a single shot that destroyed the brain and skull. He never felt, never saw anything. His thoughts continued in his head until he suddenly stopped thinking. His limp, lifeless body falls forward to the floor, blood and brain matter oozing from the fractured opening in his skull. The blood pool continues to flow freely. His brain gone, his heart hasn't yet received the message that the host is dead and the heart will pump until most of the blood is gone, the blood pressure will drop, the pulse will increase to compensate for the lack of volume, until finally the systems will shut down, leaving nothing more than a shell of a man. This work had become his life. His work also played a part in his death. The sound made by the revolver with a silencer could not be heard by those still in their offices behind thick wood doors. No one was distracted.

The shooter returns the revolver to its holster under his left armpit, hidden by his cleaning staff coveralls, the silencer removed and placed in his pants pocket. The revolver is "old school" but leaves no shell casing. He knows where the cameras are placed, where to stand, and how to exit the building, avoiding as many of the security systems as possible. Working as a cleaner for months in this building, he knew where to place his cart, which office had the least video surveillance, and where he could accomplish his mission drawing the least amount of attention. Most of the people behind those doors cared little for the support staff, didn't acknowledge them. He purposely made noise, night after night, for weeks on end, and one by one, each night another office door was closed to shut him out. He was able to pick that exact office and wait patiently for just the right time. Tonight was that night.

He reaches down, retrieves the case from the dead man's grip. He shakes the case, assesses the weight and guesses what he needs is inside. He squeezes the two sides of the plastic buckle, pulls the lid back, peers in, sees what he wants, closes the flap, and simply walks away.

He cares little at this point if security knows his face or recognizes him from the video surveillance to be viewed later during the investigation. His face, the entire life history of the name on his Government Identification Card was fabricated...his fingerprints, his family, his previous jobs, his schooling, all lies. His paced quickens. He had calculated his exit to the second, knowing where the guards would be at this exact time, how long it would take to get to the parked car waiting for him. Nothing was left to chance.

He pushes the panic bar of the steel exit door, which is supposed to activate an alarm. The system had been bypassed hours earlier. He knows they will eventually figure it out, but tonight was the only time he needed that door to be silent to grant him the few extra moments to make good his escape.

It's raining out. Perfect! Any trace evidence will be washed away. His plan is going better than expected. In the parking lot, he kneels in a puddle of rain water beside a car, reaches under the driver's fender to the top of the tire and finds a remote. There as promised. A single row of cars is parked along the north road that circles the back of Centre Block. Beyond the road, a small footpath straddles the hill that falls below to the Ottawa River. On the banks, dense woods cover the slope. He always assumed the woods were monitored, but never had the need or desire to check. Along the shore, a bike path snakes its way along the river, east to west. During the day, people are permitted to walk the grounds of Parliament Hill, just metres from the buildings.

"*Canadians!*" He thinks to himself as he walks. If this were the United States, the river would have boats patrolling the shores 24/7, the wooded shores would be levelled to prevent any covert operation, and the entire perimeter of the Hill would be surrounded by concrete walls to deter possible intrusion or access to the restricted grounds. Instead, Parliament Hill is open and accessible by boat, air, and land. Truly, Canadians have a different view on life.

"Fucking stupid Canadians!" he says just loud enough so he can hear himself speak. Secretly, he wished that the plans he held would make everyone into Americans, his way of life, his way of thinking. He works with men from different countries, not because he chooses to but because he has to.

His pace is casual at first then breaks into a brisk walk. He thumbs the auto start on the remote as he makes his way around the lot to see which car will start. The rain is coming down harder. He turns back toward the buildings; lights are being turned on in different sectors and floors. No alarm will sound. That will only alert the public and the media to the chaos inside.

He continues to thumb the remote. A dark sedan suddenly roars to life. He makes his way over, presses the "unlock" button, gets into the driver's seat, and drives west around Centre Block, then left past West Block, left again on Wellington Street, blending into traffic. It is that simple. Designed and executed flawlessly. He smiles. It is the type of smile that is usually reserved for happy times with a loved one. To him, this event was analogous to a happy family gathering.

Inside the building, Security staff run from their posts to the area where the body lies in the corridor. Others station themselves at each exit, side arms drawn, while others man the phones. Anyone left in the building is locked in. The security system automatically signals the building lockdown mode, and everyone who works here has been fully trained and instructed to follow the directions of Security.

A security guard holds a flashlight at eye level as he runs to the alarm. Seldom do these events happen on the Hill. He is breathing heavily, and sweat is flowing freely from his brow. He feels the moisture build under his Kevlar vest. He turns a corner, sees the body of a man lying in the hall, pauses and feels a wave of nausea flow from the pit of his belly to the back of his throat. He forces a swallow to make sure he doesn't vomit and contaminate the scene. The bitter sour taste of vomit lingers in his mouth. Surely, almost vomiting was just a moment of weakness, he thinks, but he continues to stare at the body before him. His stomach continues to rumble. He breathes in through his nose to calm his stomach before he does vomit. He stands tall and rests his free hand on the butt of his side arm. He has never needed to draw his weapon before.

A male body is lying face down in the corridor. Blood, dark blood, pools around the head...the scent of iron fills the air and his lungs. The blood has stopped moving. The front of the man's head is blown outwards. Shards of flesh, bone, and brain matter are scattered in front of the man. The guard does not see an entrance wound, it is small, hidden in the hair at the back of the dead man's head. The guard looks down the hall, right and then left. Even in this dim light, the contrast of body fluid and soft tissue on stained wood stands out. The even texture and symmetry of the wood panels have been peppered with tiny mounds of flesh.

Keeping the beam of light on the body, he keys the mike of his radio. "Call 9-1-1."

"Belay that order!" A voice from the darkness echoes in the hall. From the shadows, a large man emerges to stand beside the guard, large in the sense that he is rotund. His voice matches the size of his frame, a voice that commands respect. He surveys the scene, taking in the prone body lying on the marble floor. People stand in shock at their office doors to view the chaos unfolding before them.

"Sir?" The guard knows his superior, but decides to question the order to cancel the call. "Sir, is that a wise idea?" He pauses, swallows and stands square. "I mean, to cancel the 9-1-1 call. Do we really want to seem as if we have something to hide?"

The guard also wants to know how a man so large could get from his office a few hundred feet away to this corridor so fast. No sweat, not even a hint of breathlessness from the large man; something he dares not mention.

"This will be an internal matter. It will be dealt with internally." He walks to the closest office, reaches past the people standing in the doorway, forcing them inside, and closes the door. Everyone else gets the hint and withdraws to their offices; multiple doors close in unison.

"Sir, with all due respect, this administration has enough problems without having to worry about hiding a body from the press. What about his family?" His head points to the man lying on the floor.

As the conversation continues, a Medical Response Team arrives behind the guard. Defib in hand, trauma bag, oxygen, and medication bags are carried by the two guards trained as part of the medical response team. One look and their assessments are complete. The two guards look at their boss. The prognosis is clear. They push the gear to the side and resume the role of guards to protect the scene.

The large man ponders the comment. Different scenarios unfold in his head, conversations to come. Who will be fired? Who will be viewed as the person who kept this situation under control and kept the media in check? His ambitions are as large as his frame.

"Call 9-1-1 and meet them at the back loading bays. Full security detail in full tactical gear will meet the police, EMS, and any other agency that shows up. No press. I mean NO press. Understand? Restricted access. Everyone--and I mean *everyone*--gets an escort. Got it?"

The guard knows better than to question his boss a second time.

"Crystal clear, sir!"

The guard keys the mike, "Call 9-1-1."

"And," the large man pauses, "You wanted to bring in the locals; you are in charge. If heads roll, yours is the first."

With that, he turns on his heels and disappears. The guard now questions if calling in the local authorities was the best or the worst decision for his career.

CHAPTER 4

I pulled into the parking lot of Ottawa EMS, ready for my last night shift of the rotation, met up with my partner, got assigned a rig, and off we went. My new permanent partner, Bradley Chambers, was at the helm. Bradley--you have to call him Bradley, not Brad or any other possible variation, or he will not reply.

I didn't shave today. That would have sent Tom into a panic and he would have yelled at me to shave before booking on. I not only missed being yelled at for not shaving but had grown to enjoy pissing Tom off.

Brad--sorry, Bradley--is a PCP, Primary Care Paramedic who graduated the year before and, in my opinion, is still a newbie and as green as grass. The Primary Care Paramedic program is a two-year, full-time course at college. I am an ACP. First you have to become a certified PCP, then return to school for another year to get your ACP certification. It's not that being an ACP is better; quite the contrary. I have even questioned whether I should revert back to PCP status. The headaches aren't worth it, sometimes; and management doesn't take kindly to medics who relinquish their advanced status and go back to being a PCP.

Being a paramedic in Ontario is not glamorous, at least not in my opinion. The strained relationship with Fire is an ongoing issue that started long before I decided to become a medic. Firefighters have always wanted to control EMS, because new building standards are putting them out of a job and the public just loves Fire, since they think paramedics are just "ambulance drivers." A lot of medics have turned to the dark side and joined the fire service because the job is easier, the pay better, and the truth is, EMS will probably be amalgamated with Fire anyway, eventually.

The insurance industry wants a larger Fire presence, and the towns, cities, and municipalities justify the Fire budget to keep their insurance in check. EMS, on the other hand, has no such relationship with the insurance industry and therefore will never attain the same requirements placed on the municipalities that Fire has. The insurance companies value property more than human life.

For a newbie, Bradley is still soaking wet behind the ears. He gets excited on calls, runs instead of walks, but overall he's not a bad guy...just not a great medic. I wish he weren't so damn keen. I sat slumped in my passenger seat, eyes closed, driving around waiting for dispatch to call our truck number. We're on "Standby," a term used when one ambulance is sent to cover two zones or areas when there aren't many available units. We're told to park our truck at an intersection and wait.

*****

The real estate agent was showing the house while I was at work. Maddy would be so upset having strangers walking through her house, shoes tracking dirt on the carpets, inspecting our home, critiquing our choice in paint colours, furniture, the very way we chose to live. I realized Maddy would never know, but still I knew how she would have reacted. I just wanted to have the house sold, move on to--well, move to somewhere. I hadn't given it much thought. It's good to be somewhere else when strangers are viewing our home, my home.

I closed my eyes and listened to the music emanating from the rig's radio. The volume was low, but just loud enough to fill the cab with '70s music. I looked over at Bradley and saw that the music was not relaxing him the way it does me. Seniority has its privileges. I got to choose the radio station.

Rain hit the windshield. The wipers were still at rest and the water ran down the windshield like a peaceful stream. With the cadence of the rain, the rhythm of the music, and the dark night, I could have fallen asleep easily.

"Four-three-five-six." Our truck number for the day just won the lottery!

Bradley picked up the mike, "Go for 4356."

"Four-three-five-six. You've been requested to proceed Priority 4 to Parliament Hill, Centre Block. Switch to Charlie VR 1."

I sat upright in my seat. It wasn't often anyone got a call to Parliament Hill, let alone inside the building.

"Ten-four, did you say, requested?"

"Four-three-five-six, that's 10–4. We were told to assign your bus to this call."

Bradley switched radio channels, acknowledged the change and receipt of the call.

"Four-three-five-six, you are responding to a man down in Centre Block, Parliament Hill. Go around to the back. Security will meet you there and escort you to the scene. Ten-200s and Fire are tiered." Dispatch was sending the police and Fire to assist.

More information was exchanged, but at this point, even I was curious.

"Man down" could be anything. But at Parliament Hill, what was "man down"? And, more important, who was the man down?

With lights flashing, siren wailing, Bradley zigzagged his way through the streets. Most cars failed to pull to the right and stop; instead, drivers seeing an ambulance will hit the brakes hard and stop exactly in your path. For a newbie, Bradley seemed to have control of the truck and didn't drive too fast. My kind of guy! As Tom liked to say: "No call is too great that it can't wait." We both have

15

the same philosophy that it is better to arrive alive and be a few seconds late than drive like you have an Indy car on a track.

"Four-three-five-six."

"Four-three-five-six go."

"Be advised, 10–2s and Fire told to stand down. Caller stated that RCMP and internal security have jurisdiction and will assist as required."

Bradley turned, looked at me with a puzzled look. I looked back with the same bewilderment.

"Four-three-five-six. Do you copy?"

"Ottawa. 10–4."

"What the hell are we getting into?" Bradley asked, eyes forward on the road.

"Your guess is as good as mine. I've never even been in the Parliament Buildings before."

"You've got to be kidding me! Never? Seriously? Every kid in Ottawa got to go visit the Parliament Buildings."

"Sorry, partner. Grew up in Sudbury. We got to visit the Big Nickel. When you're three, the Big Nickel looks really freaking big. Left Sudbury when I was three, and still haven't had the chance to see Parliament."

The Big Nickel was just that, a huge five-cent coin. A big nickel. The Big Nickel was constructed to make the barren landscape of Sudbury in Northern Ontario have some visual appeal. Fifty years ago or so, the mining companies stripped the land from the rocks, literally. The area surrounding Sudbury at one time was bare rock, a huge mountain with no vegetation. The story goes that the mining companies used high-pressure hoses to wash away the earth and trees to expose the rock beneath for the valuable nickel held within. With little concern for the environment or carbon footprint, the companies mined the nickel and other natural resources. Since the mid-1970s, vegetation has been growing with trees, moss, and grass. In another fifty years, who knows, the mountains around Sudbury might look like they did a century ago.

Bradley drove, staring straight ahead, silent, as was I. Having the police and Fire being called off from a call is not the normal protocol. EMS lives and dies by protocol. We treat patients according to protocol: Tab A goes into slot B and so on, normal, precise, not a lot of problems, few questions. I smelled a problem.

I pulled my cell phone from my shirt pocket and sent a quick text: "Something weird on the Hill??? Idea?" Galen Hoese of the Ottawa Police should answer me shortly. I hope.

On Wellington Street, two black, nondescript sedans, with men standing on either side, blocked traffic. Expecting our arrival, flashlights in hand, they pointed where they wanted us to proceed. Bradley slowed, turned north from Wellington into the main green space of Parliament Hill. Bradley reduced the vehicle speed to a snail's pace past the Centennial Flame. All traffic, all activity had ceased on the Hill. As we drove up, we noticed that all access and egress to the Hill had roadblocks, and the entire area, West Block, East Block, and Centre Block, were being patrolled by foot. Again, silently, we looked at each other.

Forced to drive to where security wanted us, Bradley turned east and headed around the rear of the main building.

"Ottawa, 4356, 10–7 scene." Bradley indicating we were on scene. No response. In fact, no radio chatter at all.

"Ottawa," Bradley repeated himself, slowly and with a little more authority, "4356, 10–7."

Still nothing!

The driver's door opened, startling Bradley, and he jumped. As if all secret security agents came from the same mould, a tall, dark-haired man, wearing the cliché covert uniform--black suit and tie with a white shirt and a clear earpiece in his left ear--spoke with a monotone, authoritative voice. "You will have no radio or cell reception here. There will be no unauthorized communication while you're on the Hill." He stepped aside, gesturing Bradley to exit the vehicle. My passenger door suddenly opened and the twin of the man holding Bradley's door was holding my door open. He stepped to the side, making his point clear. I was to step out.

I met Bradley at the back of the ambulance. Before we could open the dual rear doors of the rig, our two gracious doormen intervened again. "Please turn and face the back of the truck." Again, kind, polite, monotone, but in no way to be toyed with.

I shrugged my shoulders, turned, faced the back of the ambulance, and outstretched my hands, letting them rest on the rear window.

"That is not necessary, sir."

"I don't want any misunderstandings, guys. Check away." The last thing I wanted was to piss these guys off. The pat-down began.

Just as the agent had his hands over my chest, my phone started to buzz. I detected a slight hesitation from the agent.

"I set an alarm on my phone. No cell phone reception, remember?" I raised my eyebrows.

He continued to cop a feel for the sake of security.

The wind picked up, and my clothes snapped against my skin. The roar of an engine could be heard getting closer. Without warning, we were awash in light and the deafening rumble of a helicopter overhead. The light swung back and forth and bathed the back of the rig as the pilot tried to keep the helicopter steady; we floated in and out of the floodlight.

"Come on! Really? A helicopter? Is anyone going to tell us anything?" I yelled at the security guy.

He stared through me, not at me, as if I had just asked the stupidest question in history. Apparently, there is such a thing as a stupid question! I returned to looking at the back door of the ambulance. Once finished with the pat-down, I decided it would be best to hold my questions and simply follow orders.

When security deemed us not to be a risk, they simply took a step back, saying nothing, indicating that this part of the security check was completed. Bradley pulled the back doors open. Inside the patient compartment, two men with the same suit and haircut were busy rummaging through our medical bags. The wash created by the helicopter blades whipped the lighter equipment around inside the truck.

"Are you finished yet?" I had to yell to be heard. "I imagine there are people waiting inside, or are you going to bring the patient out to us while we play games out here?"

The two men inside the rig turned and hopped out, leaving the bags open and much of the contents scattered about the interior of the ambulance. I jumped in and just started throwing equipment into any open bag and placed the bags on the cot.

"Can we get any patient information so we know what to bring in?" I yelled from inside the rig. Nothing! Was I being drowned out by the helicopter or just ignored?

Not knowing what to expect, Bradley and I decided to pack for the worst and hope for the best.

"You!" I yelled and pointed at one of the men in black. Without changing expression, his attention turned toward me, but he didn't move.

"Yes, you! Come over here and help us carry this shit in!" He turned, looked at another suit, who nodded. I made a mental note of that man, who was obviously in charge. The large, rotund man stood quietly in the shadows, making mental notes of the events transpiring before him.

He walked over to me. "What do you want?" Even yelling, his voice was monotone.

"Since you guys won't tell us what kind of call this is or give us any information, we have to bring everything. And that means everything in the truck for any type of call so we don't have to run back and forth for equipment. Of course, you could make my life easier and just tell me what's going on. So what's the story?"

Again, the man standing next to me, turned, looks for the approval of the fat man. For several seconds, the roar of the constant "thump-thump" of the helicopter hovering overhead, the light swaying back and forth, all of it, was suspended in reality as we all waited for a response from the man in charge. A nod, barely noticeable, granted permission for the agent overseeing us to brief us on the situation.

"Trauma! We have a man down." Typical government black-suit talk. Short, sweet, and to the point.

"We already got the 'Man Down' from our dispatch. Can you give me any more information?" My patience with the current situation and our hosts was wearing thin. Bradley was looking at me like he, too, was about to lose his cool. He noticed some loose equipment that I had missed and threw them into the gear bags with enough force to show his displeasure. Again, no more information was forthcoming from the men in black.

Bradley and I hurtled out of the back doors and pulled out the cot. Two men immediately stood on either side of the cot. The implication was clear: these two men would escort the cot to and from the scene, no questions asked. I didn't object.

Time was no longer of the essence. We had wasted so much time with our hosts in the parking lot, that if the patient was indeed critical, the golden hour was slowly winding down and we'd still had no patient contact. The chance of survival for a critical patient diminishes with each passing second. Bradley and I had danced around long enough with the security that any chance the patient had of being saved was long gone. Was the delay intentional, or did it really matter if we got to the patient in time?

Bradley had the foot of the stretcher as we followed our escorts. We walked from where we had parked the rig to a rear security door. Approaching the metal door, the agent looked up toward the back of the building, and a loud metal "Bang!" released the electromagnetic lock. I scanned the area and saw a tiny, red LED light beneath a surveillance camera. That's what he was looking at, I thought to myself. Another mental note!

From one locked metal door to a large alcove, to another locked metal door and yet another alcove. Each one required the same procedure: Present a security card to a box, insert, enter your clearance code and pass through. In each alcove was a lone camera looking down from above like an all-seeing eye granting or denying permission to pass through another gauntlet.

Through several locked doors then up an elevator found us in a section that resembled nothing of the back of Parliament...opulent offices, thick, wooden crown mouldings, and marble floors; and armed security every ten feet or so, indicating we were someplace important. A place I'm sure that normally we would not be permitted to enter. The tactical uniforms of the guards--a military-style vest with full, bulging pockets, some form of assault rifle, faces covered and a hard, dark helmet--told me these guys were not your average rent-a-cops. They stood silent, motionless, but their eyes followed our every move. Our host kept a steady pace, the sound of hard, leather-soled shoes echoed in the halls, keeping perfect time in cadence with his walk. All the halls were dimly lit. Ornate, antique light sconces with dim, yellow bulbs on either side of the halls directed us to a sharp left turn. A crowd had gathered, and the scene was brightly lit. Our destination was ahead.

The rotund man in the black suit had his back to the crowd. He watched us carefully as we approached.

"Your patient," he turned, granting us permission to pass.

"Holy shit!" Bradley couldn't have picked a better way to express himself when he saw our patient lying prone on the floor.

I followed the cot around the corner.

"You've got to be kidding me!" I looked square at the rotund man to my right. "What the hell do you want us to do with him?"

"Your job!" He knew his job; he never wavered from his intended goal. His eyes pierced mine, still cold and serious.

CHAPTER 5

As we turned the corner to the lighted hall, Bradley had stopped short. I kept walking and pushed the cot into his back. We stood stunned. Down the hall, most of the doors were closed; a few were ajar, curious eyes peeked through the cracks to see the scene unfolding in the hall. The large, rotund man turned quickly for a man of his size and looked down the hall at the open doors. Any door that had been open immediately slammed shut. He obviously demanded respect and had authority.

Our patient lay prone on the floor before us; right arm outstretched, left arm under his torso, legs straight. He wore a dark suit, expensive compared to anything I had in my closet. His shoes were leather, polished, with leather soles that appeared to be almost new, with little wear. A large, uneven, crimson halo of blood had formed around his head. The edges of the blood pool had already started to dry and harden. I'm unsure of the time required to allow blood to dry when pooled but I am guessing his golden hour had long passed. Upon inspection, the occiput sported a small opening, barely visible except for the section where the blood had matted the hair.

I bent down to examine the front of the skull. A larger section of the frontal lobe of the brain, including the left eye, had been forced out by the projectile; the skull, jagged and white, had captured raw brain matter around the edges with bits of skin, and hair hung loosely from the hairline. The entire left orbital cavity was empty except for pooled blood at the bottom. His right eye was open and bloodshot, almost completely red with blood, and stared straight forward, looking at me. No other wound was visible. Not that he needed another wound to complete the task. On the left wall of the corridor, matter that had sprayed forth from the wound driven by the force of the bullet was now dry and clung to the woodwork. It suddenly reminded me of pasta and tomato sauce that had been thrown against the wall. Sometimes I think of the oddest things at the worst possible times.

I looked at the rotund man in the black suit.

"Can I speak with you, please?" I asked politely. He nodded and simply turned and walked a few steps, expecting me to follow.

I turned back, "Bradley, can you just double-check to make sure he is dead and then call Base Hospital and dispatch and let them know we won't be transporting?"

"You won't be calling anyone!" His voice never changed tone. No sense of urgency, excitement, or panic.

"We have protocols to follow. No one changes that except for the doctors at the Base Hospital." I tried to stress the importance of our job. I stared into his eyes. Even though the scene was brightly lit, his pupils looked as if they were blown, making the colour of his eyes appear solid black. Every time I looked at him, I was amazed how cold his eyes were. I was beginning to question if he were human.

I turned to Bradley. "Assess, confirm, then call." I turned back to the rotund man then back to my partner. "Got it?" Bradley knew better than to question me at this point. No reply from Bradley, but I knew he understood.

"Do you want to tell me exactly why we're here?" I asked. "This guy has obviously been dead for some time now. Have you got a name? When did this happen?" I looked at my watch for effect and to see what time of death to give Bradley for the call to Base Hospital.

He looked forward--not at me, but through me. I felt violated, almost a little scared. The man before me was able to evoke a sense of dread and fear in me just by staring at me. It was effective and it was working. Again, I questioned if he were human. I was not about to get information from this man.

"We, too, have protocol to follow. Don't call to pronounce death. Please take this man to the hospital. Of course we realize he is dead. He's been dead for some time now, but we need to show that we have control of this building and can't risk a public inquiry."

"Please?" I was stunned. People in his position do not ask politely. They tell you.

"I was assured you would co-operate."

"By whom, may I ask?"

Another not-so-large, familiar figure approached from behind and planted himself beside me. Ottawa Police Detective Galen Hoese, a veteran cop and long-time friend, gently put a hand on my shoulder.

"Can I be of fucking service?"

"Geez, Galen. Try, please try, for me. There are more metaphors to use. Did you get my text message?"

His eyebrows raised, shoulders shrugged. "I got it right after I got the call to come here and hold your hand and make sure you play nice."

"Who called you on this? Is this even your beat?" I asked.

"I got a call from one of my bosses--"

His words were interrupted. "After speaking to my superior, I called your superior, Mr. Tennant, then I called Mr. Hoese's supervisor. Your names were given to me directly." The rotund man knew the drill. "I was assured you would comply with what needs to be done and that discretion would be your top priority."

I was out-matched, out-played, and out of my pay grade. I looked down at Bradley, who confirmed our suspicions. The victim was dead, nothing to be done.

"Fine! What would you like us to do? And, Galen, you are coming with me. This is not a request. I want my ass covered. Got it?" I was beaten but I still had to make sure that I could justify my actions if this call was ever investigated.

"Everything is arranged. Transport him to the Ottawa General Hospital. A special room is waiting. Vehicles are standing by to escort you and avoid any delays en route." Again, the fat man had all the details covered.

A security guard leaned in close and whispered something into his ear. He returned the gesture and whispered something back. Galen and I looked at each other. Bradley, noticing everyone was now in silent mode, stood and placed his right thumb and baby finger to his head to simulate a phone. I understood he questioned whether to call Base Hospital to ask for a Code 5 (obviously dead patient).

Rotund man turned back to Galen and me. "This is our head of Security, Mr. Smith. Mr. Smith will accompany you to the hospital. He will stay with the patient until I release him."

There was an uncomfortable pause as we all looked at each other, expecting some kind of response. But the silence continued as Bradley started to remove all of our gear from the cot. I joined in, placing the equipment on the floor well out of range of the restricted crime scene. Together, we lowered the cot to waist height. Since we didn't bring a backboard or spinal equipment, a blanket would have to do to. Galen, Rotund Man, Mr. Smith, and the rest of the armed security detail stepped aside, giving us room to work.

"Should we at least make it look like we have a viable patient or look like we are transporting a corpse?" I asked.

Rotund man and Mr. Smith looked at each other. Possibly they had never considered that scenario. Rotund man transmitted a silent command through his evil, black eyes to Mr. Smith.

"Make it look like he is still alive and you are doing all you can," Mr. Smith said. He seemed new to being in command, unsure of his orders or unsure of how the scenario would play out.

Bradley, already gloved, pulled out a few more pairs of nitrile gloves and handed them to Galen and Mr. Smith. Galen knew the drill and donned them. Mr. Smith accepted the gloves, rolled them over, and put them on. Galen was aware of what we were asking; Mr. Smith hadn't a clue.

I held the corners of the blanket and threw it in the air, allowing the blanket to open and come to rest on the dead man's left side. As the blanket floated to the marble floor, a corner of the fabric came in contact with the blood on the floor. Like a textile sponge, red liquid slowly infiltrated through the weave and stained the white cloth. Bradley walked carefully around the body to the feet and smoothed out the blanket and bunched a rolled end of the blanket under the dead man's left side. I grabbed the dead man's right arm and pulled it up over his head. Bradley pulled the man's leg tight and crossed his ankles. Galen, who had helped out on several scenes, knew his place and knelt beside me.

"Come on over here beside me," Galen told Mr. Smith. "Trust me, this guy won't bite."

Looking a little squeamish and possibly sick to his stomach, Mr. Smith positioned himself to Galen's right. Galen reached over the blanket and grabbed the dead man's right shoulder and his right hip. When Mr. Smith failed to get the idea, Galen pulled the security guards hands and placed one just below the hip and told him to grab the knees. Galen re-positioned his hands as before. I squatted over the blood pool, grabbed the shattered head, not really worried about a spinal injury at this point and looked at Bradley.

"Okay, guys. On three, we will roll the dead guy over onto the blanket. Try to keep him from slopping around too much. Ready?" They all looked at me with a surprised look. Screw political correctness, he was dead, after all. "One--two--three."

In sync, the body was rolled onto the blanket. I kept the head steady, not wanting any loose matter to break free from the skull. From the foot end, Bradley pulled the rolled blanket out from under the body. I repeated this from the top of the blanket under his head.

We lifted the body from the floor to the cot and kept it supine with his face covered. While Bradley was collecting our gear and handing it to Mr. Smith, who then passed it on to other guards, I hung an IV bag, plugged in a line, and simply tucked it in the blanket for effect. The defib was secured on the head section, and again, the monitoring cables were simply placed in the blanket.

As we started to pull away, Mr. Smith nodded at several guards, all of whom were carrying assault rifles, and they followed a few feet in front and behind. When I looked back at the crime scene, Rotund Man was nowhere to be seen. Galen walked with me at the head of the stretcher, while Bradley pulled and guided the cot behind the security detail assigned to escort us out of the building.

As we were about to exit the building, the armed guards pulled to the side and simply let the four of us--Bradley, Galen, Mr. Smith, and me--exit the security doors unescorted. In our absence, the building and grounds had been sanitized. The helicopter was gone, and the huge security detail had dispersed. No one was around to guard our presence on the grounds of Parliament Hill or to protect us from whoever killed our patient. We loaded the cot and stowed and secured our gear, and Mr. Smith squeezed past and sat in the jump seat without saying a word.

"Have fun on the way to the hospital. I'll meet you at the ER," Galen offered.

"Get your ass in there now!" My statement was not meant to be misinterpreted.

"My fucking car is here. How will I get back here to pick it up?"

"Mr. Smith here will have a guard drive it over to the ER, right?" I looked over at Mr. Smith to make sure he understood. "Now get in here!"

"Ethan, for one: I don't get in the back of these tin boxes with dead people. And two: do you really think I have the flexibility to climb up in there?"

"Fine. Ride up front with Bradley and let him know we can go any time."

"You will have an escort through the city to the Ottawa General Hospital ER once you leave the grounds," Mr. Smith added.

Galen and I looked at each other, smiled with raised eyebrows. No sense in arguing. Galen slammed the door and walked to the front. Bradley booked into service, and once we cleared the Hill's grounds, RCMP cruisers appeared in front and behind us with warning lights blazing and sirens wailing. Bradley and the escorts kept pace while Mr. Smith and I sat silently in the back with a dead body that we were all pretending was alive on the way to the ER to be resuscitated.

CHAPTER 6

Not long after, Bradley, Galen, and I were in the covered garage outside the Ottawa General Hospital Emergency Department. Bradley and I sat on the rig's back bumper, Galen stood before us, all with coffees in hand. The coffees were cold; no one drank. One of Ottawa's finest had brought the coffee at the detective's request.

Galen had never bothered to purchase tall dress shirts, and whenever he had to do anything that resembled physical labour, the shirt tails would free themselves from his dress pants. He always wore the same suit; either it was always the same suit or he purchased a few dozen of exactly the same suit when they were on sale. We felt the way Galen looked: disheveled and a bit worn out.

It had been almost an hour since we arrived at the General. Uniformed RCMP officers had escorted us through the night streets of Ottawa to the General ER and briskly escorted us into a waiting room. Once the body was transferred from the ambulance cot to the hospital gurney, we were pushed out of the room. Nothing was said; nothing was offered.

Dispatch knew we were out of service. Bradley and I were trying to figure out how to write our ACR, Ambulance Call Report. Discretion was requested by guys dressed in black with guns. Big guys with even bigger guns. I have a new philosophy: always listen to the guy with the gun.

I stood, tossed the cold coffee into the trash. "I don't know about you guys, but I can't sit here any longer and whine about what did or did not happen." I walked back and stood beside Galen. "We really have to get back to work, buddy. And besides, I wasn't aware detectives worked night shifts anymore."

"We don't. Or at least we aren't supposed to." Galen tipped the coffee cup, downed whatever was left, and tossed the cup in the garbage can. "I am heading off to bed and calling in 'tired' tomorrow. I know why I got out of the uniformed division again. Nights fucking suck!"

Galen walked toward the steel shutter doors of the covered garage and took his car keys from his pocket. "Have a quiet night, guys." He turned, the doors opened, and Galen went home.

I pulled the cot from the side of the rig and Bradley and I locked it in place.

Bradley was securing the bags and equipment when he picked something off the floor of the ambulance.

"Ethan, is this yours?" Bradley was holding a tiny piece of white plastic with gold connectors on one end. It was small: one-half inch wide by one and a half inches long and as thick as a credit card.

"Not mine," I replied. "Looks like a USB jump drive, but I've never seen anything that small before. Have you?"

Bradley turned it over several times. The name "GIZMO! Jr." was embossed on one side in bright royal blue. "It must be a jump drive." He tossed it to me. I had to use two hands to catch it. The small piece of plastic was so light, it tumbled in the air and floated until it landed in my cupped hands.

"I'll take it back in to the ER and give it to the guards." I turned and walked back into the General's ER to the secluded room where we had taken our dead patient. As I approached, the armed RCMP sentry at the door turned his head and watched me approach. He sidestepped, standing in front of the door to prevent me from entering.

"You are not permitted beyond this point." His monotone voice, direct and authoritative echoed in the hall.

"We found something in the rig and thought it might belong to your guys," I brought the tiny piece of plastic up to eye level. The guard stared at me, not the jump drive. These guys must all go to the same spy guy school: they all speak the same, stare at you like you aren't there, and disregard pretty much anything you have to say.

He continued to block my path and stare. I lost my case. Without another word, I pocketed the jump drive, turned on my heel, and headed out the door back to the rig.

"Well?"

"Apparently it is not theirs. I'll take it to lost and found when I come back on days."

CHAPTER 7

I woke at two in the afternoon the next day. No alarm, no forced wake-up, just got up when the body said it was fully charged and ready. The afternoon sun sliced through the opening in the drapes and cut a white swath across the far wall. Snickers and Molly were fast asleep on the right side of the bed. The eighteen to twenty hours of sleep the day before for the two felines must not have been enough! Both cats purred away; they only cared about clean litter and a freshly stocked food and water dish. Nice life!

I sat on the edge of the bed and ran my hand through my hair. Maddy used to tease me that every morning she could see less hair on my head and more on the pillow than the day before. I did notice that grey hairs had started to sneak their way in, silently, covertly, not just around the temple, but all over. It was a tactical move on their part, attack from all sides at once for guaranteed success at making me look and feel older. It was working. I rubbed my cheeks and neck and could feel the stubble. That, too, was no longer a strong single shade of solid black, but was now black peppered with invading white hairs mixed in. Getting old sucks!

I showered, shaved, and dressed in cut-off sweat shorts and a worn out T-shirt, turned inside-out so the full front logo of New Kids on the Block wasn't showing, for an easy day of housecleaning. I fixed a hybrid single-man breakfast / lunch / early dinner of cereal, coffee, and leftover hamburger patty on toasted wheat bread. I had contemplated throwing in a beer, but even I had standards. They weren't very high standards, but they were standards, nonetheless.

I sat at the table and watched Molly and Snickers playing in the backyard while I ate. I left the patio door open during the day when I was home so they had free rein of the house and the backyard. It meant cleaning out the litter box less and toxic soil in what had been Maddy's garden plot by the back fence; but I knew I would never take up gardening. My chair creaked with each move I made. This was the chair I had thrown through the patio door glass months ago when I thought the house was on fire. It was either going to have to be fixed or turned into kindling for the fireplace. I glided side to side on the chair, the squeaks keeping cadence with the music from the radio.

In the basement, I sorted clothes for laundry. I had a simple system: whites in hot, everything else in cold. Not sure if it was right, but it worked. Checking my uniform pockets, I found the jump drive that Bradley had given me the night before. Like a scientist, I lifted it up to the light and slowly turned it over and over again, trying to imagine what it was made of and what was on it. That was for later. I tossed the jump drive in the jar above the washer where Maddy and I kept loose change, buttons, and anything else found in the pockets of clothes destined for the wash.

Anyone who has ever worked shift work knows that the transition from nights to days and back again is hard...two weeks of twelve- hour day shifts, then two weeks of twelve-hour night shifts, repeated over and over again until retirement. The day coming off of nights is one of the hardest. If you sleep in too much, you can't get to sleep that night. Too little sleep, and you are a zombie for the day. My routine was simple: stay at home on transition day and do housework and spend some quality time with the cats so they remember who the man with the hair starting to go grey was and who fed them and occasionally scooped out the litter box.

Galen called and said if his workload permitted, he would stop by to update me on the situation at Parliament Hill. Knowing Galen's schedule that meant he probably wouldn't show up until after dinner for leftovers and a beer.

The iPod played my favourite selection list while I folded laundry on the kitchen table. I felt like shit: not enough sleep, too much sleep, circadian rhythm all screwed up, who knows? All I know is that all night shifts should be banned. The phone rang. I found the cordless phone and started walking to stretch my legs and stay awake. As it turns out, the conversation would set off the adrenaline and wake me.

"Hello?" Not a creative greeting, I agree.

"Ethan, it's Dave Green from EMS. We met a few months ago."

"Dave, what's up?" I remembered him vaguely from my hearing with management for chasing a murder suspect and leaving my partner Tom Lister alone with a patient. For a guy in management, he was down to earth and hadn't forgotten what it's like being on the road.

"Sorry to call you at home, but I need to get some information, and the brass said it couldn't wait." I figured it had to do with last night.

"Can it wait until I come back to work in two days?" Having work call on a day off was not normal unless the situation demanded. "I can go over the entire call from Parliament Hill with you then."

"What are you talking about?" His voice indicated confusion. "Ethan, we have a major issue at work. All the ACPs are being called in to get things sorted out."

Now I was the one who was confused. I was completely in the dark.

"Just the ACPs? Dave, I just woke up from nights. Can you give me some more details?"

"Ethan, I have known you professionally since you started here. I trust you had nothing to do with this, but we have to get a statement from everyone." Dave's voice was now more serious.

He continued, "You know the narcotics pouch you sign out every shift?" His voice trailed off. Dave was waiting for an answer.

"Yeah!" I finally answered.

"Some of the morphine has gone missing. Well, not some--lots, actually. As it turns out, it has been going on for over six months. Brass called in the city cops and an audit was done. We don't know how it happens, but either every single medic is involved in stealing narcotics from the service, or somebody has come up with a clever way to steal drugs."

"So, how is it happening?"

"I can't go over anything with you on the phone, but can you make it down here today? We have advised your union rep and they have someone to sit in on every interview with the police. They want everyone interviewed now. Something happened this morning, and the police came in with the chief's approval to find out any information. The police and our chief feel these interviews are best done when no one has any advance warning."

This sounded serious enough to wake me up. I had walked upstairs and didn't even realize how I had gotten here. My mind was reeling with the implications of what Dave was telling me.

Narcotics--morphine, no less--was being stolen from the small narcotics pouch each paramedic signs out at the beginning of each shift. Each medic is assigned a small, black, sealed nylon case before each shift. That case is to remain with the medic until the end of his or her shift, and each vial must be accounted for.

"Dave, I'm in the middle of things here at the house. I'll have a shower and head straight down. Do I need to bring anything?" I had nothing to hide, but these situations can sometimes escalate beyond a simple investigation, and the innocent can look guilty.

"Nothing! Just get down here as soon as you can. The police have set up several rooms. I've been advised to tell you not to speak with any other medic until after you've been interviewed by the police."

I could tell Dave Green was taking a lot of heat for what was happening. It was not an enviable position to be in. Some of the medics could get downright nasty even if they had nothing to hide. I assured Dave I would be there as soon as I could and hung up.

I went downstairs to get Molly and Snickers into the house before my shower. Shocked, I stood before the patio door leading to the backyard. It was closed. Had I closed the patio door while I was on the phone and not realized I had done it? I looked closely outside and could not see either cat playing. If one came in, the other would follow. Surely, I must have closed the door.

Turning to go upstairs, I was face to face with a stranger. I felt two piercing probes penetrate me, sending jolts of electricity flowing through me, and I fell to the kitchen floor, my mind out of focus, images swimming before me.

CHAPTER 8

Voices! Someone was speaking, one or more, no clue. My head ached. Flashes! Light, bright light blinding me. More flashes. It was just a split second of light, a camera?

"Smile boy-o!"

Smile? It must be a camera. I lifted my head to the voice, but all I could see was burn spot in my eyes from the flash.

A figure stood before me with a cell phone pointed at me.

"That should do for now." An accent...not French, not English--not Canadian English, anyway.

My body felt like it was twitching inside from the remaining current of the Taser that I had just been attacked with. I forced my eyes open. I was in my gym shorts, T-shirt, barefoot, and secured to one of my own kitchen chairs. Each foot had been zip tied around the front legs of the chair. I went to rub my head. Like my feet, my wrists were restrained to the back spindles of the chair. My eyes were blurry. I needed to rub them to help them focus, but instead I blinked several times to reboot and clear my vision. I raised my head to face my attacker.

Before me stood a man in a black business suit, black shoes, black tie, and dark grey shirt. Was he from the government? He looked like he had graduated from some spy college. He stood, motionless, silent, studying me. He looked out of place in a suit. His black hair was slicked back with too much hair gel, his face pocked, and his nose had obviously been broken one time too many.

My head remained in a fog. Thoughts flashed, no cohesion, my mind raced with wild images completely disconnected from the thoughts that should accompany them. I closed my eyes again, forcing my eyelids shut tight, hoping that my mind would focus.

"I will ask you the same question I asked your partner this morning. Where is the jump drive? Now, he told me he gave it to you. So, I am asking you: Where is it?" There was that accent again...Irish, Scottish, British?

My head was still down, eyes shut against the light. I couldn't think straight.

"What jump drive?" I was stalling. How long had I been out? Would Galen stop by soon to check on me? I needed information to process and right now

32

I had none. I was still looking at the floor. If I hadn't improved my poker face playing cards with Galen and his buddies, when I looked up, he would know I was lying.

Pain raced from my left temple across my brain. I hit the floor and my right shoulder, twisted around and locked in place from the wrist restraints, burnt from the pain of the sudden impact. I looked up at my house guest. He had put on black leather gloves and was rubbing the knuckles on his right hand. He'd sucker-punched me, the son of a bitch!

I closed my eyes again, trying to gather the facts and put together the scenario before me. The chair was lifted up off the floor. I went along for the ride, as the restraint held fast. The chair creaked beneath me as the chair legs slammed against the floor. The chair creaked! Months earlier, I had a small house fire and I threw one of the dining room chairs out the patio window to escape. I had been meaning to fix the chair and now I was in the weakened chair. I needed to stall.

"You're not being smart, boy-o! Tell me where it is. I looked all over the house while you were unconscious and I know you didn't hand it in at the end of your shift." My head suddenly jerked back, my neck straining against the tension of being pulled by my hair. His face was inches from mine.

"Your partner told me what I needed to know and I did as I promised; a quick, painless death." He spit as he spoke showering my face with spittle. "Of course, to make sure he wasn't lying, I made sure the pain leading up to being shot in the head was no picnic."

"What? Bradley is dead?" I couldn't believe what he just said.

With his free hand, he pulled my gym shorts open. The gun was inserted into my shorts and the end of the barrel found my scrotum. He straightened his arm and put all his weight on the gun which flattened a testicle. I felt pressure on my groin and the sound of a gun hammer being cocked back. He pushed harder. I held back the moan; it was hard to speak with my head pulled back and I didn't want to give him the pleasure of knowing how much it hurt. He pulled my head back farther.

"Pick a jewel!" He pushed harder. "Pick which one lives and which one gets blown out of your nut sack."

Even with his teeth clenched, he still managed to spit in my face. He released my hair and my head fell to my chest.

It was worse than being kicked in the crotch by a professional football punter. Sharp pain thrust into my belly and down my legs. I lost my breath. The pressure was increasing as he put more and more weight on the barrel of the gun. Even if I wanted to speak, I couldn't.

Just as I thought I would feel a bullet rip through my scrotum, I heard the man holding my testicles hostage let out a startled scream. He stood and turned as Molly ran past and out the hall. He pointed the gun.

"Molly!" I screamed with anger hoping the cat would think I was upset. Molly ran. He pulled the trigger and the bullet meant for me found its target. Blood and cat hair sprayed across the doorway.

Molly bolted and ran down the hall and found the open door to the basement. The amount of hair and blood was minor. The bullet only grazed or nicked her. It was enough to send panic into her and she ran like she had never run before. I hoped the fear would make her find a hiding spot in the basement and stay put. I prayed Snickers was also hiding.

"Fucking God damn fucking cat!" He turned to me. "I am going to find that cat, blow its fucking head off and bring it back and put it on your lap. Then I will shoot both your knees off and get what I want before I kill you."

"Hurt that cat and I will kill you myself!" A veiled threat under the circumstances but I meant it.

"Now that, boy-o, would be a neat trick indeed!" He slapped my cheeks a few times.

The intruder turned on his heel and made the doorway to the basement in only a few steps. I heard him calling, "Kitty, kitty!" Neither of my cats responds to the idiotic call of "Kitty, kitty." I figured I had only moments. My groin hurt, my neck was strained, and I still had minor jolts flowing through me from being tased.

In the basement, his musical "Kitty, Kitty" calls become angry and turned to shouts of frustration. Boxes and furnishings were being tossed and made a thunderous clamour as they hit the floor or wall. Lots of noise, perfect!

I shifted my weight back and forth several times on the rickety chair. The decision was made. I could break an arm, a leg or my idea wouldn't work at all but I had to chance it. The chair was weak. The noise in the basement was loud enough to conceal my escape efforts. It had to work.

I leaned back and then tossed my weight forward. I stood on my feet, but I was looking at the floor, still in a seated position. With what momentum I could muster, I bent my knees and threw myself up in the air, kicking my legs out from under myself and landed on the two back legs of the chair. The chair crumbled into shattered pieces of wood and kindling. I forced my back straight and fractured any remaining wood parts of the chair that were still holding out. The chair back fell apart and the spindles all fell to the floor. My feet were still firmly attached to the wooden legs and cross support. The tie wraps around my wrist allowed the back spindles to slide through now that the back arch and seat sections had fallen away.

I reached down, held the leg cross support and gave it a pull with any reserved strength I had while I forced my legs apart. The support gave way from the right leg spindle. I pulled both spindles free through the tie wrap. The four tie wraps still remained, but my hands and feet were free from their bindings.

I swept my arms across the floor so that the broken chair pieces would not be visible from the hall.

Footsteps thundered up the basement stairs. He was returning faster than expected. He cursed all the way up from the basement. Good news. Molly was probably still alive. I needed a weapon. My back was against the fridge. I didn't have time to get to the knife drawer for a weapon. I reached for a jagged piece of a wood spindle on the floor. I held the wood weapon in my right hand up along my forearm.

Looking at his reflection in the patio door across from me, his arms were at his side, nothing in his hands except for his pistol. If he was mad before, he would be furious now.

As he walked from the hall to the kitchen, his reflection was full size. Even a daylight reflection in the patio door showed the anger in his eyes and astonishment that I had escaped my bonds. As he took one more step into the kitchen, I swung my arm, left to right, with all the strength my weakened arm could salvage, belly height at an upward angle. I felt the weapon hit and push its way through soft tissue and stop. Stepping from around the corner to face him, I pushed the makeshift spear further into his abdomen. We were now facing each other. Shock and awe filled his eyes. All his strength was gone. He had nothing left and he knew it. The gun fell from his hand to the floor. I pushed harder on the spindle and felt resistance the further it went in. For an instant, I looked down and saw blood flowing freely from the wound and running over my hands.

His knees weakened and I followed him down, maintaining tension on the weapon. As he lay on my kitchen floor, I kicked his gun across the room.

"From the position and the angle I think the spindle went in, it's quite possible it lacerated your bowels, your stomach, and ruptured your diaphragm. That means breathing is almost impossible right now. You want to breathe, but you can't. Blood is filling your gut and maybe even your chest cavity and if you pull the spindle out, you'll bleed out. Tough choice: suffocate or bleed to death. Did you give Bradley that option?"

I twisted the spear and pushed it in deeper. I was terrified that such rage existed inside me. I had no idea I was capable of such violence. Flight or fight, survival mode kicks in. I had lost too much in the past and was not going to run while what remained of my life was being shot at or terrorized.

"Did you do anything like this to Brad?"

He couldn't speak, but his eyes showed the agony. His weakened hands came up and covered mine in an attempt to release my grip on the weapon. I guided him to the floor. He went down easily.

I was within inches of his face. "Who do you work for? Who sent you?" I knew he couldn't answer but I had to ask. I released my grip on the spindle and stood over him. His mouth opened and closed like a fish out of water too long trying to catch its breath. He couldn't move. I looked down at my hands that were covered in his blood, knowing he was going to die unless I did something. In the cutlery drawer, beside the spatulas and large knives, I found a roll of two-inch white medical tape that I'd left in my pocket after finishing a shift on the rigs.

I taped his hands and bound his feet. He offered no resistance. The cordless phone was where I had placed it after my call from Dave Green. I hit the talk button, but heard no dial tone. The phone had power but no signal. I went for the phone in the front room. It, too, was dead. The bastard must have cut the telephone lines. I was leaving bloody hand prints on each device as I held it. I rubbed my hands on my shirt to clean them as I went for my cell in the front hall.

I pulled open the drawer. My new flip phone was broken in two. I raced back to the man dying on my kitchen floor. A quick pat down found what I was looking for. I tapped the power button at the bottom of the phone and slid the unlock bar at the base of the screen. The numeric pad appeared. It was locked.

"I need the unlock code to call 911 or you will die!"

He knew the outcome: tell me the unlock code or die. I knew it was a lie but I hoped he was dumber than he looked. Cell phones can call 9-1-1 while locked.

He couldn't speak but mouthed the numbers: 4–8–2–4. The phone came to life. I dialed 9-1-1.

I disconnected after speaking to the 9-1-1 operator, placing the phone out of reach of the man lying on my kitchen floor, not that I feared he would call someone but rather he would destroy the phone before I could give it to Galen.

As I stood to get a towel hanging from the oven handle, nausea raced up my throat, pain shot through my lower abdomen. Every time I moved, my testicle reminded me how much it hurt.

I grabbed the towel, wrapped it around the wooden spear and secured it in place. I hoped the makeshift splint would prevent any further damage. My head was filled with conflict. Why am I trying to save the man who moments earlier had a gun to my crotch and wanted me dead? On the one hand, I had survived. Do I kill the bastard who broke into my house, threatened my life, my cat, and killed my partner? The other was training and my job: save the man who tried to kill me.

Other than calling 9-1-1, making sure his airway was clear and stabilizing the wooden weapon protruding from his belly, there wasn't much I could do with the equipment I had.

I fell backward against the fridge, sat on the kitchen floor with my elbows on my knees, watching the man in front of me fight for his life as I waited for the police and EMS to arrive.

CHAPTER 9

I sat in the front room, holding a bag of frozen peas on my crotch. Galen was on his cell phone, doing whatever police do. EMS had treated my attacker on scene and transported him to the Queensway–Carleton Hospital. His survival depended on the care of two great medics that had treated him. Whatever damage I caused could only be repaired in surgery. If the crew could keep him alive, he might just make it. I refused transport. My manhood was still intact and would survive without medical care.

Several uniformed officers milled about the house. Notes were being scribbled, pictures taken, evidence bagged and tagged. My statement had been taken before Galen arrived. Even before reviewing the statement, Galen knew the attack was justified. I may have pushed the envelope a bit, but under the circumstances and considering the attack on Bradley, I was justified.

"Did you find Bradley?" I asked Galen. I knew the answer but wanted to hear it from him.

"Yup. Just like he said, there was just one shot to the head! Your partner either put up a good fight or took a lot from our friend. There were lacerations and contusions all over. Brad would have died from blood loss eventually, but the shot finished him early. Based on your story, with the fucking shit that happened here, this cocksucker was a professional hit man. Christ, I really didn't think this fucking shit happened in Canada, let alone Ottawa. We don't have fucking mob hits in Ottawa the way they do in Montreal! Even the mob has the fucking common sense to take their mark to Quebec before plugging 'em."

Galen's vulgarity-filled diatribe was cut short.

"Good as new! Molly is one tough cat," Dave Green, Ottawa EMS supervisor, said as he came down the steps, removing the nitrile gloves and balling them. "It seems the bullet grazed her tail near the tip. I put a gauze pad on and a little self-adhesive wrap. You need to get her to a vet in the next day or so to double check my cat care skills." Dave sat on the chair facing Galen and me.

"Did you hear about Bradley?" I couldn't even look Dave in the face when I asked him.

"Yeah, I heard. Police won't even let us into his house. They let one crew in to confirm death then kicked us out. They said it would contaminate the scene." Dave gave a look of disgust to Galen, as if he was somehow the one who ordered EMS from Bradley's house. Galen refused to comment or make eye contact.

Dave stood. "Don't worry about that meeting we scheduled earlier. We can reschedule for another day. Call me when you can come in. You have enough shit to process for a few days. I can't imagine what it must be like to almost kill a guy to defend yourself," and with that he turned and walked out.

"Meeting?" Galen asked.

"Long story! We have a thief at HQ. Some of our narcotics have decided they would rather be somewhere else than where they are supposed to be. Everyone who has access to the narcotics is being interviewed and questioned. Me included." I shifted in my seat, readjusting the frozen peas.

"Ethan," I hate when someone starts a conversation with your name and then pauses. Galen continued, "I can ask the group for some input on this if you like. You're one of us, now."

The "Group" was our poker group that met every few weeks to drink, play cards, and discuss relevant issues or the hot topics of the day. Every single one of the members of our little group was not only out of my pay grade, but out of my league, but I was accepted. It was nice to have friends in high places when and if you need them. The group consisted of Liz Matyas, who was either the head of CSIS or ran some dark ops department--she couldn't or wouldn't tell us exactly what she did; Colin Peats, president of Pendergrass Software; Richard Stabenow, chief of the Ottawa Police; Judge Bill Thomas of the Supreme Court of Canada; Galen Hoese; and I made up our little group. Live in the nation's capital and powerful people tend to stick together. How Galen and I got to be part of the group is a mystery. I guessed that Galen had been invited by his boss, Richard Stabenow. Why or when, I have no idea, and they never said.

"No, not yet. I appreciate the offer and I know the guys wouldn't mind--but this is not ...well, I'm not sure what it is yet."

"So why did this guy attack you and Bradley anyway?"

Without saying a word, I stood, grunted with pain, readjusted the ice pack to the front of my crotch and went to the basement to retrieve the jump drive.

When I returned, I had the jump drive and the attacker's iPhone in my hand. Galen was standing by the front door, BlackBerry to his ear. His voice became quiet when he saw me. More police stuff, I assumed. I shoved the iPhone in my pocket. As he spoke, his shoulder arched, head hung low, he nodded in agreement to something being said from the other end. Galen's body language indicated something was wrong. He did not look happy. When the conversation ended, he tapped a key to disconnect.

"Can you fucking believe it?" Galen paced back and forth, a man with too much tension and no way to release it. "He was fucking kidnapped!"

"What?"

Galen kept walking around the furniture. This was his way to vent--otherwise he looked as if he may explode. "That was Stabenow. A car cut the fucking ambulance off, another car blocked the side, and a van came around from behind. They took the guy, stretcher, monitor, IV, the whole fucking package!" Galen added, "The two medics are having a fucking fit about the cops not protecting them, and now we have a fucking kidnapping!"

Galen kept pacing around the living room. The two remaining uniformed officers knew better than to get involved or question a detective when he was that pissed. Galen walked a few feet, turned, walked back the other way, and repeated the same path over and over again. All the while, he kept yelling, "Fuck!"

I knew Galen better than the two uniformed officers. I could interject and ask Galen what had happened. "What happened with the police escort?" Galen turned to look at me.

"The cruiser was rammed from behind. They stopped to question the truck that hit them and as they got out, the truck took off. The cruiser was so badly damaged, they couldn't give chase."

"So what happened to the rig?" I really needed to know more.

"These fucking cars cut them off. They stop, the back doors are opened, guys with guns drawn take the guy on the stretcher and load him in a van and take off."

"Did the medics give any details?"

"Like what?" Galen asked, as if the medics could hope to shed any relevant information.

"Just simple EMS shit. One: did the guys know how to disengage the cot from the mounting bracket? Two: did they know how to lower the carriage of the cot? Three: did they know how to load the cot in the back of the van? Four: did they take any other equipment?"

"Why the fuck would we need to know that?"

"Galen . . ." I paused. I wanted him to calm down. My voice lowered and I spoke slowly, "Who was the cop who told me that every little bit of information, no matter how small, how irrelevant at the time may lead to a bigger clue later on? You!" I paused again. "So why does all that shit make sense? Simple: if they knew how to unload and load a cot, it means they have field medical experience, military or civilian--but experience, nonetheless. My guess would be military, Canadian, American or British, but military for sure. Not a big clue, but a clue. This means, they may have a doctor who can operate on the guy and try to save him and get the information you wanted to get from him."

I took my seat, grabbed the now warm bags of peas and stuck them to my groin. Galen took a seat as well. I held the jump drive with my free hand.

"What the fuck is that?" Galen asked.

"This," I twirled the jump drive between my thumb and index, "is what he was after. This is what got Bradley killed! And this," I leaned to my side and pulled the iPhone from my pocket, "is the bastard's phone!"

*****

He sat in the coffee shop, alone at a table with a hot cup of tea. He hated tea served in paper cups with a thermal wrap around the midsection to protect the customer from the heat. He hated the plastic lid they put on it. Tea should be served in a Brown Betty with a china mug. He hated a lot of things but mostly he hated waiting for someone who was not going to show.

He retrieved his mobile phone, scrolled down to the number he needed, and dialed.

"He hasn't shown yet. What would you like me to do?" He spoke with an English accent.

"We have him. Not sure if he will survive, but we managed to retrieve him from the police before they could get any information from him. Get back as soon as you can."

He stood and walked out, leaving his unfinished tea on the table.

*****

My laptop powered up, Galen placed the jump drive in the USB slot, and the file came up under the "F" drive. With a simple click on the only file under F, Microsoft Word booted up and the screen came to life. A few numbers appeared; then, like magic, thousands of numbers, each separated by a comma, rolled across the screen: single digits, double digits, triple digits...they kept coming. No page breaks, simply a comma. No delineation to form a cohesive sequence. There was nothing but numbers.

"What the fuck is this supposed to mean?" Galen was not happy. More questions when what we needed was answers. Galen hit the "page down" key; more numbers; hit the "down" key again; more numbers. He leaned in closer, squinting to focus on the screen as if that would somehow change the numbers to letters.

345,67,55,254,178,1,54,30,14,24,104,87,6,59,21,48,11,98,22,35,9,203,94,32,1
27,564,358,10,29,66,74,82,219,113,220,51,292,404,195,61,84,655,24,418,216,40,5
,9,54,69,587,21,33,58,547,219,1,52,18,157,259,35,39,568,658,84,64,13,10,208,5,6
1,105,901 . . .

The numbers continued endlessly.

"What the fuck am I supposed to do with this?" Galen did have a tendency to repeat himself when under stress.

I had been looking over his shoulder and couldn't understand what I was seeing either. Like Galen, I saw a series of random numbers. I had never seen anything like this but I knew this was what the attacker was after.

Maybe the attacker's cell phone would shed some light on the situation. The phone was in a plastic bag beside the laptop. I reached for the bag, pulled back the zip lock and retrieved the iPhone. I entered the unlock code while Galen watched.

"Your fingerprints are on the phone anyway, so go ahead. Just don't delete or change anything."

The iPhone home screen came to life, and I touched the sunflower icon for "Photos" and tiny images appeared from top to bottom. At the very top, I recognized myself, sitting in my kitchen chair, bound and helpless. There were dozens of pictures of me, various shots of different rooms in the house chronicling his movements and actions. Was this a trophy or evidence to show his boss or employer what he had done?

I scrolled down further and stopped short. Photos of Bradley, alive, beaten, and after he had been shot. The bastard had photographed the entire event from start to finish. This guy is one sick son of a bitch. As paramedics, we see and are witness to some of life's most gruesome events, but seeing a colleague murdered in a series of photos on a cell phone adds a new twist on depravity. I tapped the home button to shut down the photo app.

I was about to replace the phone in its plastic bag when something struck me. If he took pictures for his boss, perhaps he also called him from this phone.

"Do you want me to call the last person he called?"

Galen smiled and turned toward me. He bobbed side to side, his way of showing the thought process at work.

"Sure, why not! What fucking harm can it do? I mean, we do have Goddamn procedures for this sort of thing, but what the hell, what you do when I'm not looking and the fact that you took the phone without my permission saves my fat ass if you fuck the whole thing up. Just put the fucking thing on speaker so I can hear."

The iPhone screen was still on. I tapped the green "phone" icon, found the "recents" page on the bottom and tapped that. A screen appeared with all the calls placed to and from this phone and who they were made to. There were no names listed for his contacts, just cities: Oslo, Sao Paulo, Cairo, Stuttgart, London; the list of cities continued as I scrolled down. The last number called was code-named "Buenos Aires."

I touched the arrow to the right of the listing and the contact for "Buenos Aires" showed itself. Blank! There was nothing more than a name and a number. No personal information, no contact pictures, nothing!

"So much for calling the last number. I don't speak Spanish."

"Spanish? Is that the language of Peru?"

"Galen, yeah, um, pretty sure you meant Argentina."

Embarrassed, Galen stood, walked over the front window of the living room, and placed a call on his cell. His tone was low, preventing me from overhearing whom he was speaking to and what was being said. This was my chance.

Turning to my computer, I slid my finger across the touchpad and the mouse moved to "file," on the top left of the screen. I scrolled down to "Save As" and saved a copy of the jump drive in "My Documents." I quickly moved away from the computer before Galen turned. I stood and went to the fridge for a Diet Coke and brought one for Galen, who still had his back to me and was speaking softly. I tapped him on the shoulder and handed him the Diet Coke. He took it with his free hand and placed it on the end table. I lifted the can and put it on a coaster. Maddy hated water rings on the furniture.

Galen hung up and turned his attention back to the computer. "That was Liz from CSIS. She wants to see the jump drive tonight and she wants you there, too."

"No poker tonight?" I quipped.

"No poker."

Galen had me place the phone back in the plastic bag.

CHAPTER 10

Liz Matyas, CSIS, headquartered in Ottawa; position unknown, job title unknown. Other than that she worked at CSIS, not much was known at all.

No one knew where she lived; Liz liked it that way. If we wanted to violate her trust, I am sure Galen and I could have figured out where she lived, but what would that accomplish? Liz is a very private person and one of the few times she is permitted to relax is when we play poker. Violating her trust would destroy the group and ostracize the offender.

The restaurant/bar was on March Road. The sun was setting over Scotia Bank Place as Galen and I pulled into the parking lot. Galen spotted Liz sitting in a booth as soon as we walked in. A hostess offered us menus when we sat down. Galen squeezed in tight beside Liz, I sat across from them. Liz had a menu, so I accepted. Galen already knew what he wanted.

"Do you have it?" Liz was direct.

From his jacket pocket Galen pulled out a small, plastic zip-lock bag with a labelled brown hang tag on it and handed it to Liz. She immediately pulled her laptop from the bench and placed it on the table. She inserted the jump drive and pulled up the file. I sat forward and craned my neck to see the screen.

"Son of a bitch! It's a Beale Cipher," Liz exclaimed.

"And a Beale Cipher is what, exactly? It's nothing but numbers separated by commas, no order, no consistency, no sentences, no breaks," I said.

"A Beale Cipher, or a Book Cipher, is simple, but effective, and hard as hell to decipher without the key. It's very low-tech, actually. Thomas Jefferson Beale created the most famous book cipher back in the 1820s or so when he supposedly hid millions of dollars in gold or something in the Southern states. To this day, two of the three Beale Cipher texts have not been decoded.

"The person who wants to hide information will take a random text-- anything, really; it can be a book or a song, a passage from the Bible, a poem, anything. The text is broken down and each single letter or word, in sequence, is assigned a number. The person who creates the code could use each letter within the key for the code or use each word. If they use the word, then the number would represent the first letter in the word. So we not only have to find the correct key text, but also have to know if the code uses each letter or each word."

Liz took a pen from her purse and started to scribble on a napkin.

"For example, if you use each letter in the key, 'the cat is black': 't' would represent the number one, 'h' would represent number two, 'e' would represent number three, 'c' would be four, 'a' would be five, and so on. The problem is that one letter, like the letter 'a' or 'e' or any vowel that we use to help break a code, is more difficult with this cipher because any letter can have multiple numbers assigned to it found in various parts of the key. In this case, the letter 'a' shows up in the word 'cat' and 'black.' Therefore, the letter 'a' could or would have two numbers: five and eleven. The code becomes harder if the creator of the code uses a larger base in the key, creating more numbers.

"The receiver of the cipher must know the key and, if it is a book, have the same edition of the book, to avoid confusion. The receiver of the cipher can translate the code by finding the correct section of the key and replacing the numbers with letters.

"We could study this, but without the key, it would take some of our best guys and computers months or years to break this. If ever! Like I said, two of the three original Beale Ciphers have never been broken and they were created over one hundred and fifty years ago."

Liz asked for the details on how I became in possession of the drive. After Galen and I went into detail of the call on the Hill and the attack at my house, she emphasized the importance of keeping this matter quiet and telling no one of the cipher.

I omitted telling them that I had made a copy. Not knowing if I was now in possession of stolen national secrets or a recipe for pad Thai, it was best I kept that secret to myself.

I needed some time to examine the code in detail when I had the chance. Until then, it would have to wait.

*****

He unpacked glass vials of one millilitre--ten milligrams--of morphine from yellow plastic bullet boxes. This was a trick he'd learned working at another ambulance service. Bullet boxes, designed to store live rounds, are perfectly suited to hold twelve one-ml vials and protect them from banging against each other when being transported. They also reduce any noise if the vials tap against each other. This makes it so much easier when he leaves the Ottawa Emergency Services Headquarters. The last thing he wants is to have the sound of glass vials clanging in his backpack as he walks out the door.

The twelve vials are placed on the table and prepped for distribution through the network he created. He never sees the users; his street level dealers sell to the users. Each vial goes for between twenty-five and fifty dollars on the street. He charges a flat twenty per vial, regardless of what the dealers get.

His network of dealers knows nothing about his identity, and he plans on keeping it that way. Orders arrive to a generic Gmail account, payments arrive by PayPal, and drugs are shipped with a fictitious return address. The PayPal account and Gmail address are under identities he created solely for the transaction of drugs. Total anonymity! His day job pays well, but even he realizes that he is pushing how much more he can steal before he gets caught. Only a few more good hauls, then he will call it quits.

Once he found a way to re-label blank vials of normal saline with a clear plastic label indicating the contents were now morphine, the switch began. He knew the morphine was meant to simply diminish the pain of the patients the paramedics were treating and didn't actually save their lives. And working for Ottawa EMS gave him access to almost unlimited quantities of morphine. Only vials used in the field would be replaced, so the count was always accurate. The medics had to account for each and every vial of any drug used on calls. No harm, no foul, and lots of profit, he justified.

He had been purchasing foam sheets from a craft store. The foam had tiny little holes that kept the vials secure and protected during shipping. He organized large Tyvek envelopes on the kitchen table before him, each one for a different dealer in Ottawa. He cut the foam pieces so that the holes matched the number of vials being shipped to each customer. This method had been successful hundreds of times.

Before going to bed, he reloaded twelve more fake vials of morphine in the bullet box. He sealed the completed envelopes and placed them in the backpack along with the bullet box. Another profitable day!

CHAPTER 11

The hotel smoking lounge provided adequate cover. It was empty except for the three of them, and a handsome tip was all that was needed to entice the bartender to lock the doors, take a long break, and leave the bottle of brandy on the bar.

All three men were dressed in custom-tailored suits, cufflinks, expensive shoes, and silk ties; and each spoke with a different accent. One of these men looked more at ease in his custom-made suit, calfskin shoes, and silk tie. The other two seemed out of place and would feel more comfortable in off-the-rack suits. The three dark brown, leather Queen Anne chairs were placed in a circle with a small marble table centered between them. Several arrangements of chairs were placed about the room, but all were empty. Snifters with various amounts of brandy sat on coasters on the table. An ashtray for the cigars was within reach of all three. The air was filled with years of smoke from large imported Cuban cigars. Beside the ashtray was a signal jammer that had been activated as soon as the bartender left the room. Any cell phones or bugs would be inoperative within a hundred feet.

"The file we obtained was incomplete. Part of it, I am sure of this, was on the jump drive we have yet to locate." He rolled the cigar between his thumb, index, and middle finger. "We don't have Cubans in Texas unless they're illegal migrant workers." He looked hard at the cigar. "I prefer these."

The Texan was large, like the state of Texas, hair creased back with a halo effect just above the ears where his cowboy hat usually rested. His belly strained the buttons on his shirt and the short length of his tie made his belly appear larger than it was. He tried to slouch in the chair and cross his legs, but the chair refused to give way to his girth. He propped himself back on his elbows and sat upright once again.

"We shouldn't trivialize the circumstances. We've placed the whole operation in serious jeopardy. Unless we can get the second half of that file, what we have is useless. Tomlinson was smarter than any of us thought. We should've taken him and made sure we had the complete file before deactivating him." His accent was indistinguishable. Not American, not Canadian; European, perhaps. His suit fit his frame well. He had been bred to wear a suit and tie. He was comfortable this way. He was vain, the type of man to have a manicure and not be embarrassed about it. He was cultured and spoke eloquently. "I wanted him taken and questioned to make sure we had the complete file, but you two wanted the hit to send a message. And where does that leave us now?" The European crushed his cigar, barely started, in the ashtray. He sat back hard in his chair to emphasize his displeasure.

"The agenda was planned far in advance." The French-Canadian accent was easy to place but his English was impeccable. "We've had plenty of time to examine the what-ifs before we acted. Don't start with your self-righteous bellyaching now. Now is the time to correct our fuck-ups and get back the second half of the file. Do we know where the drive is?" He stood, walked to the bar, and filled the snifter. He returned with the bottle and topped each of the other glasses off.

The French Canadian, the eldest of the three, had been involved in more operations than the other two combined, but still respected the other men for what skills they brought to the group.

He continued, "Did we learn any more from the asset we recovered in the ambulance?"

"We learned what we could and disposed of the body," said the Texan.

"Do we have another asset in the area?" the European asked between puffs.

"One! We can activate him tonight and go after the jump drive. I don't care how much damage has to be done. Too much money and time has been invested to lose when we're this close." The more anxious he got, the more of his French accent came out.

"Then it's agreed. Activate the asset and retrieve the drive."

Smoke filled the air, the snifters were finished, and the three men left one at a time to avoid being seen together.

CHAPTER 12

The next morning, I called Dave Green and told him today would be as good as any to go over the stolen morphine issue. Dave scheduled me for the last meeting on the docket, just before lunch. I had time to take Molly into the vet and make sure she would survive having the tip of her tail shot off. It also gave me time to go see an old friend I have been neglecting.

Tom Lister met me at his front door. He swung the door wide and stood before me with only a cane to aid with his balance. The last time I saw Tom, he still required two canes and had difficulty standing even for a few moments without losing his balance.

"You dumb shit, why didn't you tell me you were walking?" I asked.

"I wanted to surprise you."

I followed him down the hall to the kitchen.

"My physiotherapist said I am making great progress. It won't be long before I can swing a golf club again. She said if I keep up the pace, I can start riding third on the rigs in a month or two."

He grabbed the back of the chair with one hand, held the cane firmly in the other, and lowered himself to the chair. He hung the handle of the cane over the edge of the table.

"You know the worst thing about the accident?" I shook my head side to side.

"I think I've put on about twenty pounds. I haven't worked out in over four months. I feel like a fat piece of shit." Tom reached down and grabbed a large belly roll and shook it. Since his motorcycle accident, Tom has been unable to lift weights, run, or follow his scheduled workout routine. His once solid body, without an ounce of body fat, was now looking like a normal man for his age.

"Christ, I'm starting to look like you! You want a coffee? I could use another."

"What? You drink coffee now?" I wasn't surprised that Tom had relaxed his workout routine, but was surprised that he had also given up his protein shakes and water-only diet. He grabbed the table and chair and pulled himself up to a standing position. I knew better than to offer help. He was able to walk over and pour two coffees without the aid of his cane. He was making amazing progress.

"I have dreams of going back to work and living my life again, buddy. Not just spending countless hours in the gym."

"But the doctors said you being in such good shape is probably what saved your sorry ass. Why give that up?"

"You look like a worn-out piece of shit and still you had a great wife and enjoyed living. I had a series of superficial girlfriends who cared more about image than substance. Time to start living, my friend, and from now on, you are my inspiration. I have been keeping up with protocols and training. I do my assignments online to stay current and once I get medically cleared, it won't take long to get paired up with you again."

"Nice that you are keeping up on things, but in what world am I an inspiration? Are you on crack?"

For an hour, Tom and I caught up. I brought him up to speed on my home invasion and Bradley's death. I promised I would pick him up for the service.

I sat outside Dave Green's office at Ottawa EMS headquarters, bottle of water in hand, with unknown feelings of guilt. I was unaware of the stolen morphine until Dave told me about it. The rumour mill had been kept surprisingly quiet about it.

The door opened and Dave stuck his head out.

"Ethan, you ready?"

With that invitation, I entered his office. The last time Dave and I spoke was in an interview room, sterile, white, and not at all accommodating. Dave's office was small, but well appointed. Industrial tile floor, but the wall and décor were uniquely his. Most of the pictures were of his family, kids, dog, and travel photos from around the world. Three chairs were placed in front of his desk. One was occupied by an older, stern-looking woman who obviously was the union rep. She did not look like a happy person.

She stood and extended a hand, "Lilly Hargreaves." She smiled broadly, her voice musical, totally contrary to her appearance.

"I am here only to listen and advise," she offered. "And at the request of management and to ensure your rights are protected." She continued to smile.

Instead of sitting behind his desk, Dave pulled one of the chairs out and sat between Lilly and where I was to sit. I joined them.

Dave informed me that over the course of the past few months, several medics had complained that the morphine they were giving under the standard Advanced Life Support Protocols was not having the desired effects on patients. The medics would call Base Hospital and ask the attending physician for permission to administer more morphine outside of the standard protocols. One call would be understandable, but this had happened several times and was beginning to form a pattern.

Without the knowledge of any of the staff, and only key people in management, the pharmaceutical company was called in to perform an audit of the morphine. Under secrecy of night and without any employee aware of the situation, the entire inventory of morphine was pulled and replaced with new vials. After several days, the pharmaceutical company found several vials of fake morphine.

The vials were too small to check for prints, but the telltale sign was a very high-quality clear sticker applied around the vial of unmarked normal saline.

It is normal practice that each medic be assigned a small, sealed pouch at the beginning of each shift that contains the morphine; it must be worn by the Advanced Care Paramedic throughout the shift, and he or she is responsible for the contents.

"Ethan, are you aware of any calls or situations where you had a patient that didn't respond to a standard dose of morphine as per protocol?" Dave Green read from the sheet before him.

Lilly looked right me, pen in hand, ready to record my response.

"None that come to mind; in fact, I haven't used morphine in quite some time."

Dave continued asking questions...questions that had obviously been prepared by a professional...the same question asked multiple times in various ways that could cause a guilty person to give a different answer.

For over an hour, Lilly watched, Dave questioned, I answered. Once the questioning ended, Dave asked how I was handling the home invasion. I was sure Dave had heard about the patient abduction from the ambulance, so there was no use rehashing old news. I thanked him again for the care he had provided to Molly and for checking on me.

As I was about to leave, Dave asked Lilly if we could have some privacy. Lilly looked at me, silently asking if I thought union representation would be needed. Dave picked up on our voiceless communication.

"I can assure you," Dave looked at both of us, "this is not union business and more personal in nature."

Lilly stood and walked to the door, offering her service if I felt I needed it.

"Ethan, you are supposed to start your rotation again tomorrow. After what happened on the Hill, Bradley, and the home invasion, are you sure you want to go back to work tomorrow? We can offer a few days off for stress leave."

"I appreciate the offer, but honestly, I don't have a problem. It seems lately my whole life has become a shit magnet and this has become my norm."

For a few more minutes, Dave tried to convince me that a few days' paid rest might help, but I argued that being home alone thinking about what had happened would be the worst thing for me.

Dave spoke to scheduling and reminded me that my new Algonquin College ACP student that I was supposed to preceptor would be starting tomorrow. And

I would have another new temporary partner.

"Under the circumstances, it might be time for me to apply for a supervisor's position, so I don't keep scaring partners away! Working with me is not exactly healthy," I added.

"You apply when you feel comfortable. In the meantime, I can reassign your student to another preceptor if you want."

"Nah! This might be just the change I need."

CHAPTER 13

The next morning, I reported to work early, shaven; uniform clean, pressed, and crisp; and sporting a double/double coffee with another in reserve. I tracked down the shift supervisor for the names of my new partner and ACP student: PCP Adrian Moss and ACP student Michael Abbott. Most ACP students have several years of Primary Care Paramedic experience under their belts before deciding to take the extra step to becoming an Advanced Care Paramedic. Mr. Abbott had had no such experience. He'd finished his PCP program and decided during the course to apply for the ACP program. His marks justified the application. The shift supervisor warned me that his arrogance was surpassed only by his marks in school.

Mr. Abbott was passed on to me from another ACP preceptor because she refused to work with him. Due to my now justified history of going through partners, either by accident, kidnapping, or death, it was felt that Mr. Michael Abbott could learn something from me. What, I wasn't sure!

Adrian arrived ready for work on time, and personal gear was stowed in the rig we had been assigned. Our shift started at 6:30 that morning, and with two minutes to go, Mr. Abbott was nowhere to be seen.

"You're supposed to have a student, right?" Adrian asked.

"Supposed to, but if he doesn't show in the next minute or two, we leave."

"I heard about what happened to Bradley and what you had to do to the guy who busted into your house. You okay to work? You should be taking time off to deal with this."

"Funny thing is, this is actually the worst of the stuff that has happened in the last little while. This shit is now my norm." I smiled a little smile, trying to make Adrian believe what I said was true. He smiled back.

Adrian decided to book us on and take our first call. As we were pulling away from the base, a sharp rap on the back doors caused Adrian to brake. Mr. Abbott had decided to grace us with his presence.

Without introducing himself, Michael opened the side door, hung his gear bag from the crash netting, climbed in, and took a seat.

"Can we stop at Tim's? I need a coffee."

"Not a chance--we have a call. Come prepared and on time tomorrow if you want to ride with us," Adrian said, staring straight ahead. He glanced over to me to get my approval which I gave him by smiling. Mr. Abbott was actually my student but I was glad Adrian had put him in his place.

"And put on your seatbelt!" Adrian said with a smirk.

*****

The Texan, the French Canadian, and the European stood in the lobby of the same hotel. As always, any conversation mandated that the signal jammer be turned on. They each waited for separate taxis to take them to the Ottawa International Airport. Other than meeting before going their separate ways, their individual itineraries were confidential.

"The asset has been activated. We learned late last night that the jump drive is now in police custody. We have been assured by our contact there that gaining access to the property room will not be a problem. Access will be gained today," the French Canadian said with confidence.

"I look forward to your report," the Texan said quietly for a man from Texas.

"I trust there will not be another fuck-up like we seem to be having lately. Frankly, my confidence is more than a little shaken, not only in the whole operation, but also with your reckless approach to the process. I have people to report to and they demand results." The European raised his hand and a taxi stopped for him. "I expect a positive report by the time my plane lands at Heathrow." The taxi driver overheard the tone of the conversation and decided it was best to simply take the man's suitcase and place it in the trunk without asking. The European tossed his briefcase in the back seat and slammed the door shut hard.

The Texan looked at the French Canadian. "He needs to be eliminated."

The French Canadian nodded in agreement and switched off the portable signal jammer.

*****

Galen woke shortly after seven, rolled out of bed, and walked naked to the bathroom. His wife, Ellie, simply rolled over and paid no attention. He stood before the mirror, turned sideways, and hated that he had gotten so fat. He grabbed his belly and shook it. He knew he had become this way because he ate what he wanted, when he wanted, and how much he wanted. He was happier doing that than denying himself the things that made him happy. Abstinence or moderation was not his style.

Galen stood in the shower, arms outstretched with his palms flat against the wall, his eyes closed, facing the thundering water pouring from the shower head. He liked to think this way. He and Ethan had met with Liz last night and discussed how the home invasion, the killing at Parliament Hill, and the jump drive were all connected. Galen tried to piece the facts together, but what little he knew didn't make sense.

Over a breakfast of fried eggs and bacon, he spread the Ottawa Citizen, the Ottawa Sun, and the National Post on the dining room table. He knew the bacon and eggs should be fruit and plain oatmeal, but again he was not about to deny himself one of life's luxuries. He flipped through each paper, reading the stories on the death of one of the prime minister's aides, thirty-two-year-old Kyle Tomlinson. Galen thought to himself that surely Mr. Tomlinson would have had a complete and thorough screening by CSIS before making it up that high on the Hill.

He tore the related articles from each paper and stuffed them in his suit jacket. He would reference them again when he got to the office and see if Liz Matyas had any more information to share. Like all things in Ottawa, it was whom you knew that got things done. One day, he would have to buy some new suits for himself. He thought they all had the same style and wondered if others had noticed that.

Galen's wife still slept soundly as he left for work. His mind raced with murder, home invasions, suspects, and clues during the entire commute to the Ottawa Police Department. Kyle Tomlinson was high on that list of things to follow up on. That was his first priority this morning.

*****

Marcel woke up with Josie lying in bed next to him. He woke in the same clothes he had fallen asleep in. The room was dark, barren. An old bed sheet hung from two nails where a curtain should be, and there was no television or phone. Those were extra amenities that neither could afford. He rubbed his eyes and scratched his beard growth. Shaving each morning had been a ritual for him that now seemed destined to die with his previous life. That life was now in the past.

Marcel walked down the hall to the washroom everyone shared, entered, and locked the door behind him. He wasn't even sure if the lock worked. The bathroom had a single light bulb hung from an extension cord from the ceiling, was windowless, and smelled of dried urine, feces, and sweat, the kind of smell that causes most people to retch the first time they smell it. Each morning, the odour would trap itself in his clothes and remain with him all day. The toilet was stained so dark, Marcel wasn't sure if the original colour was white or beige or some other colour unknown to him. Not that he worried about hygiene; he was only concerned about his next fix. He had enough money saved today to pay for five more nights in the room they rented by the day and a fix for him and Josie.

His morning bath consisted of washing his face and using his wet hands to wipe the sweat from his body. There was never any soap in the bathroom. No one dared use the shower. It was used more as a second toilet than a shower. Occasionally, the landlord or caretaker or whoever sat in the front lobby and collected the rent, would pour a bottle of bleach down the toilet and another down the shower drain and run the shower for a few minutes to wash down any residue that remained on the shower stall floor.

Marcel walked back to the room and found Josie sitting on the edge of the bed, arms clutching herself as she rocked back and forth.

"I hurt so bad!" she told Marcel.

Marcel looked down at Josie. Marcel cared for Josie, deeply. She wasn't his girlfriend, wife, or lover. They just looked out for each other, like a brother and sister. They'd met on the street and instantly bonded. Perhaps in another place and time and without Marcel being more than ten years her senior, they would have been a couple who celebrated their fiftieth wedding anniversary with children and grandchildren around them in their old age. Instead, they seldom knew where they were going to sleep.

"I need a fix, Marcel."

"I know. Me, too. My back hurts so much I can barely move today."

Marcel used to work construction, fractured his pelvis at a work site, and became addicted to the medication that kept him out of agony. Josie got hooked on methamphetamines in college. Both addicts were now on the streets of Ottawa living one day at a time.

"I'll pay for another few days and be back shortly with some stuff." Marcel looked at Josie, saddened he couldn't do more for her; upset with himself that he was partially to blame for her addiction.

He left her alone in the room and locked the door behind him. In her state, some of the other tenants might see her condition as an opportunity for quick sex in exchange for a drag of a joint. Marcel wouldn't stand for that.

One day, Marcel thought, he would be clean and help Josie do the same. Then, perhaps, he could show her how much he cared for her.

CHAPTER 14

Galen sat at his desk, the three newspaper articles laid out before him, each one detailing the events at Parliament Hill, each with its own viewpoint of the events that transpired that night. The National Post viewed the murder from the political aspect and what it meant for the party in power and what it meant in the polls. The Ottawa Citizen looked at how the events would impact the city and what it will do to the image of Ottawa. The Ottawa Sun took the common man's viewpoint and blamed the party in power for failing to live up to the expectations of the people who had elected it.

Galen wanted to piece all three articles together like a puzzle that didn't belong together. He sat staring at the torn sheets of paper, reading, then rereading each article. He began to highlight the relevant points of each one in bright fluorescent colours, hoping something would jump out at him. The phone rang and startled him.

"Detective Hoese?" the female voice on the other end said. "Galen, it's Liz. We need to meet tomorrow night. We can't talk on the phone."

"Our usual?" he asked.

"Yes. Richard will join us. Call Ethan for me, please."

"Time?"

"Ten." With that, the line went dead.

*****

Adrian guided the rig around the police cruiser, close to the curb. He booked 10–7 with dispatch, indicating we had arrived on scene. Michael bolted from the side door and surveyed the scene with an air of superiority. Adrian and I calmly exited the vehicle, went around to the back, and pulled the stretcher out with the equipment we needed already secured to the mattress. I looked up at the building. The brick façade was stained with decades of pollution, spray paint, and neglect. The windows appeared to still be the original windows from when the building was constructed. Paint peeled, revealing the rotting wood beneath.

In a city like Ottawa, these windows were only slightly better than having a piece of plastic food wrap to keep out the winter cold. Garbage was strewn along the base of the building, and bags of unclaimed garbage bags were stacked high, certainly not the image the city wanted to project to tourists or visitors to the National Capitol.

A police officer approached and asked us to follow him. I guided the foot end and Adrian pushed the head of the cot. Michael walked alongside the stretcher instead of assisting with the equipment. The officer guiding us walked with a steady pace, which seemed to irritate our student. Michael wanted to walk faster, but was kept in line by the speed of the police officer. The officer walked up the crumbling concrete steps and held the door open for us.

Adrian and I lowered the cot down to half height and started to release the straps that held the equipment on the cot. I looked to find Michael to hand him some of the equipment and help share the load, but he had already passed the police officer and was bounding up the steps.

"Fucking newbies!" a familiar voice said behind me. I turned to see Galen Hoese walk out from behind a cruiser. A crowd had already started to form across the narrow street.

"Let me give you a hand with something." Galen reached for the ZOLL defibrillator. "Christ, this weighs a fucking ton! You guys have to carry this shit in on every call?"

"Yup. Now follow me, if you can keep up." Adrian was already inside the foyer and making his way up the stairs.

"How did you know I was here?" I asked my friend.

"We're the cops, remember? We know everything." I stopped short on the steps and let him bump into me as my way of showing what I thought of his humour.

"We got the call first. I called EMS dispatch and they told me you were assigned to the call, too. Oh, Liz wants to see us tomorrow night." When I looked back, Galen had fallen behind already. He was already breathing heavy.

"Do I need to use that defib on you?"

"Shut the fuck up! It's hot in here and smells like a hockey bag on steroids. It's hard to breathe. What the hell is that smell?" Galen passed the defib to a uniformed officer and pointed up the stairs. The officer trailed us up the stairs.

Galen was right; the house smelled foul. The building was once an opulent home and, over time, it and the once-affluent neighbourhood had fallen on hard times. The large, stately home had been converted into a rooming house in which rooms were rented out by the day or by the hour. The large front foyer had nine-foot-high solid wood pocket doors leading to grand rooms on either side. One room now held a reception desk; the other looked like a depository for junk. Like everything else in the house, the staircase was solid wood, but the centre of each stringer had worn over time. The banister was loose and was missing spindles. The walls in the foyer and up the stairs were carbon copies of the outside: dark, peeling paint. A single light fixture with a low-wattage bulb illuminated the entrance. The smell reminded me of a mixture of cat litter box ammonia mixed with decomposing flesh left out in a hot Dumpster in a back alley with hints of lilacs! Someone had obviously sprayed the entrance with cheap air freshener before we arrived.

At the top of the stairs, our excited student motioned us to hurry. Galen and I were keeping pace with Adrian, who was only a few steps ahead of us.

"Dispatch was vague," I said to Galen. "What have we got?"

"Suspicious death, possible suicide. You never know with EMS dispatch. You guys just want us to confirm death? Is anybody working on him?"

Galen shook his head side to side.

"Dead is still alive until someone says he is legally dead. I don't want any fucking uni thinking they know your job any more than I want ambulance drivers thinking they can do my job."

Galen knows I hate being called an ambulance driver, probably as much as uniformed officers hate being called a "uni" by detectives.

At the top of the stairs, the corridor broke off into different directions. Each featured several doors on either side. Most of these doors were closed. It was easy to tell which direction to go; uniformed Ottawa Police officers lined the hall. Michael stood at the entrance to the washroom and waited for us. Adrian walked past Michael without saying a word.

As I approached him, I asked Michael, "So what do we do now?"

Michael stood frozen, staring at the walls and ceiling, looking for the answer as if it were written in the air.

"Patient contact," I suggested.

Michael took the hint and walked in behind Adrian.

"Jesus fucking newbies! Honestly, where do you pick these fuckers up?" Galen asked.

"You don't want to know."

Galen and I followed. The male body was in a seated position, suspended in the shower stall, with his buttocks only a few inches from the floor, and the noose still around his neck. Two uniformed cops were already standing in the large bathroom, careful not to touch anything, not because they didn't want to contaminate the crime scene--they didn't want to touch the toilet, sink, or walls for fear of contracting some as yet unknown virus. It was obvious the police knew he was already dead.

The deceased had used a bed sheet and twisted it tight into a long, rope-like device. Crude, but effective! The bed sheet was tied around the shower head pipe, and the length ended around his neck. He simply sat down and let gravity do what it does best, his full weight pulling on the sheet and cutting off oxygen to the brain. Eventually, he would have passed out and, as long as he didn't stand or kneel, the pressure remained constant and he died. It was a risky move: once he passed out, someone could have found him and cut the sheet or the antique pipes could have easily pulled from the wall.

His skin was cyanotic, purple, from the neck up; his lips were swollen; his heels and part of his feet were also cyanotic from blood pooling. This was a good indication he had died in this exact position. After death, the blood stops flowing and will pool in the lowest parts of the body within a few hours.

While Adrian looked at the surroundings before entering the shower, Michael was anxious to examine the body. Before he could begin to confirm death, Adrian glanced back at me. Michael was my student and Adrian was asking if I wanted him to do the examination.

"Michael," I said his name loud enough to break his trance on Adrian.

"Yeah!"

"Do you know what you have to do at this point?"

"I have to make sure the guy is really dead. Right?" He continued to stare at me.

"Well, then?"

Adrian stepped aside and let Michael into the stall. With a gloved hand, he reached for a radial pulse. "No pulse. The body temp is below normal, not warm, not cold. We need to get a temp, right? I don't think rigor has set in yet, so this happened fairly recently, probably a few hours." He looked back at Adrian and me for approval. Michael turned his attention back to the body.

"If we want to make sure he is dead, really make sure, we can always do a full set of vitals: pupils, ECG, blood pressure, and temp. That way, if this is a crime scene and goes to court, we have covered ourselves. Right?"

We gave no indications he was right or wrong. We simply let Michael take the lead. He hooked up the monitor and found that, although rigor had not yet set in, the arm was just beginning to show signs of stiffness.

Michael was busy taking a set of vitals on an obviously dead man. For whatever reason, the dead man thought death was better than life. His choice!

The silence was broken by the desk clerk running into Galen. He held onto Galen for support. He could barely breathe.

"Come quick!" His voice was deep and throaty from years of smoking. He turned and ran back down the stairs.

"Stay here!" Galen pointed at the two officers already in the bathroom. He looked at two officers in the hall, "You and you, you're with me. And medic-boy, grab some gear in case we need a Band-Aid applied." He looked at me and smiled.

"You okay here with him?" I asked Adrian, nodding at Michael.

"Sure! You have your portable radio turned on?"

I rarely remembered to turn on my radio. I twisted the power/volume button, heard the radio come to life, and followed Galen with a trauma bag in hand.

Galen had already left me behind, which was fine with me. I heard their voices and followed those downstairs, past the front lobby desk, and farther down the hall in the common area kitchen. The door leading to the back alley was open, and Galen was blocking the door. Bright light from the early morning sun poured into the dusky kitchen, casting a large shadow that was Galen. He turned as I approached, giving me a view of the scene outside the kitchen door.

The two uniformed officers knelt beside the body of a young, white female. She was dressed in a dirty white T-shirt and jeans, dishevelled hair, far too young to be dead and left with the garbage in an alley. The two officers stood aside as I emerged from the kitchen doorway. The body lay supine, looking serene, eyes open as if staring up into some unknown expanse. In her right hand, she clutched a five-cc syringe with a small-gauge needle still attached. Several clear vials with the caps snapped off lay beside her.

I reached for a carotid pulse. Nothing. I tugged at her fingers. Stiff! Rigour was already setting in. Her open eyes had a thick mucus-like glaze over them, the pupils fixed and dilated.

"Send pictures of those vials to me, will ya?"

Galen nodded in approval. "Today's special: two for the price of one. Oh, staff meeting tomorrow night, remember, usual place and time."

CHAPTER 15

That morning, I sat at the dining room table drinking my coffee and pretending to read the morning paper. News articles went unread, pages were turned without even a glance at what stories they told. Molly and Snickers ran after each other with all remaining thoughts of the trauma a few days earlier had passed and were now being replaced with thoughts of the backyard, food, squirrels running across the yard, and birds in the trees.

This was the day we were going to Bradley's funeral. I hate the very thought of funerals, the concept, the morbid send-off. Since Maddy's funeral, I hadn't been able to attend another until now.

A short while later, I turned from Baseline Road into the parking lot behind the church close to the main entrance. Tom swung his legs out of the passenger door of the Neon, grabbed the door for support, and planted his cane down. He pulled himself out, stood upright, and tugged down on his dress uniform jacket. He positioned his peaked cap, squared it, tugged at the cuff of his white cotton gloves, and coughed to catch the attention of the crowd who had gathered outside St. John the Apostle Church. Several friends and older medics who knew Tom came by, surprised to see him after all these months of seclusion. A small circle formed around Tom, and even though the reason for the gathering was sad, it was always good to see old friends and colleagues again.

Bradley did not die in the line of duty, but the circumstances behind his death were directly related to the job. Bradley would have a full honour guard funeral. Everyone knew what had happened, and even in private, no one dared speak aloud in case a family member overheard.

I found a parking spot at the back of the lot. Perhaps a dozen or more school buses had been used to shuttle medics in from various sites. Even with the buses, finding a parking spot was difficult. Mixed in with the buses was a lone ambulance, lights covered with black cloth. It would be used to transport the casket to the cemetery. Cars continued to drive around until they found a spot or parked along the long driveway leading in from Baseline Road.

The walk from the car was quiet, and I fidgeted with my dress uniform. I hate, despise--no, loathe--dress uniforms. I refused to wear my peaked cap until the last minute. In the meantime, it remained under my left arm and would stay there as long as possible. Men and women in cloned dress uniforms from different agencies walked around the parking lot in groups: fire with fire, police with police, medics with medics, and so on, but they all came out of respect for a fallen co-worker.

There were hundreds of paramedics from services across Ontario and Quebec, and, from the service crests on the jackets, the Eastern and Western provinces were represented as well. Mixed in were Ottawa Police, Ottawa Fire, and police and fire from across the country as well. I didn't recognize all the shoulder patches, but it looked like some American medics had come to pay their respects as well.

I joined the group standing around Tom and caught up on the news around HQ and the different shifts. No one mentioned the morphine thefts. Not the place or the time. The mood remained casual and jovial, but I knew that would all change once we entered the church.

Men and women in dark navy dress uniforms, caps, and white gloves entered the church in small groups. There were only a few people in suits or civilian dress--family, I surmised. I wanted to approach them, talk to them about Bradley, about working with him, and tell them I wished I had gotten to know him better, but I felt sad for not getting to know him, for not being there when he needed me as a work partner. It wasn't my fault, but I felt a wave of nausea run through me as I thought of how he died and what I did to the man who killed him.

Nausea turned to anger then back to nausea. Maybe if I told his parents what I had done to the man who had killed their son, they would feel better. I decided against it.

The conversation around me went on without my input and didn't hold any interest for me. I felt out of place. Looking around, Galen stood in a group with other Ottawa Police officers in his official police dress uniform; nothing worse than a fat man wearing a jacket with a belt that makes him look even fatter! His jacket hung out in front and draped over his belly. His pants were strategically positioned under his protruding gut, making his inseam look too long and the cuff gathered around his shoes. More people entered the church. No one had said anything, but as if on cue, our group made its way to the front door.

*****

At Heathrow Airport, Terminal 3, the limousine driver stood beside the back door of the vehicle. The European man had had a long flight and wanted only to relax and acclimatize to a time zone he knew. He recognized the waiting vehicle as his own; the driver he did not. As he approached, the driver walked toward the back door and opened it for his employer.

"Where is Mr. Thiede?" questioning where his regular driver was.

"Family issues today, sir. I am Mr. King."

He handed his briefcase to the chauffeur and entered the back of the car. As the back door was closing, the European stuck his foot out and blocked the door from closing.

"Is traffic bad today, Mr. King? I think I will make a quick visit to the loo before we depart."

He exited the car, calmly walked toward the front entrance of Terminal 3 and was swallowed by the crowd. He walked directly to the washroom and, just before the entrance, darted off in another direction. He reached inside his suit jacket, retrieved his mobile phone, and removed the battery. He pulled the SIM card from its slot, bent it in half, seeing it crack, and tossed the two pieces on the floor as he walked. He tossed the phone into yet another trash basket. He removed his overcoat and hung it over his arm. With his free hand, he loosened his tie and tugged at the free end until it slid around his neck. He discarded the expensive silk tie into the trash.

He had transformed his appearance from formal to casual, hoping he would be harder to spot if they were in fact looking for him. He continued to walk, never looking back.

*****

That night, Galen, Liz Matyas, Police Chief Richard Stabenow, and I sat around a small table barely large enough to fit all four Venti-sized cups. Liz and Richard used to meet here for years before bringing Galen, then myself and the others, into the fold.

"Does the name Kyle Tomlinson mean anything to you?" Liz asked as she scanned her male guests for a reaction. Galen and Richard looked at each other then back to Liz. Both Galen and Richard seemed to recognize the name. I looked at Galen, puzzled. The name meant nothing to me.

"Mr. Tomlinson is the one who was killed in Centre Block on the Hill two nights ago." She directed at me. Next time, I should actually read the newspaper instead of skimming over it.

Liz blew across the small opening of the cup lid to cool the coffee and took a long sip. I pulled my cup from the table and cradled it in my hands. I was never one for fancy coffees. I sipped the beverage and found it too strong for my liking.

Liz continued, "It seems Mr. Tomlinson's real name is James Percy Kautz. Now does it ring familiar?"

"What? Not THE James Percy Kautz! Holy fuck!" Galen exclaimed, realizing his voice was too loud.

Galen's outburst caused a few people in the coffee shop to turn and look our way before turning their attention back to the laptops or tablets before them.

"James Percy Kautz was killed in Cardston, Alberta, in 2005, in the Arian shootout with the RCMP at their family farm. He and his father were the leaders of the whole White Power movement in the West. Three members of the Kautz

63

gang were killed, and one RCMP officer was injured. That was the last we ever heard of the Kautz clan," Richard added.

"We thought so, too," Liz said. "During the shootout, the barn mysteriously caught fire, and the bodies found inside were identified with what information the RCMP had available. One was almost definitely the father, another body was a cousin, and they thought the third body was the younger Kautz. Apparently, they were wrong.

"We've been busy on this since you and Ethan pulled the body from the Hill. We tracked down the records of the real Kyle Tomlinson from British Columbia and created a timeline to when Kautz, aka Tomlinson, appeared. The identity was real, not a fake one as we initially thought, and Kautz got away with using the real ID because they actually looked a lot alike.

"Kautz must have disposed of the real Kyle Tomlinson and taken his place. James Percy Kautz never resurfaced, never was a blip on the radar. His friends and family claim they never heard from him again, but that is probably all bullshit anyway. By all accounts, he was dead. Our contacts in Alberta have never recorded any further sightings of Kautz since the shooting. Everything pointed to him being dead."

Liz took another generous sip. "After a little digging, it seems that the new Kyle Tomlinson appeared after the real Tomlinson went on vacation in 2010. While on vacation, the new Tomlinson quit his job in B.C., cancelled his apartment lease, and paid a moving company to pack up his gear and move it to Ottawa. The new Tomlinson never contacted his old friends or family again. We assume the real Tomlinson is dead and buried somewhere in Mexico or is fish food off the coast of Cozumel.

"It was only a few months later that year that Kautz/Tomlinson showed up working as an aide for an MP in an Ottawa riding. He worked his way up from there and managed to get an office in Centre Block. Kautz did pretty well considering his background. We know there was no way he did this alone. We have a team working on the MP now."

Liz paused for a moment and sipped her coffee again. We all sat back in stunned silence, contemplating how easily James Percy Kautz had assumed the persona of Kyle Tomlinson and infiltrated Parliament Hill.

Liz went on to tell us that CSIS would now be responsible for quietly investigating the member of Parliament to determine if anything illegal had taken place and why the RCMP background check failed to pick up on James Percy Kautz's, aka Kyle Tomlinson's, fake identification.

Liz had asked that we all keep the information confidential, but remain vigilant.

"Any news on the cell phone I got from the guy in my house?" I got the feeling that most of the group had planned on leaving before I changed the subject.

"Actually, the phone had a lot of information." Galen paused, pulled out a notepad and flipped through until he found the right page.

"The phone is registered with Vodafone in Ireland. That part was easy to figure out. Who it belongs to is another fucking matter! It is not a burner or disposable phone. The SIM card held an encryption program that we can't break. The numbers are still on the card, but the names associated with each number are scrambled. This is way over our IT guys' heads. Our guys called your office, Liz, for some help. Hopefully you will be able to crack whatever they are using to scramble the fucking phone. I think whoever stole his body knows we have the phone; if I was them, all the numbers should have been cancelled, leaving us with a pile of shit to work with."

"I thought you said you had a lot?" Liz said as she sipped the last of her coffee.

"I said I had a fucking lot of information. No fucking details, but a lot of shit."

"Out of curiosity," interrupted Richard, as he hid behind his mug of coffee. Galen knew this was not going to be nice. "You kiss your wife with that mouth, don't you?"

"Among other things, too, and don't you fucking forget it!" Galen was smiling so hard he dribbled coffee onto his tie as he drank.

*****

Back home, I stood before the mirror and ran one hand through my hair, making the grey hairs reveal themselves. With the other, I was brushing my teeth, amazed at my multi-tasking skills. The house phone rang, breaking my self-adoration. A quick rinse and I ran for the phone at my bedside.

"Hello."

"Ethan, it's Becky."

I fell backwards and landed hard on the edge of the bed.

Becky was a voice from my past. I hadn't seen or heard from Becky for several months. We'd never really dated, but the connection...no, attraction...was strong. Becky was a new-hire paramedic assigned to work with me after Tom had his injury. It didn't take long for the mutual attraction to build; after Maddy's death, I had found it hard to let myself be attracted to another woman without feeling guilty.

"Still there?"

I must have drifted off.

"Hi." I felt like a tongue-tied teenager speaking on the phone with the most popular girl in high school.

She laughed. "Nice that you remember me."

"Kind of hard not to after I was responsible for you getting kidnapped." I felt misplaced guilt.

"Ethan?"

"Yes?"

"Have you met anyone yet?"

"No."

"Good. Open the front door. It's a bit chilly outside."

I ran downstairs, taking the steps two at a time. I pulled the door open so hard, the handle almost slipped from my still wet hand. Becky pocketed her phone and walked past me into the front foyer. Her scent drifted past. She smelled so good. Old feelings burst to the surface. She stood before me, smiled, wrapped her arms around my waist, pulled me in tight and kissed me.

We sat on the couch, talking, bringing each other up to date on what we had each been doing for the last few months. I learned that after Becky had been abducted, she'd moved back to Kitchener to recover from her experience. Her injuries were more psychological than physical. Her parents had provided the emotional support she needed, free of any pressure from work or friends in Ottawa. Ottawa EMS had granted Becky a six-month leave of absence from her paramedic duties. Due to the extenuating circumstances of Becky's leave, Ottawa EMS had given permission for her to work part-time for Waterloo EMS in Kitchener to keep her skills current. Becky's parents wanted her to make the move to Kitchener permanent. She had moved to Ottawa to take the Paramedic program and after school she'd made Ottawa her home. Her leave was almost up, and a decision had to be made: stay in Kitchener with her parents or return to Ottawa.

"That's why I came to see you, Ethan. It isn't fair of me to ask you, but I need you to help me make my decision."

"What can I do?" I was puzzled by her request to include me in her decision making process.

"I want to know if you want me to come back to Ottawa."

I was about to answer and realized my answer, either way, could have serious consequences. I stood, walked around the coffee table, put my hands on my hips and was about to say something and nothing came out. I was stunned. She was considering me in the equation.

CHAPTER 16

The ambulance from Quebec pulled into the Ottawa Civic parking lot. The two medics exited the vehicle and rolled the cot from the back of the rig. The Ottawa crews waved to acknowledge them as they walked past. The Quebec medics smiled and nodded back. It is not an uncommon site to see ambulances from Quebec at Ontario hospitals. For all its faults, the Ontario health care system far surpasses that of Quebec. The Quebec hospitals will often send Quebec residents across the border for treatment at Ontario hospitals and ambulances from Ottawa will respond to calls across the river in Quebec if requested and one is available.

One of the Quebec medics fumbled with the keypad and entered the wrong code several times trying to gain access to the emergency department. An Ottawa medic, seeing his out-of-province counterpart having difficulty, walked over and entered the correct code in the keypad; the sliding glass doors opened, granting them access to the ER. The Ottawa medic wondered why the Quebec crew had their trauma bag and oxygen bag on the cot going into a hospital. He assumed that was their protocol; or perhaps they were picking up a patient to return to Quebec. He dismissed the thought.

Pulling the cot through the ER foyer, they walked through the hall unobstructed, gaining access to restricted areas because they looked the part. They passed through the double doors just to the right of the ER reception desk by pressing the large, circular, stainless-steel disk on the wall and headed down a corridor to the main section of the hospital. Once past the doors leading into the main section of the hospital, patients, hospital staff, and the public walked past them without giving them any thought. Two paramedics walking in a hospital corridor is a sight seen countless times in every hospital across the county. The medics paused and looked up and down the hall to get their bearings. They turned right and blended in with the traffic. They followed the signs leading to the maintenance area and left the crowds behind.

They located the locked closet and paused, looking up and down the hall for signs anyone might be close by. Sensing they were in the clear, they inserted the key they had acquired, entered with the ambulance cot, and locked the door behind them. One of the Quebec medics unzipped the main flap of the trauma bag, removed the false lid of the suction unit, reached in, and flipped a switch. A red light is activated, and he set the timer for twenty-four hours. He closed the false lid of the suction unit so the red light and timer would not be visible to anyone unless they knew the suction unit was not what it seemed. The bag was zippered closed.

They exited the closet, closed the door, locked it, and squeezed an entire tube of Super Glue into the keyhole, jamming the lock.

The Quebec medics walked down the hall, retracing their steps back to the ER. At the hall door leading back into the ER, they found it locked and only accessible with a pass card.

One of the medics appealed to a female nurse walking past. "Excuse me--is this the way back to emerg?"

"Yes, it is."

"Could you let us in, please? We went for coffee, got lost, and can't find our way back."

She smiled at the two young medics and waved her card past the sensor. There was an audible click, and one of the medics pulled on the unlocked door.

They walked past the Ottawa medics in the ER on off-load delay, waved at them, asked how things were going, and headed out to the ambulance parking lot. They entered the Quebec ambulance and drove away.

*****

I paced outside Dave Green's office, cell phone in hand. Galen had emailed me the crime scene pictures with the morphine vials taken the day before. Over the past few months, working with Galen, I learned that coincidences don't really exist.

Dave spotted me wearing away the tiles in front of his office. I didn't hear him come up from behind.

"Morning, Ethan. What's up?"

"Yesterday, we talked about the medication issue," I began, unsure if anyone else might be listening. Dave unlocked the door and invited me in.

"You not supposed to be on the road?"

"I managed to weasel my way off the road for a few hours. I really need to show you something."

Dave sat down behind his desk, deposited his coffee mug, pulled his laptop from his messenger bag, and offered me a seat.

"What have you got?"

I had the photo readied on my phone and I turned the screen toward him. "I had an OD yesterday. These were on scene. The police emailed me the pics this morning."

Dave took the phone from my hand and zoomed in on the photo.

"Is there any way to trace the lot number or the vials to see if this is some of our missing meds?" I asked.

"I'm not sure, but can you email me the pictures? I'll bring this to the assistant deputy who is in charge of the matter. Thanks for keeping this quiet."

"No problem. I lied to the shift supervisor and said you were the one who authorized my time off the trucks so we could talk. Back me up on that, okay?" I smiled.

Dave smiled, but his eyes never left the tiny screen. He finally handed me back my phone and I immediately started forwarding the pictures to Dave's email address as I left his office. I still had difficulty texting and typing on my phone.

The truck was still idling when I jumped into the passenger seat. Adrian was behind the wheel, looking at me as I finished texting. Our student, Michael, sat quietly in the Captain's chair in the patient compartment. Adrian had had a little chat with Michael before the end of his shift. Even though Michael was taking his ACP course and I was officially his preceptor, Adrian had taken the lead and put our student in his place. Tom was being kept updated with regular texts or as often as I could remember to send them.

"All set?" Adrian asked.

"All set."

"Dispatch 4129, back in service."

Seldom did crews receive the same truck two days in a row. In Ottawa, equipment technicians checked the stock, cleaned each rig, and readied them for the crews when they showed up for their respective shifts. It is an efficient system that allowed the crews to book on, ready to respond, knowing that the same piece of equipment would be in the same location in each and every truck. When a crew showed up for the start of their shift, they took the next truck in line.

Traffic was normal as we drove west on the Queensway. The morning calls were routine, exactly what a seasoned medic wants but not really what an ACP student is looking for to practice his skills.

It was mid-morning and the sun was at our backs, reflecting in the side-view mirrors. Traffic was normal on the Queensway, Highway 417, a four-lane artery that runs east-west through the north end of Ottawa and connects towns like Arnprior and Renfrew, northwest of the city, turning into the rural bedroom communities of Ottawa. For those who didn't mind the commute, you could work in the city and enjoy life in a small town less than an hour from the city. East of Ottawa, at the 417 split, the south extension of the highway runs through beautiful, untouched farming land, primarily French communities, to the Ottawa River, and then into Quebec. The north extension continues past Orleans and, at Trim Road, becomes a two-lane bordering the Ottawa River and takes you into the province of Quebec.

The unique, hexagon-shaped bronzed-glassed Corel offices reflected the day's sunlight and created an aura surrounding the building, sending spears of light into the sky, as we approached. Everything seems so much better in the sunshine. Dispatch broke my daydreaming.

"Four–one–two–nine Ottawa."

Adrian picked up the mike to respond. "Go for 4129."

"Code 4, 1742 Bromley Road and Sherbourne Road. Police and fire also dispatched. Domestic assault. Husband is no longer on scene. Take Maitland exit from your current 20."

"Ten–four. Ten–eight."

Dispatch provided us with a few more details and asked us to switch to our working radio channel.

Adrian reached down and activated the lights and siren. He pulled over to the far left lane as traffic became aware of our presence. Bright, sunny days played havoc with the emergency lights. They proved ineffective at warning drivers. They were unable to see the red and white strobes against the sun in their rear-view mirrors. On days like this, the siren blared constantly; some vehicles pulled right and gave way, but most ignored us, like they usually do. Adrian skillfully weaved the rig through traffic, keeping his speed constant and within reason, nothing that would cause me any concern. Some new medics feel that turning on the lights and siren gives them carte blanche to drive like one of the Andretti's on public streets with a five-ton vehicle. Ambulances do not drive or respond like, or have the control of, a passenger car, and many of the new young medics have never driven a rear-drive vehicle. However, Adrian had complete control of the rig.

I looked back through the opening to the back patient compartment. Michael Abbott was squirming in the captain's chair, straining to look forward. A broad smile appeared on his face, eyes widened in anticipation of what lay ahead.

Looking at Adrian, he sensed my stare and looked at me. I nodded my head toward the back, and he smiled. Voiceless communication!

Adrian pulled north on Maitland Avenue from the Queensway. At the lights, he turned north and continued straight. Traffic was lighter on Maitland Avenue, with residential homes and less traffic noise. Surprisingly, every car pulled to the curb, giving us clearance to pass safely. It was only a few blocks north before we came upon the Carling Avenue intersection, turning Maitland Avenue into Sherbourne Road on the north side of the intersection.

One block north, Bromley Road continued east and west off Sherbourne. Adrian turned left when he saw two police cruisers parked in front of one of the houses. The police must have arrived in a rush. The first cruiser was parked in line with the curb; the second blocked traffic from coming or going in either direction on this residential street. Adrian turned and backed into the driveway, leaving the front cab on the street. We booked 10–7 scene, letting dispatch know we had arrived and that the police were already on scene.

As I exited the passenger side, an Ottawa police constable walked from the house, his bare hands covered in blood. Michael had opened the back door and saw the officer holding his arms up, hands in the sterile surgeon position.

"Mike, give him the towel off the cot and a bottle of hand sanitizer."

"Got it!"

"Scene secure?" I asked.

"She's in the tub in the basement. Husband is gone. We can't find him. Backup is coming." The officer was out of breath and apprehensive. He wanted the blood washed from his hands as quickly as possible.

"What happened?" Adrian released the locking bar and began to pull the cot from the restraint.

"Multiple stab wounds. She isn't responding. Partner is doing CPR." The officer was only capable of short, direct sentences. He walked to the back door, where Michael stood.

Michael had already donned his nitrile gloves. His blue gloves were at odds with the bright red hands of the officer's. The officer presented his outstretched hands as Michael draped a towel over them and began to wipe them down vigorously.

Adrian and I moved the cot close to the front door, lowered it to working height, and released the defib, med bag, and trauma bag from the cot. With gear slung over our shoulders, we entered the house. Even for a bright day, the house was dark. All the curtains were drawn, air stale, ashtrays overflowing on the coffee table, furniture dated. First guess: elderly couple.

We walked through the living room into the hall, which turned left and right. To the right, an open door welcomed the light from outside, cutting through the darkness.

"Down here!" a voice screamed, demanding we comply.

Adrian led the way downstairs. The narrow and steep wooden steps permitted only one person at a time. I had to turn sideways to keep the bags from hitting the walls and pushing me off balance.

The basement had been converted to an apartment. Area carpets covered most of the painted concrete floor. Like the upstairs, the furniture came from decades long past. Adrian continued to the open door. Heavy breathing, panting, and shouts for us to hurry beckoned.

Inside the tiny bathroom, directly facing us, a large, elderly woman lay supine, rolled slightly to the right, in the tub. A police officer stood over her, breathless. The entire tub was red, blood red. He had his left foot outside of the tub on the bathroom floor. The other foot steadied against the wall and the side of the tub. His hands, like his partners, were covered in blood. His right hand braced his weight against the shower wall. His left hand pushed hard and fast on the patient's sternum, between her breasts, as she bounced in the tub. Blood-soaked clothing pooled fluid around his hand with every compression. The constant movement caused by the violent compression as the officer performed CPR created swipe marks against the porcelain.

Already gloved, Adrian reached down and felt for a carotid pulse. The patient's large jowls prevented locating a pulse caused by the compressions. Blood had saturated all of the clothing, preventing us from seeing the cause of the massive blood loss. He searched for a radial pulse. Nothing--or else the blood pressure was very low, making it impossible to find a pulse.

"Don't just fucking stand there, take over for me!" The officer was exhausted and did not enjoy his current task.

A quick scene survey revealed a toilet with the lid closed to my right and a sink between the toilet and the tub. A large, wooden-handled knife lay peacefully at the base of the sink. Blood, still wet, covered the silver blade and darkened the wooden handle. I guessed the blade was about four to six inches long.

Adrian stepped out of the bathroom and started setting up the equipment in the room beside the bathroom. I heard him call out for Michael to "get his ass down here with the spinal gear."

"Did you see this?" I asked the officer as I pointed to the knife.

"See what?"

I pointed without saying a word. He continued compressions, never missing a beat and strained to see the object in the sink. A nod indicating he had not seen it was all that was needed.

"There is no way we can work on her in the tub." Adrian looked at the officer. Perspiration poured freely from the officer's brow. "Ready to switch?"

"Please, anytime! The sooner the better!" His tone had changed. He was happy to rid himself of the responsibility of caring for the patient. With that, the police officer stopped compressions, stepped from the tub, and exchanged positions with Adrian. Adrian assumed the same position as the officer, bracing himself to do compressions. Adrian started CPR, fast and hard. The sound of blood being compressed between the patient and the porcelain tub echoed with wet gurgling sounds.

I turned to the officer, "How long has the patient been here?"

"We got the call as a domestic disturbance from dispatch. When we got here, the front door was open. We walked in, looked around, found her, and secured the scene. I couldn't find a pulse, so I started CPR. The other officer and I tried several times to pull her from the tub and get her on the floor, but she kept slipping out of our hands."

Adrian interjected. "I can see a few stab wounds from here. One in the left side of her shoulder...and the shirt has a few slice marks. I am guessing those are wounds, too. Porcelain tubs make everything feel cold. I can't figure out how long she has been here. Call for a Code 5 or TOR?"

Patients who are obviously dead and meet certain criteria are deemed to be Code 5 and can be left at the scene. These patients can be in full rigor mortis, have been decapitated, or exhibit other obvious signs where they can safely be classified as deceased. A TOR, or Termination of Resuscitation, is a field pronouncement of death in someone who does not meet the Code 5 criteria, but is in cardiac arrest secondary to severe blunt or penetrating trauma.

"Nope. Besides, we can't determine death in there."

Michael finally joined us and, from the eager look on his face, wanted to get involved.

"What do you want me to do?" Michael had the spine board and collar kit in hand. He dropped them in the hall at the entrance of the bathroom.

"We need help getting her out of the tub!"

With that, the cop stepped from the bathroom and observed from the hall. He continued to wipe the blood from his hands with a towel he had pulled from the backboard kit.

"How are you guys gonna do that?" Over the years, experienced medics have learned a lot of tricks to do things most people wouldn't think of doing.

I placed the plastic blue backboard a few feet short of the tub. The spinal kit was already opened, and I pulled the black foam rolls used to immobilize the cervical spine, tape, and quick-connect straps from the kit. The defib and oxygen were on and primed for action. I tossed Michael a towel from the rack and told him to drape it over his chest.

Michael climbed in the tub and maneuvered himself behind the patient's head. Adrian stopped CPR just long enough to grab her thick, blood-covered wrists and pull her forward. Michael reached from behind, grabbing her right wrist with his left hand, her left wrist with his right hand, pulling her in tight to his chest. The white bath towel draped over Michael's chest turned red as soon as she made contact. Adrian bent down, reached under her knees, and readied himself to hoist her out of the tub. I positioned myself at the tub and let Michael call the shots.

"On three: one, two, three." Michael lifted with his knees and stood upright with the large patient hugged in close to his chest. He appeared unsteady on his feet in the slippery tub. The patient slid down Michael's chest, and he pulled her wrists tighter, preventing her from sliding any farther. I looked down into the tub. The entire surface of the tub was covered in watered-down blood. Michael's black boots stood in stark contrast to the bright red sea surrounding each foot.

Adrian had both his arms under her knees and had stood in unison with Michael. I grabbed Michael by his shirt to help support him. He bounced once, twice, then lifted his right leg over the edge of the tub. His left foot slipped on the wet blood covering the floor of the tub. I caught the shifting weight and kept Michael and the patient from falling. He planted his foot on the floor, heaved the weight up higher and hopped to get his left leg out of the tub. I supported the patient under her buttocks and walked backwards as Adrian lifted her legs and stepped from the tub.

The weight of the patient, the lack of a strong footing and the slipperiness of the blood caused the patient to hit the spinal board with a little more force than planned. A soft moan emanated from her as she made contact with the board. We all paused and looked at each other, wide-eyed. She was alive. We moved into fast forward. Michael kept control of the patient's cervical spine. His protective towel fell to the floor as he flattened her jowls and searched for a carotid pulse.

"Shit! Found one--weak, thready, but its there."

Adrian felt the opposite side of her neck and felt a faint pulse. He grabbed the defib and applied the monitoring electrodes.

The patient was still unconscious, unresponsive, but she had a palpable pulse. A carotid pulse in the neck meant the patient had a blood pressure of at least forty mmHg. Not great, but a pressure, nonetheless. It would fall fast if we didn't hurry.

"Get a pressure while I check her injuries." I cut through the bloodstained shirt and bra. As soon as I exposed her chest and abdomen, we all stopped and focused our attention on one laceration on the left side of her chest above her breast. Small, almost indiscernible from the other cuts on her chest and abdomen, this one laceration gurgled and bubbled as the blood reached the surface. I pulled my stethoscope from around my neck, closed my eyes and auscultated for breath sounds. Breath sounds were absent on the left side, diminished on the right. Heart sounds muted. The head of my scope was now also covered in blood, but I threw it around my neck anyway.

"Did you notice the trach?" I looked at both Adrian and Michael.

They looked at each other then back to me. They both shook their heads, "No!"

I flattened the skin around her neck while Michael moved to the side, maintaining control of the c-spine. He turned on the oxygen tank, attached a non-rebreather, and turned the regulator to twelve litres per minute.

"Shit! She has a pneumo." The trachea was shifted and leaning toward the right side. Air was filling her chest because the knife wound had punctured her left lung. With each inspiration, air would not only be drawn in from her mouth, but also from the opening in her chest. The pressure had collapsed her left lung and was now filling the chest cavity with air and increasing the thoracic pressure. Her heart was being pushed from its normal position, to the right side, which in turn would put more pressure on the right lung. Our patient would eventually suffocate. Michael placed the oxygen mask on her face while we worked on her chest wound. In this situation, she needed the concentrated oxygen.

Adrian wrapped a cuff around the patient's upper arm, attached an oxygen saturation sensor on her blood-soaked index finger, and pressed the NIBP button on the defib. The internal pump started inflating the cuff around her arm to obtain a blood pressure. Adrian then opened the IV kit and tore a one-litre bag of normal saline from its plastic container and primed the line.

I frantically looked for the towel that was supposed to be in the backboard kit and remembered that the cop had taken it to wipe his hands. Adrian looked behind the door and pulled the towel off the hook. He knew what I was about to do and prepped her left chest, ensuring it was free of blood.

I tore the package of the Asherman Chest Seal, removed the dressing and the protective wrap and placed the one-way valve directly over the bubbling wound. The one-way valve immediately started to work. The chest seal forms a tight seal around the wound, leaving a small opening that permits air inside the chest to vacate the pleural space when the patient breathes out, and collapses onto itself when the patient breathes in. This simple device would prevent the right lung from collapsing any further and hopefully balance out the thoracic pressure.

We all noticed the change. Her breathing improved, but was still laboured. Michael opened her mouth, reached for the suction unit, pressed the power button, moved the oxygen mask to the side and inserted a yankauer suction tip to the back of the oral pharynx. We watched as the tube filled with red fluid.

"She probably has a bleed we can't see. There's a lot of blood down there. We are going to have to suction her all the way to the ER. Give me a number 5 oral airway. Have you got vitals yet?" Michael looked concerned as he asked Adrian for her vitals.

Adrian was busy wiping down the patient's right antecubital area to start the IV before her blood pressure dropped any lower, so Michael looked at the defib.

"BP 55 over 30, pulse 45, respirations eightish and shallow, SpO2 76 percent, ECG is all over the place, too much artifact from the blood and paroxysmal breathing."

I inserted the oral airway and attached the oxygen line to the bag. I immediately started to assist the patient's breathing. The oxygen would help her saturation levels.

The police officer, seeing our predicament, had run upstairs and found clean towels for us to use.

Thunderous steps could be heard coming down the basement steps. Several firefighters forced their way past the police officer to look into the bathroom.

"What can we do to help?" one of them offered.

I said, "Get the stretcher ready outside, clear the path from here to the front door, and turn on any lights so we don't trip on anything. Have a couple of guys ready to help us lift."

Adrian and Michael had put a collar around the patient's neck. Black head foam immobilizers were taped in place on either side of her head, and straps crisscrossed her chest, one across her pelvis and one around her lower legs. Adrian had the IV started and running wide open. He hung the IV bag from the towel bar. Both her hands were secured alongside and tucked in to the strap around her pelvis. I kept the airway patent; and ventilation and oxygenation were maintained throughout.

"I'm an ex-Ottawa medic. What can I do?" I turned to see one of the firefighters at the door offering assistance.

"We already have three medics in a cramped bathroom. Get a couple of guys to help us lift." I felt like I was repeating myself.

The cop standing with them got the point. He casually moved directly in front of the firefighter's path to block his view. "When these guys are ready to move, just be ready to help them lift!"

The police officer turned back toward us, "Goddamn hose handlers! They think they own the world. Christ, what a jackass!" The police officer echoed our sentiments exactly. I doubted that the working relationship between Fire and EMS would ever improve during my tenure.

A quick glance at the defib displaying the current set of vitals showed we were fighting a losing battle. Her heart rate was only slightly slower, but her blood pressure was dropping, and I noticed her respiratory rate was down.

"Can you get the fire guys down here? We're ready to get her out of here." I didn't have to ask the cop twice. He barked orders and four firefighters entered the bathroom, two on my left and two on my right. Adrian and Michael stood back and directed Fire to lift the backboard on my count. I maintained the airway and ventilations while firefighters grabbed each corner of the board and lifted in unison. Michael and Adrian fell back, were handed towels from the police officer, and began to wipe themselves clean. Adrian retrieved a bottle of alcohol hand sanitizer from the trauma kit and the two of them used it liberally as they followed us.

The firefighters maintained the patient level on the board across the basement apartment, up the stairs, and through the house. The cot had been prepped in advance, and the board was gently lowered into place.

When I looked up from the patient, the street had been transformed into a parking lot for emergency vehicles: police, EMS, and fire trucks, parked at every possible angle, blocked access and egress from the house. Bystanders stood at the edge of their respective lawns, arms crossed, some held their children, others pointed and spoke to one another. Some held cell phones up and recorded our every movement. Eventually, YouTube would host the video of the scene playing out before them or they would show the video at work the next day.

The patient was loaded. Michael and I hopped in the back, Adrian jumped into the driver's seat, and the police cleared a path for us to leave. An idling cruiser was parked in front of our ambulance to provide an escort en route to the hospital. This was still an assault, and potentially a murder, if our patient didn't pull through. The police officer would stay with the patient in the ER up to surgery, if she made it that far.

Adrian craned his head from the front, looking into the back. "Ready?"

"Whenever you are!" I answered.

Michael donned new gloves, put on a face shield, and took control of the airway. He maintained c-spine on the patient, suctioned as required, and bagged the patient to assist with her breathing. Her vitals stayed constant; didn't improve, didn't deteriorate. I cut the blood-soaked shirt and pulled it to the side. Her skin was now a mixture of flesh tones with brush strokes of crimson. Tiny marks, puncture wounds--I counted seven over her chest and abdomen--no longer flowed freely with blood. I placed a gauze dressing over each one and taped them in place. Lacerations, defensive wounds, on both forearms, no longer bled. With my shears, I sliced up the fronts of both pant legs. There were no lacerations or stab wounds on her lower extremities.

The siren overrode our status updates to each other, only to be repeated when Adrian turned it off. The vehicle shifted left, then right. We adjusted our balance to compensate. It's like attempting to do surgery on a patient while on a cruise ship in rough seas.

The defib was set to take vitals every five minutes, and as long as she maintained a blood pressure and a pulse, and we assisted the patient's breathing, I would be happy to get her to the hospital alive.

Michael compressed the bag, forcing concentrated oxygen into her lungs, coercing the body to breathe and improving her blood oxygen saturation levels. As part of his training, he directed patient care, and we discussed the anatomy of the injuries sustained and what the consequences were of each location of the stab wounds on her body.

*****

We walked out of the Queensway–Carleton Hospital Emergency Department into the enclosed ambulance parking garage, exhausted and ready for a shower and a change of clothing. Our patient was still alive. The doctors and nurses took over for us and did a great job of stabilizing her in the ER before sending her up for emergency surgery.

Adrian, Michael, and I sat down, leaned back, and breathed deep.

"Was it good for you?"

"Yeah, we should do this more often," Michael said with a wide grin.

"You're not as big a dick as everyone says!" Adrian cut in.

"Who says I'm a dick?"

"Well, just me! But you did good back at the house." Adrian smiled at Michael.

I placed my hand on my knees and went to stand. My back cracked, my knee buckled, I stood and arched backwards to work out the kinks.

"I really am getting too old for this shit." I closed my eyes and groaned.

Footsteps and voices broke my concentration.

"Do you have your radio turned on?" A police officer came running up. I looked back at him.

"I don't know."

"Turn on your fucking radio!"

Adrian reached down, realized the portable radio volume was turned down. More officers came running outside. Doctors and nurses followed close behind.

"What the hell is going on?" Looking at the faces in the crowd, it was evident that whatever it was, it was bad.

A nurse from the emergency department screamed, "Didn't you hear? An ambulance exploded outside the Civic ER!"

CHAPTER 17

The crowd started talking over one another. The sound of the police radio buzzed with chaos. My heart skipped a beat; epinephrine burnt my sides as it exploded from the adrenal glands. My heart rate increased, my palms became sweaty, and I could feel moisture forming on my brow. My entire body tensed.

"Everyone, quiet!" I yelled. The only sound was now coming from the EMS radio on Adrian's belt and the police portable radios.

The police dispatcher called for more officers to respond to the Civic Hospital. Fire had been dispatched as well. Uniformed officers, including tactical officers, were responding from all over the city. EMS tactical was also deployed.

Adrian and I and some of the medical staff huddled around the lone EMS radio. Michael ran to the rig for the second portable radio. Dispatch called for radio silence. Crews were being called in from across the city to the hospital. Casualties were high, numbers dead or injured unknown.

I ran back to the group listening to the police radio: An ambulance parked at the far side of the ambulance parking lot had exploded; it was simply caught in the blast. The explosion was powerful enough to tear part of the ER overhang off and collapse the section onto the pavement below. Several rigs were on fire. At full capacity, eight to ten ambulances can be parked at the ER at one time. If rigs were parked under the overhang when it collapsed, medics could be trapped under the rubble. The only entrance for ambulances into the Civic ER had been completely destroyed.

Adrian grabbed my attention and summoned me over.

"They are calling in every available medic from across the region. I just heard we had six rigs at the Civic when the explosion went off. No word on any injuries yet. I can't see how all the medics could have escaped. Radio chatter is already saying it was a planned attack. We really should head over."

"Have you tried getting through to dispatch to see if they want us there?"

"I tried, but no luck. Dispatch is redirecting rigs from Prescott–Russell, Renfrew, Leeds and Lanark Counties until we know what hit us. Shouldn't we just head over? The city is going nuts, Ethan!"

"They have enough confusion to deal with. Try the land line. I'll try calling

HQ." Michael paced back and forth, wanting to do something, anything...looking helpless.

"Mike, clean the truck. Get it ready to roll. It will help if we are cleaned and stocked if they need us mobile." A simple nod from Michael indicated his agreement.

Adrian went inside the ER to phone dispatch for directions as Michael ran to the rig. Getting clean uniforms would have to wait. So would completing the electronic Patient Care Report form for this call. We were the only rig at the Queensway–Carleton Hospital. All the other rigs would have been on calls or responding to the Civic ER.

I pulled myself away from the crowd to collect my thoughts. I couldn't recall if EMS had ever been the target of a planned, coordinated attack.

Adrian came running into the garage from the ER, "Ethan, dispatch wants us ready to roll, but we stay put until we hear . . ." His words trailed off.

My cell phone started to vibrate and ring inside my shirt pocket.

"Hello."

"Do I have your attention, Ethan?" The voice was calm, assertive and authoritarian.

"Excuse me? Who is this?"

"We tried earlier to retrieve our property from you, but you proved to be more resourceful than we anticipated." There was a slight deliberate pause from the caller. "We sent one of our best men to speak with you and have you return property that is rightfully ours."

"You sent him to kill me, not have a little heart-to-heart about current affairs!" My voice rose above the level of conversation of the crowd that had gathered to listen to the radios. Heads turned, a few walked a little closer. The bay door to the ambulance garage was open. I walked to the open door. I had to squint against the afternoon sun.

"Nonetheless, you still have my property, and I want it back."

"What happened to the guy at my house? Is he dead?"

"Would it make you feel better if I told you if he was alive or dead?"

"Neither. I just want you to know what I am capable of."

"That's a poor attempt to intimidate me. Now, what about the code?"

"If you're talking about the jump drive, I gave it to the police. They have it. I don't. Go ask them yourself. Maybe they'll give it back." Sarcasm!

"Then you better hope you can get it back. What time have you got?"

I looked at my watch. "One-ten."

"You have until ten tomorrow morning to get it back from the police and call me. Listen carefully, Ethan. Do you have call display on your phone?"

"Yes."

"Read the number I'm calling from back to me."

I pulled the phone away from my ear. Looking at the number on the display, I repeated it out loud, "It's 613–555–0803."

Nurses, doctors, and police officers started to gather around me. The tone of my voice and the topic of conversation had attracted unwanted attention.

"Good. When you get the jump drive back from the police, call this number. And don't grow a brain; don't try to be smart! This number is a burner phone, so you can't trace it. If you don't call before ten a.m. tomorrow, another hospital may experience the same fate. Or maybe a nursing home, who the hell knows? It may even be a grade school, for all I know."

"What if I can't get it back?" I looked at my watch. It was already 1:12. I was purposely dragging out the conversation to see if the caller would slip and disclose some minor detail or reveal an accent, or I would hear a noise in the background--but nothing so far.

"Don't test me, Ethan! If we blow up part of a hospital just to get your attention, what do you think we will do if you don't get the drive back?"

I walked outside into the sunlight and was pacing around the parking lot, thinking of something to say to get more clues as to who the caller was.

"I know where it is, and getting it is going to be hard, but not impossible. Where do you want to meet?" I knew I had a copy of the jump drive on my computer at home.

"When you get the drive, call me by ten tomorrow morning if you want to avoid a repeat of today." The line went dead.

I stared at the phone. The phone call timer read over four minutes. The time across the header on the phone read 1:14. Time was on my side, but I needed to know what my options were. Only one person could help me with that.

I began to thumb a text to Galen. He shouldn't be at the Civic Hospital incident. Not yet, anyway.

Within a few minutes, my phone beeped a reply.

I called Dave Green, our shift commander, with a request to go mobile and explained we would still be available and that dispatch had enough to worry about without going through them.

Permission was granted.

I looked over to see Adrian speaking with several police officers. The entire group looked far too serious and quiet for there to be any good news. I got Adrian's attention. Michael was still in the back of the rig cleaning.

"Mike, Adrian! We're leaving!"

CHAPTER 18

The ride from the Queensway–Carleton to the electronics store was silent. No one dared speak for fear of missing news coming over the radio. We headed west on the 417. Traffic was light, the mood sombre. Michael and Adrian listened for updates from dispatch or the crews. Radio chatter was confusing...talk of casualties and injuries. But worst of all, no one made mention of whether any of the injured were medics, cops, hospital staff, or civilians.

I turned north from the 417 onto Terry Fox Drive and into the business plaza on the east side of the road. The business complex was an intricate weave of roads around stand-alone grocery stores, small shops, restaurants, and tiny strip plazas, carefully designed to create confusion and keep you in the area and take you to the next shopping experience instead of to the exit. I found what I wanted, came to a stop, grabbed the portable radio, said nothing, and exited the vehicle. No one offered to join me. Perfect! I would not be a great conversationalist. I felt tense, my jaw clenched. Sunglasses hid the anger in my eyes and my mood was best described as anger surrounded by a thick layer of "totally pissed off."

I walked over to the aisle where they kept memory cards and storage devices. Looking around, I saw nothing that resembled the tiny white stick I had given to Galen. There were various styles of jump drives, flash drives, and USB drives. All did the same, but each one was unique in shape, colour, and make.

A young sales representative saw my confusion and walked over, smile ever present, eager to earn his commission. Thin, pale, too much time playing video games and not enough time outside, smarter than I ever will be when it comes to technobabble, he looked confident in his ability to help.

"Having a hard time deciding which one you need?" he asked.

"Yeah! Looking for a specific type." With thumb and index finger I showed him the approximate size of the jump drive. "White, thin, had the name of a movie character on it, like E.T. or Teddy Ruxpin, or something like that." I was showing my age.

"Gizmo drives, from the movie Gremlins, remember? We have them over here." He turned, indicating he wanted me to follow. "What size do you want?"

"Shit!" I hadn't thought about the capacity of the drive. What if they actually knew how many gigabytes the drive was capable of holding?

"What?"

I had to make an excuse. "I borrowed my wife's drive and lost it. She keeps telling me to be more careful with things and I will never hear the end of it if I don't replace it with the right one." I pulled my glasses up onto my head, figuring my lie would be more believable if he could see my eyes.

"No problem. How old was the drive? An older drive will no doubt have a smaller capacity. So how long have you had it?"

Think! If you were putting an encrypted file on a drive for some covert operation, would you risk using an old drive or buy a new one?

"It was only a few weeks old. Pretty new, I guess."

He pulled a blister pack off the rack. The pack said, "Gizmo Jr. 8gb." The price tag read $14.99. I handed him a twenty-dollar bill and turned. "I gotta go."

"Sir, what about your change?"

"Keep it."

Adrian stood outside the passenger door of the rig. He looked nauseated. Adrian had taken a phone call from one of the other medics reporting that four medics had been seriously hurt in the blast, and one toddler in a stroller had been killed by flying shrapnel when she and her mother were walking past the ER on the Carling Avenue sidewalk.

The whole event was hitting home. It was one thing to hear about the explosion over the air, quite another when colleagues and civilians were killed because of something I was involved in. Could this have been prevented? Was I somehow indirectly responsible for the death of a little girl and my injured co-workers?

I gave my head a good shake and realized I was not the one who set the explosives. I was not the one who planted or detonated them. I was not the one who plotted to...Plotted to do what?

I sat in the driver's seat, placed both hands on the wheel, paused, and stared straight ahead.

"What?" Adrian asked.

"Nothing. All this shit is getting to me."

A few years ago, I was married, quite happily, to a beautiful, wonderful woman, working a job with the best partner a guy could hope for, and a house almost paid off. The most exciting thing to happen in my life had been the cable going out in the middle of a hockey game! In the past year, I have been shot at, wrecked my car in a high speed chase, had my house catch fire, and stabbed a guy with a wooden stake. Now this! And I still have to pass along an encrypted file to some guy who might blow up...something, if I don't get it to him in time.

"Ethan, Ethan, you okay?"

My mind was far off in a distant cloud, my thoughts murky; I was staring straight ahead, seeing nothing.

"Hey, Ethan, wake up! You stroke out or something?" Adrian was pushing my right arm with enough force that I rocked in my seat. I turned to look at him. "You've been sitting there staring for over a minute. Just staring!"

"You okay, bud? You're scaring the bejesus out of us!" Michael peered through the window from the patient compartment of the ambulance. I pulled the rear-view mirror down to see Michael looking at me with concern.

"A lot going on right now, that's all," I reassured them.

2:05. Time was passing fast, and I still had a lot to do. I put the vehicle in drive and headed for my house.

*****

Galen sat in the living room, nursing a headache by rubbing a Diet Coke across his forehead. A strange woman sat in front of my laptop, looked up from behind the screen long enough to acknowledge my presence, and went back to work on the keyboard. Galen had the look of someone stressed beyond his limit and wanting to call it a day. He looked like he had aged years since the last time we spoke. The lines around his eyes were more pronounced, and condensation from the pop can had formed tiny canals in the wrinkles above his eyebrows.

"Would you mind telling me how the fuck you got a copy of this fucking code while I was sitting in the same fucking room as you?" He stood, slamming the pop can down hard on the coffee table, sending liquid shooting up from the opening.

"I made a copy when you were on the phone. Hi!" I walked over to the computer technician working on my laptop and extended my hand.

"You can't be making illegal copies of police property--" Galen's voice echoed in the background. He kept yelling at me while I introduced myself.

"Nice to meet you!" She reached up and shook my hand.

"I'm Ethan, and you are?"

"Nicole."

I smiled at Nicole and walked into the kitchen. She looked all of twenty, pretty, geeky, and was tapping away on my laptop, which was connected to another laptop beside it by cables running in and out of various ports. I returned with four bottles of water. I glanced at Galen, "I can always tell when you're stressed by the amount of colourful adjectives you use in your sentences." I opened the front door. "I won't be long."

Adrian stood waiting for two of the bottles, thanked me, and walked away.

When I returned, the IT technician looked up from her keyboard at me, over at Galen, back to me, then back to the keyboard. Clicking sounds started again. I placed a bottle of water on the coffee table next to Nicole.

I sat across from Galen, cracked my bottle and drank most of the contents. Nicole looked at me again, then back at Galen.

"Done yelling at me? I feel like I'm about to get whacked, here. What's going on?"

Galen explained that he'd had to tell his chief, Richard Stabenow, and that Stabenow had ordered some changes to the code. If the Ottawa Police IT technicians or CSIS couldn't decode the book cypher, they certainly would not simply hand it over without ensuring they had the upper hand.

"I'm almost done." She didn't even look up from the computer. Galen and I joined her on the couch, sitting on either side and watching as she did her magic.

"All done! This was fun. I've never done this before, but it was actually quite easy."

"What did you do?" Galen asked. Galen had problems downloading music to his MP3 player.

"I embedded a steganography virus within the numerical code used in the book cypher."

We looked at her inquisitively. Nicole was now fully aware we were not computer literate.

"Come on, guys, this is basic stuff. I took the code you found on the jump drive and inserted a Trojan horse concealed within the numbers that mimics the original text, but I encoded the virus to email us the whatever-it-is written in code, once it has been opened or broken."

"You can do that?" I asked.

"You would be surprised what you can do with computers! If it were an image, it would be easy-peasy, but text is a little harder, although not much. Let me explain: Companies that make printers insert tiny dots when you print a picture. Those tiny dots include information telling you what type of printer was used and date-stamp the image. Same idea, here--I inserted tiny parts of the numbers to conceal code, which, when broken down and reassembled, gives their computer an order to send an email to our office--well, my office--with the final message. And they don't even know they did it. Like I said, easy-peasy!"

"The bad guys get the actual encryption, so you aren't trying to fool them. Even if we don't know what it is right now, when they insert the jump drive into their computer, it uploads the virus, and when they open it or decode it, we will know all about it."

She turned to me and put her hand out.

"Oh, yeah!" I took the new Gizmo drive from my breast pocket and handed it to her.

She inserted the drive into my laptop and downloaded the book cypher and the steganography virus. When she was finished, she ejected it from the USB port and handed it to me and smiled.

"Really guys, the Internet can do more than porn!"

"I still haven't learned to set the clock on my VCR." My eyebrows rose.

"VCR! Really? No one uses VCRs anymore."

I turned and pointed. Under the TV was a blinking "12:00" in red. I'm a total technotard.

"If it's a Betamax, I'm stealing it!"

"Sorry!" I shrugged my shoulders.

She looked sad that the VCR was VHS, smiled, gathered up her gear, threw it all in her messenger bag, and departed. She left her water bottle behind, unopened.

"Now what?" Galen asked.

"It's 2:45. Now I have to call and arrange a meeting."

"Just to lighten the mood, if Liz finds out about this, we are totally, completely fucked in every way; she will get fucking mad and kill us. Not figuratively, I mean literally, we are fucking dead."

"Thanks for the pep talk, big guy."

CHAPTER 19

I drove east on the 417. Adrian and Michael must have thought we were heading for the Civic Emergency to help with the wounded. They had no clue I had already spoken with my mysterious caller and arranged an appointment to drop off the USB jump drive. As we headed east, not a word was spoken. We listened to the radio with details of the explosion. It became extremely apparent just how desperate these people were to get back the jump drive with the cypher. Whatever the code would reveal was important enough to kill innocent people for no other reason than to get my attention. I began to feel responsible, as if, somehow, my actions or inactions had caused the events to unfold the way they had.

I began to go through the details of the past few days, the strange happenings that resulted in the death of one paramedic, people who were simply living their lives, hurt or killed by a group of individuals determined to do whatever was necessary to get back whatever it was on that drive. One group wanted their property back; one group determined to take it away; and then there was me, not wanting anyone to get it. The information on the jump drive in my pocket was so important that it was worth the taking of lives. Maybe that was the point.

My mind raced with details: Events repeated themselves, playing forward in slow motion, backwards, then they all seemed to flow together in one jumbled mess of death, destruction, and chaos. Maddy suddenly appeared in my thoughts, standing beside Becky. They were talking to each other. Talking about me? Images I couldn't, and didn't, want to think about at this time. I narrowed my eyes, forcing the pictures from my mind, choosing to focus on the road before me. The explosion had caused the Queensway to become a stalled parking lot. We were travelling at less than fifty kilometres an hour. The line of traffic going east and west on the Queensway was endless. On a good day, traffic was bad; today, traffic was hell.

The Woodroffe Avenue exit was coming up. I banked along the off-ramp, heading south on Woodroffe then east along Baseline Road.

I always enjoyed the ride along Baseline Road. In the middle of a major city, Ottawa has an experimental farm framed between Merivale Road on the west, Carling Avenue to the north, Prince of Wales to the east, and Baseline on the south. Urban living borders the entire farm, creating an off-kilter effect of rural and urban life in the nation's capital. Ottawa is the only world capital with a working farm within the city limits. For several blocks north of Baseline, in the middle of Ottawa, farmers grow various crops, host school visits, and house the Canadian Agricultural Museum.

Driving along Baseline Road, seeing the city on the south and the country to the north, the perfect balance always made me feel comfortable somehow; and today, I needed that. At Prince of Wales, Baseline Road turns into Heron Road, crosses the Ottawa River, and continues east until Heron ends at Walkley Road. The Ottawa Paramedic Services Headquarters is only a kilometre away, on Don Reid Drive.

"Are we not going to the Civic?" Adrian was looking at me from the passenger seat, disappointed that we weren't going to help out.

"They want us back at headquarters. I'm dropping you guys off then heading out again. I've got some stuff to take care of."

"Stuff to take care of!" Adrian voiced his displeasure. "What about our guys who got hurt? You have some personal shit to take care of?" He had turned in his seat and was now yelling at me.

I held in my anger. Adrian and Michael had no idea that I was possibly the cause of the events that were transpiring today.

"This does have to do with what happened at the Civic." I turned to face him. "All right?" I screamed back. "I'm sorry, I have to leave, but really, this has to do with what happened. I just can't tell you about it, okay?" I said, dealing with traffic.

There was silence in the rig. The calming effect of the Experimental Farm had eluded me. The tension was high in the cab. Even Michael sat silent in the patient compartment.

The rig slowly banked right along Baseline Road through the Prince of Wales Drive intersection where it becomes Heron Road on the other side. The sun shot rays of the golden domes of the Ukrainian Catholic church on the north side of Heron. Turning my eyes back toward the road, a large plume of dust cut through the rays, brake lights turned bright, tires squealed on the hot, dry asphalt, and traffic came to an abrupt halt. A large ball of dirt settled on the south bank of Heron, a huge grass section along the south of Heron Road where evergreens stood firm a hundred yards from the road.

Adrian looked at me. Whatever tension existed within the cab was now gone. Work mode kicked in.

An SUV was lying on its passenger side, the vehicle pointed toward the trees. Two tire tracks marked the spot where the driver had lost control, hopped the curb, and began to flip the vehicle in the grass. People had stopped their cars, jumped out, and started to run to the overturned vehicle.

Adrian picked up the mike. I activated the lights and hit the air horn to grab everyone's attention.

"Ottawa, 4129."

"Four-one-two-nine."

"We've just witnessed a rollover on Heron Road, just east of the Prince of Wales intersection. Roll Fire and 10–2s, please."

"Ten-four. Please be advised we have no other available vehicles at this time. In service 15:10."

"Shit!" I should be dropping these guys off and heading out to make the jump drive drop-off at 4:30. That gave me only an hour and twenty minutes to do the call, get back to HQ, and make the rendezvous.

Adrian looked at me, "You expecting there to be more than one patient?"

"If there are, the Civic is just up the street, and we'll have to bring the patients to either the QC or the Ottawa General." I had to explain my outburst with some excuse.

Stopped traffic had blocked both lanes going east on Heron. It was easier to drive onto the grass and avoid the vehicles. The rig hit the curb, the front tires bucked for a moment and landed hard on the grass. I drove beside the original tire marks in the grass to leave evidence for the police. I pulled the rig just south of the curb, and stopped about forty yards from where the SUV had come to rest. This would give the fire department plenty of room to bring their rigs into place and secure the vehicle if necessary.

Adrian and Michael exited the vehicle, donned their helmets and safety yellow vests, I went to the back of the rig, and pulled the cot out with the defib, trauma bag, oxygen, medication kit, back board, and spinal immobilization bag loaded on top.

A small crowd had gathered around the SUV. The driver's door was already open and a young man was lifting himself up through the door with the aid of bystanders. Adrian called out to the crowd asking them to stay back from the scene. As they approached the overturned vehicle, Adrian, who had the foot of the cot, turned, looked at Michael and, without saying a word, they lowered the cot to half height.

The man had pulled himself from the driver's side and jumped from the top of the SUV to the ground. He limped toward Adrian.

"My mother's in the passenger seat. She was talking to me and then nothing. I mean nothing. She was staring forward like a freaking zombie. I reached for her, lost control." He leaned forward, put his hands on his knees, paused, took a deep breath and continued, "And the car hit the curb and flipped. She never wears her seat belt. She wasn't talking when I got out."

In the background, fire sirens could be heard. They would be here shortly. I stood beside the young driver, placed my hand on his shoulder.

"You hurt?" He stood tall.

"What are they going to do? My mom . . ." his words trailed off.

"Your mother's in good hands. My partner knows his job. What about you?" I stared him in the face. "What's your name?"

"No, no, nothing." He stared forward at the SUV lying on its side in the middle of the field. "No, no, nothing."

"You said that already. What's your name?" His eyes were blank. He kept looking ahead without really seeing.

I turned to Adrian and called out to him.

He turned and held up a single finger indicating one patient. "The windshield is shattered. Mike is treating her through it, but we can't get in until Fire secures the vehicle."

I motioned him to join me. When I turned my attention back to the driver, his face was pale, eyes blank, without warning, he simply collapsed into my arms. I caught him and helped him slowly to the ground. Adrian rushed over, knelt and carefully placed both hands on either side of his head. With one hand, Adrian reached forward and felt for a carotid pulse on the side of the unconscious man's trachea. The patient's chest rose as he took each breath. No answer or look of panic in Adrian's eyes indicated the patient was only unconscious.

"Collar kit?" I asked.

"Over on the cot. There's more gear in the back? No more help coming, is there."

"Nope!"

I stood, looked over at the SUV, and saw that Michael already had the defib attached to the driver's mother, to get a set of vitals, and a green oxygen line was visible alongside the rest of the cables. He was on his knees, reaching through the fractured windshield as far as he could to treat the unconscious female patient. There wasn't much he could do until Fire had secured the vehicle, making it safe to enter.

I went inside the back of the rig and retrieved a blood pressure cuff, cervical collar, cervical immobilization device, and a blue plastic backboard and straps. The equipment was laid on the ground beside our male patient. First we applied the cervical collar. Adrian held the patient's head, and I slid the back half under his neck then folded the front under his chin. The Velcro strap held the collar secure and in place. I reached inside the tracheal hole for a carotid pulse. He still had a good, strong pulse.

Although the patient was up and walking as we arrived, what I needed now was a set of vitals. I wrapped the cuff around his left upper arm, placed the diaphragm of my scope over the brachial artery, and took a quick blood pressure: 96/52. Hypotensive! That could be the reason why he passed out. We didn't have another oxygen bag so we had to get the patient into the back of the rig quickly.

Several fire trucks arrived on scene, and the firefighters spread out to secure the SUV.

Adrian and I logrolled the patient onto his right side, and I performed a quick spinal test, examining the thoracic and lumbar vertebrae from the base of the cervical collar to his pelvis. After the exam, I placed the board against his back and we rolled him back down. We crisscrossed two straps across the patient's chest, one strap across his pelvis and one across the lower legs. A firefighter in full turnout gear approached to lend a hand.

Adrian instructed him to get inside the back of the rig so we could hand off the board and secure the patient to the bench seat. On the count of three, Adrian and I lifted the patient secured to the board and walked him to the back of the rig. We hoisted him high to the waiting firefighter who helped pull him up. I held the foot end of the spinal board and Adrian went to the side door to enter the patient compartment and assist with hauling the board up. The board was secured to the bench seat. Adrian, with the assistance of the firefighter, took over the care of the male patient, while I went over to give Michael a hand.

The scene had changed with the arrival of the fire department. Large planks of wood, placed in strategic locations along the undercarriage and the roof of the car, kept it stable. Hoses had been laid out in case fire broke out; and the hood was opened and the battery cables disconnected to reduce the risk of the air bags deploying.

I touched Michael to let him know I was standing behind him. He pulled his head out from inside the cab of the SUV.

"Whatcha got?" I asked.

"Elderly lady, unconscious, no seat belt, no air bags deployed, so they rolled side to side. I managed to reach in and attached the three-lead, O2, glucose 5.7, can't reach in and get an IV in from this angle. I got a set of vitals, but I can't do a stroke test. Shit, I can't do a lot, no collar yet. The airway is patent, wide open. She has been snoring, even with the oral airway in, and her sats are hitting 100. Now that you're here, what do you want me to do? Give you a hand with the KED and prep for extrication?"

"You're in charge of the call, bud! What do you want?" I wanted Michael to take full control and direct the care and treatment of the patient.

"In that case, get your ass in there and give me a hand with the IV and spinal." He smiled.

Turning around, I bumped into a firefighter who was standing right behind me. He must have been listening to our conversation about the patient.

"I'll climb in there and give you guys a hand. There's personal shit all over the place and the squeeze will be tight." His offer surprised both Michael and me.

"That's okay, we got it." Michael went to step around him.

He didn't take kindly to being rejected. "I used to be a medic for Ottawa before I got into Fire. I know what I'm doing."

"Once again, thank you, we can handle the situation from here. If you want to help, get a ladder and hold it while he climbs in!" Michael's voice raised an octave. I moved to step between them.

"You guys have enough to worry about. Let me help," the firefighter insisted.

Michael stepped into the firefighter, causing him to back up and hit the roof of the SUV. Michael had fire in his eyes. They were inches apart. "We got it. Are we clear?" Michael was in charge of the patient and wasn't afraid to show it. Stress from the day's event also played a part in Michael's outburst.

The firefighter shook his head up and down so fast I thought his helmet was going to hit Michael in the face.

"Is there a problem here?" A voice with the air of authority spoke behind me. One of the fire commanders on scene came over to investigate.

"Is there a problem?" Michael's gaze never left the firefighter.

"No, not at all." Again, he shook his head to indicate he understood. Nothing more was said on the matter. He disappeared and returned with a metal ladder. With two hands, he spiked the ladder into the ground, pushed it firmly against the overturned vehicle and placed his foot on the bottom rung without saying a word.

I tightened my helmet strap before ascending the ladder. The back passenger door had been too badly damaged in the roll-over to be opened without major effort from Fire, and, since the driver's door was undamaged, no efforts had been made to release the back door. Several firefighters had just finished forcing the driver's door back against the front fender and tied it securely to the front tire. From the top of the SUV, I could see the carnage on the grass. Small vehicle parts had fallen off the SUV each time the vehicle rolled and made contact with the ground. Dark, muddy furrows marked each spot and stood in contrast to the green where the grass gave way.

My foot pressed against the centre console to brace myself. I reached in and grabbed the steering wheel to hold my weight as I lowered myself down. The moment my weight shifted from the door sill, the front tires had enough slack to drop to the earth causing the steering wheel to spin in hand. My balance shifted and I dropped a foot or so until my other foot found the centre console.

The elderly lady was directly beneath me, her two arms and head were framed by the fractured windshield. Michael turned his head enough to see where I was and covered the patient's face in case debris fell from my boots or off the console.

With both feet secured, I placed both hands on the back of the front seat and wiggled my way into the back seat. The firefighter was right: Fruit, vegetables, boxes of cereal, and meat had been freed from their grocery bags during the rollover. I pulled one leg through and found a ledge to place it on where the centre armrest tucked away when not in use. I pulled my other leg and let myself drop down to the back passenger window below. I knelt on the window and felt cool fruit juices from freshly squeezed produce penetrate the material of my pants. I looked down to see a medley of orange, banana, grape, and apple puree covering the back window.

Pulling myself over the side of the passenger seat, I finally reached the patient and held her head in place to minimize any further possible complications. The best of a worst-case scenario.

"Have a good trip down?" Michael asked.

"Peachy!"

"Yeah? Haven't seen any peaches in this mess."

"Funny man! Okay, let's get her out. Again, airway good, vitals stable, unconscious, but from this angle, no way to tube. What size oral airway did you insert?"

Fire started up a generator, making communication difficult. Michael answered by holding up four fingers.

Our conversation had become a yelling contest.

It was easier to communicate with hand gestures or with a single word. Michael reached in with a collar, I held her head, and the collar was positioned to keep the cervical spine as straight as possible.

A blanket had been tossed through the open driver's door. We covered ourselves and the patient. It was obvious from the noise that they had begun to cut away the roof, and the blanket would protect us from flying hot metal shards. Under the cover, we wrapped our patient in a KED, a green nylon vest with slats to keep the spine in perfect alignment with the head and reduce the risk of movement during extrication.

The "A" pillar--the support for the windshield and the driver's door--and the "B" pillar--the support between the driver's door and the passengers--were cut away by powerful pneumatic tools. Michael excused himself as fire began to cut the "A" pillar on the passenger side. I remained inside, under the blanket, protecting the patient, while my partner watched the monitor from outside the vehicle.

The roof was slowly being winched back, and sunlight now filled the cab of the SUV. By the time I came out from underneath the blanket, a spinal board was already knifed into place under the patient's buttocks, with the head of the board resting on the edge of the cot. Michael directed the firefighter where to stand and hold the board. He asked another to reach in and grab hold of the patient and haul her up in one motion once I gave the "Go" signal.

I stood, placed one hand on the dash, and inspected her legs to ensure that they were free of any entanglements or anything that would interfere with the move to the board. I looked at Michael and gave the all go.

"On three, guys! One, two, three!" On three, the patient went from the cab of the vehicle to resting supine on the board. She was secured with straps. Foam tube CIDs were positioned on either side of her head and taped into place. Michael completed a full secondary survey to see if he could find any further injury. I finished my tasks at the same time as Michael. We had enough hands to pick up the cot and carry it over the rough terrain instead of rolling it to the ambulance. Four firefighters assisted us lifting and carrying the cot.

The patient was now placed beside her son, who lay on the bench seat inside the ambulance. He was now conscious and talkative. Adrian explained that the son had regained consciousness shortly after I left and explained he had a history of fainting during times of stress.

Michael connected the oxygen line to the wall port, ran another set of vitals, and the two patients, with the two medics, were ready for transport.

I closed the back doors and walked to the driver's door. As I pulled it open, a hard object was pushed into my back. It was only a few days earlier that I'd had the same feeling of cold steel against me.

CHAPTER 20

"Give me the jump drive!" He pushed the gun harder into my back. His voice was not familiar, but the feel of the gun was.

"I was supposed to meet you at 4:30. I still have time."

The crowd that had gathered around the accident paid no attention to two men casually having a discussion by an ambulance. They were focused on the SUV that had rolled and the firefighters still working.

"I think you have me confused with the other guys. I'm the owner of the code and I want it back. Kautz works--or should I say, used to work--for me. It was stolen from me, so hand it over. Now!" The unmistakable sound of the hammer being cocked back was enough to make me obey.

I peeled back the Velcro on my breast pocket flap and reached in. "You wouldn't shoot me in front of all these people would you?"

"Actually," pause, "I would."

My fingers found the tiny drive. "Would you mind telling me one thing? What's on this thing?"

"If we had time, I would. Hand it over!" He sounded as if he was ordering me through clenched teeth. Even in the afternoon heat, I could feel his breath on my neck.

With the jump drive in hand, I reached back over my shoulder and felt the drive being pulled from my fingers.

"Who are you talking to?" I heard Adrian call out from the patient compartment. I stuck my head in and yelled back. "No one."

I never noticed that the pressure had disappeared from against my back. I turned, hoping to see the man who took the jump drive. There were dozens of people moving about the scene behind the ambulance. No one stood out; no one was running or didn't look like they fit in.

"Shit." Had I just handed over the jump drive to the wrong guy. Or did I? I was getting confused about who each side was. I didn't have a scorecard to keep track and had no clue who the players were.

The vehicle was already idling, the engine warm. I put it in gear. "All set?"

With two approvals, I made my way slowly off the grass, booked with dispatch, and headed for Ottawa General Hospital Emergency.

*****

I paced around the covered ambulance parking garage of Ottawa General Emergency Department. Galen had me on hold. I looked at my watch. I had less than ten minutes before I was supposed to meet the other party and give them the jump drive. I could feel the tension rising in my chest, my stomach was sour, and my mouth dry.

Music designed to soothe irate customers on hold played loudly in my ear. One song finished, another began. Nine minutes until my meeting. The music continued. My pace quickened.

The door to the garage opened and another ambulance parked beside mine. The driver exited the rig, walked to the back door, and opened it. Another ACP hopped to the ground and acknowledged my presence. The phone was still stuck to my ear.

"What've ya got?" I asked as the wheels of the cot hit the concrete floor.

The ACP was someone on the same rotation as me but rarely worked with. I knew her, not well, just enough to say hi and chat. She had been an ACP for only a little over a year but was well respected.

"Chest pain, more morphine problems! I called Base Hospital and asked to give twice the protocol, and still no effect. Do you know anything more about this than the rest of us?"

With the phone still firmly affixed to the side of my head, I shook "No" as they wheeled past me through the glass doors. Seven minutes.

Galen broke the piano music. "Call him. Cancel the meeting. Make up some bullshit, piece of crap story, anything believable to delay the meeting. We're putting together another drive and getting it over to you in less than twenty minutes."

"You want me to lie to a guy who blew up the Civic ER?"

"The alternative would be what exactly?"

I hung up on Galen, found the number in my phone history and hit redial. The voice on the other end of the phone answered almost right away.

"Do you have it?" he asked.

"Not exactly!" I immediately felt how stale the air was in the garage.

"What does 'Not exactly' mean? Either you have it, or you don't."

"It'll be a few more minutes, then I can meet you. What's a few minutes?"

"Why? Don't you have the jump drive, Ethan?"

"Something came up, something unavoidable." I decided not to tell him I didn't have the jump drive and was pacing around the Ottawa General Emergency garage. The tension felt heavy on my chest. I kept wiping my brow, inspecting the amount of sweat that had gathered on my hand between wipes.

"What came up that was so important that you can't make the drop-off?"

I really had to come up with something fast. My mind played scenarios in

96

fast forward, rewound, played from different angles but seemed plausible. I didn't realize I hadn't spoken for almost a minute when he broke the silence.

"Why don't you just say you're on a call and you're now stuck in the ER? Tell the truth instead of trying to come up with some bullshit excuse."

I was dumbstruck. He knew I was in the Ottawa General Hospital ER. But how? I was being followed, and if he knew I was still in the ER, he would have to be close by. I ran for the automatic garage door. I frantically waved my hand in front of the sensor and the steel door rolled up.

I was already out of breath when I exited the garage and onto the open section of the upper ER ramp. The emergency department ramp is comprised of two sections; the ramp meanders from the ground level up to an elevated level looking down on the main entrance below. The first open section of the parking structure is for drive-in patients to the ER. Just after the car turnaround, a large enclosed garage is controlled by a keypad restricting access to emergency vehicles and the police only.

The phone grasped tight in my hand, I ran across the open parking lot and looked down to the road below.

Cars drove in slowly and pulled under the main entrance overhang to drop off visitors, employees or pick them up. Across from the main entrance was a small row of short-term parking, a hundred or so feet from where I stood.

I had to catch my breath. "You're right. I shouldn't lie. We got assigned to a call and we can't refuse emergencies." I gulped fresh air. I scanned the road, the drop-off zone, the short-term parking for any sign of the person on the other end of my phone. "With what you did at the Civic Hospital, the city is short on rigs. A car accident came in. Refusing was not an option."

"Next time, just say that. I hate fucking liars."

My eyes went from one person to the next, to the next. No one seemed out of place, no one stood out, speaking on a cell phone. I peered over the concrete rail to see the crowd below under the main entrance overhang, and my feet left the ground. A hand grabbed my belt and I was suddenly jerked back, my feet landing hard on the parking lot. I turned. Adrian stood looking back at me, full of questions. I held my index finger perpendicular to my lips. Adrian shrugged his shoulders.

"Yeah, well, I hate people who blow things up just to get my attention. You may have killed some of my friends at the Civic." I held the phone in front of me instead of against my cheek. I wanted the full effect of yelling to be caught by the microphone.

"Don't tempt me, you fucking little prick, or I'll--" Gotcha! The voice kept speaking, but I paid no attention. A figure sitting in a car that had backed into the space was yelling into his phone. The voice matched the lip movements of the person in the driver's seat. From this angle and distance, I couldn't see his face.

I cut him off, "I just realized...you really--I mean really--need whatever is on this drive, don't you? Otherwise, you wouldn't be so fucking pissed right now, would you?"

Dead air. There was no response. The man in the car sat still. I turned to Adrian and pointed at my phone. He replied with a puzzled look. I pointed at my phone then back to him. He understood and pulled his phone from his shirt pocket.

"You need this drive for something and your plans got all fucked up and you keep screwing things up trying to get it back." I pulled the phone from my face and the blue phone screen appeared. I pressed the "mute" button.

"Does your phone record conversations?" Adrian nodded.

"Great! Start it now and keep quiet, please." Adrian fumbled through the apps and activated the Voice Recorder and held it up to my phone. Instead of releasing the mute, I pressed the Speaker Phone button.

"--you little shit. You'll give me that jump drive, you puke, or I'll set off another bomb, and better yet, I'll set it off at the EMS headquarters or maybe a school. How would you like to be responsible for the death of children?"

"You set off the explosion at the Civic, didn't you?"

"Yeah." Got him!

"Now you're threatening to blow up a school and you're trying to play some sick psychological game saying it's somehow my fault if you don't get what you want."

Silence.

"Why don't you tell me what's on this thing and I'll decide if I want to give it to you?" I watched the lip movements carefully and I knew I had the guy. I pulled out a pen and yanked Adrian's hand toward me, palm up.

"Give me the drive and no one else has to die!" I was now in control. I squinted and focused on the licence plate below, C....or O, N, E or F, 7 or 9, 1, 0 or 8. Adrian stared at me, watching me squinting at the cars below. He grabbed the pen from my hand, gazed hard and realized what I was staring at. He ran a stroke through the O, 9 and the 8; CNE 710; Ontario plates; blue, blue what? Was it a Ford or a KIA? There was a silver logo in the centre of the grill.

"Tell you what, let's call it a draw and we each go our separate ways!" I turned and ran toward the garage. Adrian followed close behind, arm outstretched in a vain attempt to keep his phone close to mine to continue recording. The voice on the other end grew louder, but I was unable to hear exactly what he was saying.

"Yeah!" I said when there was a pause on the other end. I pushed in the code to re-enter the covered garage, opened the driver's door to our rig, jumped in, strapped myself in and brought the engine to life. I pressed the "Mute" button on the cell phone.

"'Yeah?' You fucking idiot! That's your answer?" I could hear the voice scream at me.

I had no idea what I was answering to or at this point what he was talking about. Adrian stood in between me and the driver's door. My raised eyebrows were enough of a question.

"What do you think you're doing?" he asked.

"I'm going after him."

"Not unless I go with you."

I unmuted the phone, held it up to my ear and caught him mid-sentence, "-- you think you can get away with that?"

"Gonna try my best." Again, no clue to what I was answering to. Mute.

I hissed at Adrian, "Plausible deniability! If you don't come with me, you can say you didn't know what I was doing. Or tell them I hit you!"

Adrian cocked his head to one side. He was at least four inches taller and fifty pounds heavier than me.

I reached for the door handle. Adrian stepped aside.

"Call it in! Give them the guy's plate number and type of car."

I put the rig in drive, rolled forward, and pulled the driver's door shut. "Tell them you saw me drive away before you could stop me," I yelled through the open window. The phone was still connected, but I pocketed it in my shirt.

The aluminum garage door rolled up as I approached and drove under before it was fully retracted, almost scraping the bottom of it. My speed accelerated as I approached the ramp down to the main level below. The speed of the ambulance caused the front tires to become airborne and slam down hard on the concrete surface. The back tires did the same when they crested the ramp.

The sight of an ambulance speeding down the emergency ramp caught the attention of the man on the other end of the phone. He looked up and for a moment we stared at each other as I drove down the ramp. My intent was to block him in, smash the front end of the car, something...anything!

I was less than twenty feet away when his car pulled right from the parking spot and accelerated, causing the rear of the car to swing wildly into the oncoming lane. Since no one was coming or blocking my way, I pressed hard on the gas. Where the ramp meets the road, the front end of the ambulance hit the pavement and bucked, forcing me back in my seat. I turned left, and the rig jerked hard.

The sound of squealing tires and metal scraping on asphalt caused visitors and staff walking in and out the Ottawa General Hospital to turn and stare at the flurry of activity. He sped through the service road intersection that connects the Children's Hospital to the Ottawa General and increased his speed as he came upon Smyth Road. The red light stopped traffic from exiting the OGH turning east onto Smyth. The blue sedan turned left through the red light and headed east on Smyth Road. Cars slammed on their brakes, skidded, and jumped the curbs to a halt to avoid causing an accident. He blew through the four-lane intersection and accelerated faster than I could ever hope to do in a heavy diesel cube ambulance.

Blindly, I reached down, activating the emergency lights and siren. More heads turned, cars blindly pulled over or simply kept driving. When I arrived at the intersection, I cranked the wheel hard, making the rig lean hard to the right. The back tires skipped around the turn, and I had to correct my steering to avoid spinning out of control.

The blue sedan continued to increase speed. My only advantage was the vehicle's lights and siren. Hopefully, drivers would pull over, allowing me to maintain or increase my speed to cut the distance between us. The car ahead kept to the east-bound lanes and avoided going into the oncoming traffic. He weaved around cars, sometimes forcing cars out of the way, causing some to brake and stop in traffic, others refusing to move until I approached.

Dispatch repeatedly called my vehicle number, giving orders to stop, but I didn't answer. By the time the car reached the first intersection on Smyth, it was almost half a kilometre in front of me. Dispatch continued with their barrage of orders to discontinue the pursuit. The police had been notified and were en route. I knew that if I did end the chase, the car could turn onto one of the residential streets, pull into a building complex, any one of the driveways, and the driver could make a run on foot and disappear forever.

St. Laurent Boulevard was approaching fast. There were several blocks of residential housing before Smyth intersected with St. Laurent. If he went north on St. Laurent, he could head for the Queensway or continue into Vanier, a francophone section of the city. South would take us through the Hawthorne Meadows division before crossing Walkley Road into the industrial section. North or south, there are dozens of secondary arteries to take and if he knew the area, the driver could disappear down a back road or hide behind a building. I floored the accelerator. The engine revved hard but produced little results. Ambulances were never built for speed or precise driving.

I kept my eye on the target before me. The car had difficulty passing other vehicles at times, but he refused to go into the oncoming lanes. From his less-than-aggressive driving skills, I doubted he'd ever had to speed through traffic before.

With the lights flashing and siren wailing, traffic continued to part for me. I made up ground--not a lot, but enough to close the gap. I was confident he would turn left onto St. Laurent Boulevard. He maneuvered his car into the far left lane, trapping himself against the median and the rest of traffic. Even with the siren, I could still hear his car horn ringing non-stop. He rear-ended cars, slamming into the car in front, forcing it to move. The intersection had become chaotic. Here was my chance.   I pulled into the two oncoming lanes of traffic. With the lights and siren, traffic facing a large white ambulance will always forfeit the right of way. They pulled to the north shoulder. I pressed harder on the gas pedal, even though it was already against the floor. Drivers of the vehicles in front of the blue sedan became confused. Car horns blared, ambulance siren yelped, each sound echoed off buildings, making it impossible for commuters to discern from which direction the sound was coming. Many cars just froze in their tracks. The blue sedan was trapped. His only escape was to jump the median. The front tires scraped alongside the concrete median. The driver turned hard left and the tires bounced off the curb. The car leapt into the air and landed hard over the barrier. He continued to press his car, and the back tires made their way over. Sparks flew, metal trim was freed from his car and bounced along the road. He lost control of the car as it bounded and slammed into one of the parked cars along the north curb. He turned and looked directly at me. I was closing in fast.

He righted the car and was about to accelerate through the intersection. He turned the wheel to the right and headed for the open road. His tires, already hot from the chase, spun, bellowing white smoke behind them. He had lost traction and was driving desperately now. There was no telling what he would do. The sedan's rear went left, smashing into another parked car, recoiled off, and was now free. I was only a few dozen feet behind him.

Off in the distance, on the northeast corner of the intersection, sat the lighthouse of the Museum of Science and Technology. I aimed for the lighthouse, knowing he would cross my path, hoping we would collide as I drove straight toward the lighthouse to cut him off.

I closed my eyes as the front of the ambulance hit his driver's door. The ambulance nose rose and fell from the impact. The steering wheel air bag exploded. The sudden stop hurled me forward into the air bag, crushing my chest, forcing all the air from my lungs from the sudden impact. I opened my eyes for a split second to see the under carriage of the car across the windshield.

The rig stalled, but continued to roll forward. The crash caused the car to roll from the passenger side and onto its roof spinning around like a top. The ambulance's slow momentum kept the rig moving until it came to rest against the overturned sedan. My lungs begged for air. I couldn't breathe. I'd failed to attach my seat belt and knew I had forgotten only milliseconds before the impact. I looked up, saw the carnage, opened my mouth and gasped for air. My diaphragm lowered, causing negative pressure to fill my lungs with new oxygen. I inhaled. It felt good. The rush of air filled my chest, my lungs expanded, and I could breathe again. I looked through the fractured windshield and saw what I had done and knew I had done right.

I removed the ignition key and threw it on the dash. I pulled on the handle and the driver's door creaked open. People were already out of their cars, coming over to help in whatever way they could. When my feet landed on the road, my right leg sent pain signals to my brain and I collapsed. I looked down, bright red blood flowed freely out from my right pant leg onto my boot. A large tear in my pant leg showed the cause of the bleed. I reached up to grab the mirror frame as a crutch to help me stand. "Stay down, you're hurt!" A female voice.

Ignoring the request, I grabbed the mirror and pulled myself up. A bystander bent down and positioned himself under my right arm and helped me up.

"I have to get over to the car." I pointed with my head. Another bystander repeated the action of the first. I was now between two men, both larger than myself, as they carried me over to the overturned blue sedan. As we walked over, the crowd in the intersection grew larger. Some stood and simply stared, some were on their cell phones, and others took photos or videos with their phones. I always wondered why there are always people in a crowd who feel it's necessary to call someone when they witness a tragedy.

"I have to get down." I was at the driver's side of the car. They helped me down so I could look in. The driver wouldn't need my help.

I used my hands to push myself up and around so I could sit and rest against the driver's side door. My leg hurt, my new boots were covered in my own blood, and I had a wicked headache. The sound of sirens could be heard getting closer.

I looked at the remains of the ambulance, and realized...Man, am I ever in a pile of shit!

CHAPTER 21

I sat on a stretcher in a private ER room at the General Hospital. The door was closed. Raised voices outside the room were barely audible, but I could still make out some of the words as one person spoke over the other.

My head was still throbbing but getting better fast. After I had been brought into the ER by EMS (which, by the way, is the biggest form of embarrassment for a paramedic), my wound was cleaned, and I had been given some medication for the pain. I was fast-tracked through triage, assessed, and then left to ponder my fate.

It sounded like Galen was either being yelled at or was yelling at someone else. His voice was always distinguishable from others. The size of his voice was only matched by his waist size! The voices continued to argue, but grew fainter. The door suddenly opened and was closed just as fast.

"What the fuck did you do?" Adrian stood at the door. He looked scared. "I told you I should have come with you. Christ, some of the crap flying around here says you killed a whole family in their car, others are saying you just killed one guy. What the hell did you do?" The look of concern on his face was sincere.

"I didn't kill anyone. The guy was unconscious and brought to another hospital under police guard. It was just him! No family, no deaths."

"Him him?" He pointed backwards with his thumb. "The guy in the parking lot, on the phone--him?"

"Yes, him, him!" I said with a touch of sarcasm. "Did you save the voice recording?"

"Save it? My phone was confiscated by the cops. I'll be lucky if I ever get it back. My girlfriend is gonna flip. She just sent me some great pics in her new bikini." His eyebrows went up and down. "She'll kill me if she finds out someone else is going to see those pictures."

Adrian walked over and pulled the dressing off the wound on my thigh. "Let me see."

My pants had already been cut off my right leg to visualize the wound. I had a large six-inch laceration on the lateral aspect of my right thigh. The whitish-yellow fat tissue just below the surface of the skin looked like it was being forced out around the edge of the wound and the red muscle tissue beneath had finally stopped bleeding. The wound was deep, the pain real. But the pain was minor compared to the shit storm brewing outside this room and what I would get after I left.

"I gotta go before I get caught. I was told by the cops not to talk to you. I was never here." With that, he opened the door a crack, peered through, and slipped out.

I sat alone for some time before a female doctor in a lab coat opened the door carrying a suture tray. She positioned herself beside the stretcher and placed the tray on a stainless steel rolling table and pulled it in close.

"So I hear you're the hero that caught the guy that bombed the Civic ER!" With her head still down, she looked up at me with approval.

"Caught? I think you could use a tad bit stronger word after what I did. Did you hear how he was doing?"

"Nope! But there are lots of cops all over the ER. Either way, I hope he gets what he deserves. You want any extra morphine for that wound? This is going to hurt."

Morphine! I had completely forgotten about the problem with the morphine back at HQ. I had to talk to Galen about that. My head began to swim with the events of the past weeks: Who wanted that jump drive? What information was so important it was worth killing over or being killed for? How many different parties were involved? Did the missing morphine play a part in this?

I went through the events as I remembered them, but they started to jell into one solid memory with no firm starting point or ending.

"All done!" She patted my leg. "And you didn't even flinch." She covered my leg with a large, white dressing and taped it in place. "You know the protocol, but I think you can take out your own sutures in about seven to ten days."

"Done? Already?" I was so completely lost in thought that I didn't even feel her suturing my leg.

"I was told to tell you that there was someone here who wanted to talk to you after I was done." Becky? She flipped the towel over the equipment tray, rolled the table to the corner, and walked out. Galen walked through the door before it closed.

His jacket was missing, tie loosened, sleeves were rolled up, and shirt tails hung free from the front of his pants. He looked like he'd just gone three rounds of mixed martial arts and lost. Beads of sweat flowed freely off of his forehead onto his cheeks and off the tip of his nose. He kicked the same stainless stool the doctor had just sat on over to the edge of the bed and dropped onto it.

He placed both hands on his knees, breathed in slowly, then cupped his hands over his face to wipe the sweat. Galen had a history of dramatizing the obvious to prove a point. My guilt was never in question; the amount of trouble I was in was the only variable. I'd seen Galen take less time letting a family member know a loved one had been killed. This was not good. I couldn't play a scenario in my head where I didn't get fired. Galen stood, walked over to the wall, turned and stood directly before me.

"You have a fucking horseshoe up your fucking ass!" He fell back against the wall with only his shoulders touching the wall. His head went back against the wall. He looked extremely upset. What was it, good news? Bad news? I couldn't tell.

"The guy wasn't hurt, you lucky son of a bitch; you just rung his fucking bell when you T-boned him. You'll never believe what the fuck we found in his trunk."

"Three. Three sentences and what, you said 'fuck' three times."

"What are you, my priest? You know I fucking swear when I'm pissed."

"And happy and hungry and tired and watching the Preds beat the Sens." Galen is an Ottawa Senators fan; I cheer for the Nashville Predators.

"Anyway?" I continued.

"My chief wants to pin a fucking medal on your chest. Your chief wants your ass tossed before you even leave this room. The media think you're a fucking hero. Every medic and cop out there thinks the same. So they can't go and fire a hero for saving more lives and catching the bastard in the process, now can they?"

"What do you mean: 'Saving more lives'?"

"We found another explosive device in his trunk. Good thing it didn't go off when you decided to crash into him. The one that blew at the Civic was this motherfucker's little brother. We figure from the blast pattern and debris disbursement, the one we found in the trunk was easily twice the size. Again, you are lucky this didn't blow when you nailed him."

"Speaking of him, what happened to him?"

Galen went on to explain that the medics treated me first, even though they should have extricated the driver trapped, hanging upside down, still unconscious. I was in the ambulance with my leg dressed when they went back. The driver was already conscious and trying to free himself from the car before the police arrived. The medics already knew who the driver of the other car was from the EMS radio chatter. With the help of the bystanders, the medics kept him secure until the police arrived. He wasn't in any condition to put up much of a fight.

He was taken to the Montfort Hospital under heavy guard. The police didn't want the unknown driver and me in the same ER at the same time.

Adrian's phone and the phone from the driver were confiscated as evidence. The car and its contents were transported to a secure compound almost immediately. They weren't leaving anything to chance. The case would go by the book, all the i's dotted and all the t's crossed. The chain of evidence would be intact and could not--would not--be questioned. And if it were, there would be a solid paper trail to prove their charges.

The suspect would be taken into police custody once he was cleared medically. The RCMP even wanted in on the action to see if the events were somehow related to any open cases with them.

Galen had texted Becky to give her an update on my condition. Becky had asked Galen to pass along her concerns. I missed having someone "concerned" about me. It felt good. My own phone was still either somewhere in the rig I'd crashed on St. Laurent, or, since the police also wanted it as evidence, it could be in their custody.

Galen pulled out a notepad, slapped it on the steel table, rolled it over to the bed and asked if I could complete an incident report. He held a pen out in front of me. I pulled it from his hand as if I were pulling straws to see who had to volunteer for a deadly mission.

"While you write this bullshit diatribe, I'm gonna go get a coffee. You want anything?"

"Sure. You know, writing this thing is going to put me to sleep! Make it an extra-large, please? I'll pay you later. You know I'm good for it."

The automatic closer slammed the door shut behind Galen. I slammed the pen down on the table with a rattle that could have woken the dead in the morgue a few floors down.

I fell hard back onto the bed and put my arm over my eyes. What did I get myself into? Last year, I never would have done anything like this. My life had changed so much since Maddy died. I lay in bed, eyes closed, and my leg started to pound where I had the wound sutured. The morphine must be wearing thin. I just wanted this day to end and wished I weren't so impulsive. Me, impulsive? My parents would laugh if they heard me say that. Maddy is probably listening and laughing, too. I was the one who insisted on planning the vacations, checked and double-checked the reservations for the resort, plane, and pretty much everything else. Maddy would pack the night before we left, if she forgot something, she would buy it or do without.

The door opened and I heard the now-familiar hissing sound of the pneumatic closer and the sound of the metal door against metal frame.

"Can you put the coffee down beside the pad? I haven't even started yet."

"I didn't bring you a coffee." I recognized the voice and shot up to face my deputy chief. If a man could have a permanent scowl and always look pissed off at the world, it was EMS Deputy Chief Marcel Coskey. However, his scowl quickly disappeared if anyone from the media was around. The man had moved up the ranks fast. He wasn't much older than me, but he was smart. Short in stature, short in temper, with a Napoleon complex: that was Coskey. He played the political game well, and in a city like Ottawa, he had what it took to get ahead. Most expected him to run for municipal or federal office, but he never did. At least not yet...

"How's the leg? I heard you got quite a few stitches. I hope they hurt!"

"What?" I was surprised by his candor.

The onslaught continued. "Since no one saw me enter, you don't have a union rep, and no one even knows I'm here yet. I wanted the chance to tell you exactly what an asinine, idiotic, stupid move that was. Of all the dumb-ass things to do, that was it! We lost a huge part of our fleet today, and you go and intentionally destroy another rig. In the process, there will probably be a few lawsuits against the city for vehicle damage that you caused." He pointed his index finger at me, pumping it back and forth to emphasize my guilt.

"I don't know what you have on people, blackmail or whatever, but before I even found out about what you did, I got a call from a council member, who got a call from a federal judge telling me that it would be in my best interest if you did not get into any trouble for the accident."

I was stunned. I knew who'd made the call. It had to have been Bill Thomas of the Supreme Court of Canada. I had a million questions going through my head as the verbal barrage of profanity continued. Why would he stick his neck out for me? I knew the guy through poker night. I go over to his place, watch the occasional hockey game with the rest of the group, but I was never particularly close to him. Chief Coskey's lips moved but I heard nothing, I only heard the voice in my head. He paced around the room, arms behind his back. I assume this was his method of self-control.

He moved closer to me, stood over me and said nothing. If the stare-down was his way of intimidating me, it failed miserably. I was in pain, my leg hurt, my head hurt, and I would have accepted a suspension just to get a few days' rest. He continued to stare.

"You may not care about yourself. You may think you're invincible. But you may be forgetting one thing: you have friends. And I assume those friends work in the department and don't have the same protection you do. If I can't get at you directly, I'll get to you through them. Do you understand me?"

He stood, continued staring down at me. I stared at him. My eyes did not waver. He hardly blinked. With his slow, unwavering monotone voice, threatening those that I care about, I wondered how often this tactic worked on some of the other medics and management?

"Yes, sir. I understand completely, and you have to understand, sir, I did not ask anyone to call you on my behalf. I take responsibility for my actions and feel what I did was right under the circumstances. I think the wounded medics and anyone else who was hurt would tell me they would do the same." I was still sitting, playing the sympathy card, voice firm, back straight, staring at him, unblinking. Countermove.

Deputy Chief Coskey smiled. Two can play that game.

He placed his hand on my shoulder. "I have two hats to wear, chief and former medic. On the record, I should fire you; off the record, I wish you had run the son of a bitch over and backed up and run him over again. If you ever repeat this, I will personally fire your ass. Don't fuck with me."

He tugged the door handle and pulled it open. Deputy Chief Coskey walked out.

Before the door closed, Galen walked through the open door, turned, and looked back at Coskey.

"He looked pissed. Get your ass burnt?"

"You have no idea."

"You've been discharged. I had your personal shit from the rig brought here before it went to the lot. I'll take you home and have your car driven over later by a uniform."

I stood, put a little weight on my right leg, felt the pain, and put more weight on it until my foot was flat on the floor. The pain levelled off and I was able to walk out with only a minor limp.

CHAPTER 22

Galen offered to buy me dinner and walk me into the house, but I just wanted to sit in front of the TV, grab a beer, let the alcohol and meds kick in, and pet the cats. Galen returned to the station. I dropped my bag in the front hall, threw the keys in the key bowl, unbuttoned my shirt and let it fall to the floor, and kept walking to the living room. As I turned to enter the living room, I stopped dead in my tracks. A man sat quietly in a chair, looking directly at me. He was older, impeccably dressed in a custom-tailored suit, tie, and cufflinks.

"You really should upgrade your security system." English accent.

"I'll do that first thing tomorrow. I'm not really in the mood to put up much of a fight. Should I be worried?"

He smiled, closed his eyes, shook his head gently the way someone with years of formal upbringing would.

"Can I get you anything while I'm up?"

"Thank you, no! May I be of assistance?" He stood to help me find a seat.

I sat down, placing both hands on the arms of the chair to slow my descent, lifted my injured leg and placed my foot on the coffee table. I put my head on the back of the chair waiting for the pain to subside. When it did, I boosted myself upright.

"I do have my cell phone, you know, and the officer who brought me home shouldn't be too far."

"Your mobile won't work and your home line has also been disabled."

My head was still resting on the back of the chair, eyes closed. "Should have figured that! Will I have to get Bell in to fix the land line?" I turned to look at him.

Again, a very distinguished nod to indicate I would need to place a repair call to get my land line working again.

"So I shouldn't be afraid, even though you cut my home line, jam my cell, ah, mobile. Besides, I can't see you wanting to get blood on that suit. It probably cost more than my car."

He smiled, stood, placed a pillow under my foot and sat back down. "I've seen your car. It wouldn't take much for any suit to be worth more than your car." He smiled.

109

"True. Since this is my house, I'll go first. I assume you're not from around here, that accent is way too thick for someone who has been living here for a while. My last house guest was Irish, I think. I didn't have time to ask or even to offer him a drink. Was he working with you?"

For some reason, a strange man breaks into my house, makes himself at home, and I have no fear. He somehow made me feel very comfortable and at ease.

"Not with me, but he was working with the group."

"Was that your associate today in the car?"

"No," he replied.

"But you knew him."

"Of him, yes. Mr. Tennant...Ethan...may I?" Very formal.

I nodded in agreement.

He continued, "Ethan, we all used to work for the same group years ago. As it turns out, things are quite different than what we all initially planned. Do you have some time to hear a story that goes back quite a few years?"

My arms went out to the side, "I'm all yours."

"You have been on our radar since you picked up a member of the team whom we had planted in your Parliament. It takes time to cultivate moles, and for that reason, he was vitally important to the program. He was able to obtain information that would have been difficult to access outside of government channels without raising suspicions.

"After his death, you came in possession of the codes on the drive. We do our research on people who come to our attention and we have come to know you very well, Ethan."

He paused. His mannerism, the tone of his voice, reminded me of a politician, his speech seemed well rehearsed, polished. He likely had told this story more than once.

"In the beginning, many years ago, Hitler thought that the only way Germany could be great again was if the state forced the philosophy of racial hygiene and eugenics. Those of strong and pure German blood should be encouraged to have children and those weak, invalid, homosexual, or impure would have forced sterilization. In fact, Nazi Germany had eugenic marriage laws to ensure that couples be tested for any hereditary diseases or insanity before marriage.

"Hitler did this to try to create a master race, the Aryan race. The master race would be pure. Pure of blood, pure genetics, unspoiled by mixed blood. Hitler may have had a plan, but it was decades ahead of science. Hitler, however, did not originate the concept of eugenics. The Americans did!"

I sat, stunned, not sure if what I was hearing was the truth or a fabrication to deflect the truth.

He continued, "The Nazi eugenics program, called Action T4, was inspired by the American program that forced sterilization first brought into law in the state of California. The state of California eugenicists promoted eugenics and sterilization and sent the program results to Nazi scientists. Before the war, California had forced sterilization on more people than all other U.S. states combined. The United States had their own purification eugenics program before the Germans. Makes you wonder who the evil empire really was, doesn't it?

"Immediately after the Second World War, the United States, England, and the USSR, now Russia, separated the brightest minds from the Third Reich. In the final days, military officers of the Reich fled to South America, defected to Russia, or to the West. Hitler, Joseph Goebbels, and Heinrich Himmler took the cowardly way out and committed suicide. Young men like yourself, those truly loyal to Hitler, fought and died in the last few days of the war. Of those who lived, they faced a mock trial at Nuremburg, Germany, were executed, or sent to jail to die as old men.

"All the scientists of the Reich knew their fates were sealed, but in order to save themselves and for the love of science, they went where they were told if they wanted to continue their research. The United States held and controlled this trial against the doctors who committed crimes so horrific, that even today in Europe, we honour those who died."

He had my attention. Instead of my head resting on the back of the chair, I now sat fixated on my unnamed guest.

"During the war, Hitler ordered unspeakable things done to the Jews and prisoners of war in the name of science. Those experiments, even by the standards of the Crusades, would be considered vile and evil.

"After the war," he had to catch his breath. Even for someone who knew the truth, telling the story again must bring back thoughts and images of what really happened.

"After the war, many of the Nazi scientists stayed in contact with each other from their adopted countries, secretly of course, and their research continued covertly, funded by their new homelands. As the older Nazi regime scientists died off, new, younger, brighter minds took control. The Human Genome Project, DNA, led us to this point.

"Hitler's Master Race was to be pure. As the world changed, immigration evolved, foes became friends, new enemies emerged; there was never a better time to re-attempt the idea of a new Master Race."

My house guest had become excited. He truly enjoyed telling me this part of the story. I too, became enthralled. I could barely move as I listened to what he had to say. More than half a century and Hitler's name and legacy were as fresh as it ever was.

"Each country that harboured those scientists in the forties, fifties, sixties, and even now, continue with the research in seclusion, working for a new world order. Not an Aryan race, but a pure race, from each country. Each country would be pure, free from all other foreign blood, and could limit those who could reproduce with their citizens. Purity was born from the ashes of Action T4, from the mind of Hitler, conceived by the Americans. Purity is the name of the group I used to belong to."

He stood. "I will take that drink now. Do you have Scotch? Would you care for one?"

"I have beer and Diet Coke."

"Ah! Beer it is."

As he walked to the kitchen, I retrieved my cell phone and quickly checked for a signal to call Galen.

From the kitchen, my guest spoke loudly, "The signal jammer won't permit a call until after I leave." I returned the phone to my pocket.

He placed a glass and open beer bottle on separate coasters by my foot. "Shall I pour for you?" I nodded. He even poured beer with class, glass tilted, minimal foam, just how I like it.

"Shall I continue, Ethan?"

I was mesmerized. Of course I wanted to hear more.

"The original intent of Purity was to permit each country involved in the program to prevent cross-culture breeding. The same way cross-species breeding is currently impossible...well, for the most part. Asians could breed among themselves, but not with Caucasian or Blacks, Blacks with Blacks, Caucasians with Caucasians, Indians with Indians, Spanish with Spanish, and so on. We recently isolated a gene that would fight off an invading foreign gene if it did not match the host DNA. Believe me when I tell you that several countries were contributing to our research and they all were excited by the find.

"All was going well until we also discovered that we could isolate character traits: hair colour, ethnicity, desired physical attributes, and so on. If we wanted to, we could eliminate disease, abnormally low intelligence, dark hair, blond hair, short people, overweight people, anything we wanted. Anything for a price! We could do exactly what Hitler envisioned, create the perfect race, the Master Race. The Master Race for your country, engineered and developed by Purity. Customized eugenics at a price! Imagine ordering your country's gene pool the way you order a combo meal at a fast food restaurant.

"The discovery tore Purity into two factions, the Eagles and the Sparrows. The Eagles wanted to have the Master Race, while the Sparrows discovered what we had become and knew it was all wrong. Each side held the science, but the final equations, the ones that seek out character traits in the DNA, were stolen. You had that equation and lost it today, it's now back in the hands of the Eagles. The Eagles want to implement the science, the Sparrows want to destroy it. I used to be an Eagle, but had a change of heart. I saw what the world could become if that science became mainstream. I saw the future, and believe me when I tell you, it frightens me to my very core. That, and they want me dead.

"The man you picked up from Parliament was an Eagle, the man who killed him, a Sparrow. The man who attacked you, here in your house, he is or was an Eagle, hired to be an enforcer. The man who blew up the hospital, he is a Sparrow. We are a violent group, both sides. Not unlike a group of paranoid Nazis, trusting no one, finding fault in anyone who disagrees with us or our ideology. It is not a bad idea to trust no one, Ethan."

He went to the window and looked up and down the street. Paranoid!

"The science is sound, Ethan, the methods perfect. The reasons, that part is less than perfect. Human testing has been ongoing for years. Test subjects, some willing for the right amount of money, others unwilling and unknowing, have been impregnated and given birth to babies brought to term and studied. Some of those infants were born right here in Ottawa. Unfortunately, none of the infants have lived longer than a few months, but new research has proven that we can eventually achieve our goal."

I sat up straighter, my whole body tensed. My mind flashed back to the young baby Clara adopted by the family who cared for her and loved her. To them, she was their child, not an experiment. "You get women pregnant, deliver a child, watch it grow and develop, and see how long it will live? I saw one of your experiments and what it did to the family that was raising your test subject! You, the group, you're no better than the Nazis."

"I realize what we are doing may sound barbaric to you, but it will happen, it is happening, whether you like it or not."

He turned, rubbed his face and sat back down. The actions and those of his group weighed heavy on him. He sipped his beer.

"Too cold! I should have asked if you had any beer that wasn't refrigerated. Would you mind if I took another?" He put the bottle down on the table and went to the kitchen.

CHAPTER 23

I sat back, sipped my beer, knowing full well not to mix alcohol and pain meds, but the thought that the Nazi Fourth Reich could be a reality and I may have contributed to its success was hard to grasp. My head ached.

"Found the case of beer in the pantry! I never understood Canadians and Americans with their cold beer! Beer is so much better when it's cool, not cold; more flavour. Of course, British beer is different, more subtle, much better when the beer is not so cold." He placed the glass on a coaster.

My guest went on to explain that Purity was now a group of men and women from around the world who controlled the science first started by the Third Reich. Members knew only a select few, and the head of each cell reported back anonymously to the head of another cell via email. Most meetings were held electronically, and not one cell kept any records on meetings. Notes were forbidden: secrecy ruled above all else. Scientists working for Purity conducted research alone and correspondence with other scientists was strictly against protocol.

"Paranoid!" I thought to myself each time he mentioned the level of covert operations required to maintain the program. But it must have worked. For over sixty years, a plan hatched in the mind of a madman has continued into the next century.

"Why Eagles and Sparrows? It seems like an odd choice for such an enigmatic group of people. I would have thought tigers and lions or elephants and gorillas?" There was a bit of sarcasm on my part.

He took another sip of his beer, "It wasn't such a stretch. The Americans have always controlled the majority of the group and they were the ones who wanted to proceed with further DNA testing. We knew the Yanks were truly always in control of the project and the direction the research took. The U.S. controlled the Nuremburg Trials, the Doctors' Trial, forcing their will on the rest of the world.

"When our opposing ideology forced us apart, we still worked together on some level, but the Eagles became the code name by which they referred to us. It wasn't until later that they started to call their counterparts Sparrows for their meek reaction to several of their plans. The taunting actually escalated to the point where they started to fight back to where we are today. The code names stuck."

"What? No uniforms, no pinky ring, no secret handshake? Come on, at least you should wear black and white hats to tell the groups apart!"

"We all know who belongs to which group." He bowed his head a little. "Well, for the most part we know who is who. In my case, I have to prove myself to the Sparrows."

The beer glass empty, he put it down on the coaster and sat back into his chair staring at me, no words spoken. Whether this was a British trait or something learned from Purity or his own conscious getting to him, he almost looked sad.

Several minutes went by without a word being said. What started as a curious pause became an uncomfortable, tension-filled silence. I felt like a specimen being examined. His stare never left me.

I broke the silence.

"You know me, but I don't know you."

"Not knowing me may save your life one day, young man."

"If I need to get in contact with you . . ." my words trailed off.

"I will find you." His voice was still polite and calm.

"So I tape a large X on the front window like Mulder used to do?" Sarcasm! "I need to know. You break into my house, serve me drinks, tell me a wild and possibly totally bullshit story about Hitler, eugenics, and custom designing the future of the human race, and you won't tell me your name. I need to know why you told me this."

"The world is changing--getting faster every day, exponentially faster, to the point where I seriously doubt in fifty years we would recognize it with today's eyes. Not all those changes will be for the better; this, this . . ." His words trailed off. His face went blank.

"We are meddling with powers that we never should have invented, tampering with things God never intended us to know or create. I am telling you because you have the key to that power and I want you to make sure no one ever acquires it from you. No one, do you understand?" He seemed genuinely concerned, maybe even scared.

"If you have it, destroy it. If you don't have it and can get it, destroy it. Again, do you understand?"

I nodded in agreement.

With that, he stood, picked up his empty glass and bottle and carried them into the kitchen. He returned, replaced the coasters and walked toward the front door.

"I was my pleasure meeting you, young man. I hope we get to chat again sometime soon. If I need to speak with you, I'll call your mobile. It will reconnect to a tower shortly after I leave."

He simply walked to the front door, never looking back. The door closed softly behind him.

*****

I retrieved my laptop and booted it up. As I watched the colourful logo dim and brighten, waiting for Windows to start, I thought back to what my unnamed guest had explained: selective breeding, altering humanity to suit whoever has the price to pay for the technology, the continuation of Hitler's research. It all seemed so far-fetched, something from the X-Files, more of a case for Mulder and Scully than me...a story from a science fiction movie...but it was real; and the way he spoke about it, it was as if it were commonplace, something we should expect in a few years. And he was probably right. It would be coming, but I found it hard to fathom that it would be here within my lifetime. It was not something I wanted and certainly did not want to be a part of.

Start...Documents...scroll down to find the file, move the mouse over the right file, right mouse click, slide down to "Delete." My index finger paused, hovering over the mouse, unable to push the button. Something in my mind fought the action. I was having an argument with myself: delete it and it would be gone forever. CSIS had a copy, but I doubt they would ever release it to the public. Galen and the tech had made an encoded copy, which I lost. Galen was too scared to make a copy for the Ottawa Police, even though he should have. So the argument raged on: delete the one--and possibly only--public file of a code to break the DNA sequence that could alter research and cure disease or worse? I'm not religious, but this sounds like playing God.

I plugged in the printer cable and right-clicked on the file and hit "Print." The printer whirled to life. Page after page were lifted, run through the printer and deposited into the tray. I picked up the first page, random number after random number appeared on the page. The second revealed more of the same; the third, and it went on and on. I never realized the size of the file on the computer, or how it related to the printed sheet. By the time the printer completed its run, a total of seventy-three pages lay in the bin.

I deleted the file on the laptop, went to the Trash Bin and deleted the file again. I grabbed a new ream of paper and carefully cut the glue seal of the package fold with a knife, measured the thickness of the seventy-three pages and pulled out approximately the same from the stack of paper. I inserted the printed seventy-three pages in the centre of the ream and used a glue stick to reseal the paper wrap. I placed the package of paper in my desk with the repaired end facing away to make it look unaltered. The blank sheets were stacked in the printer tray.

Satisfied with my covert abilities, I decided it was time for a quick bite and then off to bed when the doorbell rang. It was Becky!

Galen had called her about the accident and she'd rushed over to nurse me back to health!

After scrambled eggs, stale bread made edible by the magic of the toaster, Becky led me upstairs to the bathroom and sat me down on the toilet seat. She pulled off my torn and bloodied pants and tossed them into the trash basket. She looked at the wound and counted the sutures using her index finger to guide her.

"Seventeen! Seventeen stitches! I would have let you bleed to death for doing something that stupid." Her voice showed concern. The slap I felt on the side of my head showed anger.

"Okay! Ouch!" I pointed to the left side of my head.

"Next time, it'll be a lot worse if you ever do anything that idiotic again! I think you like doing Galen's job! Considering a career change, are we?" She pulled off my T-shirt and dropped it on the floor.

"Do you want me to wash the blood from your leg or do you want me to tape up your leg in a bag so you can have a shower?" The site around the laceration was red and tender. The last thing I wanted was to have anyone, even Becky, touch my leg.

"Shower, please."

My left hand braced against the wall under the shower head, my right hand rubbed my right leg above the bag. My thigh hurt like hell. Eyes closed, I let the water hit me directly across my face, washing away the thoughts of the day: Eagles, Sparrows, Hitler, DNA. Do I burden Becky or Galen with the details of Purity or keep it to myself?

Good questions; questions that needed answers, tomorrow. Tonight I just wanted to sleep. I was hoping tomorrow would bring clarity and insight into the events of today. For now, Purity would be my secret.

I dried myself off, wrapped the towel around my waist, brushed my teeth, took an Advil and walked into the bedroom. Becky was already asleep as I lay down beside her.

Sleep came fast, but was not restful.

CHAPTER 24

The next morning, Becky was off to Ottawa EMS HQ for an interview for any position in any department except working on the road as a medic. With all the various departments--Training, Public Relations, and Administration, I was certain they would find a position to bring her back to Ottawa.

I showed up at police headquarters with my hands full of coffee and donuts. The large coffee box carafe and dozen donuts for Galen and the guys working in the office would get their blood sugar up, increase their caloric intake, and eventually turn more than a few detectives into diabetics. Over the past few months, bringing treats in for Galen usually meant I needed something. Today was no different.

Galen sat at his desk. Newspapers were scattered across his desk, with some pages pushed onto the edge of the other desk butted up against his. Oblivious to my presence, he flipped from one page to the next, circled an article or highlighted a line, different colours having different meanings. He was fixated. Pages went one way, then the other. He had several different papers from different cities. This was Galen's old-school method of Internet searching.

I placed a donut on his desk. Without looking up, he reached over, grabbed a bite, wiped his hand on his pants, and went back to work.

"Whaddaya want, and where's the coffee?"

"Over there." I pointed. He never looked. "Where's the techie you brought to my house?"

Again, without breaking his concentration, "Second floor," and carried on working.

"They have the Internet now, you know. Type in a keyword and you get hundreds of hits."

"I can review each article faster, pick up things you just can't get from off a screen. Flipping between screens, going back and forth, you lose your place. It's easier to view them side by side. Now stop fucking with me!" Not once did he look up at me.

I needed to stretch my leg and decided to take the stairs carefully--very carefully--, my leg still feeling the effects of my accident. Planting my left foot,

I followed with my right while gripping the hand rail for support. Each step reminded me that the wound was still fresh. I should have picked up a cane from the hospital.

Walking past each office on the second floor and looking in to see who was working in each office was causing a little more than a few looks. After receiving more dirty looks, I scanned down the hall and noticed tiny blue and white signs above each door frame. Farther down, "IT Solutions" stood out from all the other signs.

The door was closed. It was the only closed door of the all the offices on this floor. Nicole sat behind three large LCD monitors, lined up side by side. It was her way of hiding from the world outside. The layout reminded me of Galen's newspapers.

She made it known that she preferred the virtual world to the real world. Nicole's office door was closed, monitors blocking people from seeing her when they entered the room, and no personal effects of any kind on or around her workstation. When I entered the room, she merely raised her head to peer over the top of one of the monitors to see who it was and went back to work.

"Hi! Remember me?" A poor way if there ever was one to start a conversation.

"Yeah," the keyboard continued to click.

"Can I ask a favour?"

Silence...assumed the lack of a negative response was a positive response. I pulled my laptop from my backpack and placed it in front of her.

"Delete the Beale Code from this thing, please! I deleted it and emptied the trash but I heard that you guys...um..." I fumbled for words, "techies, smart people--you can retrieve it." I opened the laptop, "Please make sure it is gone and gone for good. I don't want anyone coming back and trying to get a copy." I also wanted Galen, Liz, and everyone else to think that I no longer had a copy.

"Sure." Nicole pulled the laptop toward her. Fingers started to type faster than I could ever hope to; her index finger would swipe across the touchpad, move the cursor, and screens appeared and disappeared faster than my mind could process.

"Done." The lid was closed and she slid my laptop back to me.

"Why are you really here?" Nicole looked over the rim of her glasses as she continued to work. "What I did was basic shit. You could Google how to delete files."

"I need to know if the file you bugged was opened yet."

"Nope. Next time, just ask."

Galen still sat flipping pages at his desk. Articles torn from various editions were collected in folders marked by case file numbers on his desk.

He closed the last of the newspapers on his desk, stacked them, and walked to the large recycling bin. The papers had been used, read, and now were unceremoniously dumped into the bin. He pulled his chair out, sat, and leaned as far back as the chair would allow without toppling.

"Nicole called me before you got back. I would have told you if the bug had been activated." He stood again, grabbed his suit jacket, and pulled his car keys from his jacket pocket. "I'm heading over to the detention centre to talk to our new friend. Wanna come?"

I grabbed my backpack and followed Galen. His office phone rang. He turned, looked at it, looked at me, and picked it up.

His eyes lit up. A smile formed, "You bet your sweet ass I want in!"

"We're not going to the jail?" I asked.

"Better. Nicole just got an email from the virus on your jump drive right after you left her office."

Police Chief Richard Stabenow stood directly behind Nicole. A half-dozen officers stood to his right. Galen pulled in close to the chief's left side to see the monitor. I positioned myself away from the group and stood just inside the doorway with an angled view of her monitor.

Richard looked over at me and, with the skill of a seasoned politician, nodded his head ever so slightly to indicate that I could join the group. I pulled in close to Galen.

Nicole was typing away, guiding the mouse pointer over different fields and moving screens from one monitor to another. Another technician had joined her and was working the station to Nicole's right. They typed away, looked at each other, knew what the other was thinking and did what needed to be done.

"They are trying to pinpoint the exact location where the email emanated from." Richard said, his eyes never leaving the screen.

"We had their IP address, but they bounced the email off of several proxy servers. Every time I try to pin them down, the path ends, and it gets bounced to another server. Either they knew something was on the drive, which they could have suspected, or this is just their safety protocol. If it is, these guys are flipping good." Nicole had a smile on her face that showed how happy she was playing their game.

I followed a tiny dot on the map. The dot moved from one sector of the map to another every few seconds. Not knowing exactly what I was looking at, I tried to decipher what they were saying. I gathered that whoever opened and viewed the jump drive either knew it was tagged or they were following their own way of securing their computer system. When the jump drive was opened, the computer they viewed it on connected to the Internet and sent out a signal that would tell us where they were. But that signal was being bounced around the globe like a beam of light reflecting off of mirrors all over the world. Nicole was trying to pin the signal down to its originating location, if she could move fast enough, but from what I could see, it was a losing battle.

As Nicole and the other IT technician played catch-up, the dot moved faster and faster between points on the map until it stopped and disappeared completely.

Nicole slammed her fists on the keyboard. "Shit!" She looked over her shoulder, up at the chief. He gave Nicole a puzzled look. "What? I hate stupid hackers. That, and losing!"

Chief Stabenow placed his hand on her shoulder and invited everyone on the team to follow him. "You too, Mr. Tennant!" He stared right at me.

Like a human chain, we followed the chief up one flight of stairs to a conference room. The room was sparse, furnished with rectangular wooden tables with metal collapsible legs and chairs that looked extremely uncomfortable, purposely designed to keep the sitter awake during boring speeches. The tables were organized in a "U," with a DLP projector suspended from the ceiling. The chief walked around to the head of the table and stood there, waiting for everyone to take a seat. I stood in the doorway, again, farthest away from everyone, and tried to conceal myself from the rest of the group. There were a few free chairs. My leg hurt, but I felt more at ease being at arm's length.

A loud commanding voice took control of the room, "Okay!" That was all that was needed. All movement ceased, all talk ended, and the attention was focused solely on Richard Stabenow.

Chief Stabenow placed both hands on the table and leaned forward. His expression changed from casual to serious. The pause was possibly intentional, but certainly assisted in demonstrating the severity of what was forthcoming.

"Everyone in this room is fully aware of what has happened in the city in the last two days. The prime suspect in the bombing at the Civic Hospital is in custody, thanks to the totally moronic driving of one of Ottawa EMS's finest."

All eyes turned toward me. Immediately, I felt uncomfortable. I squirmed while standing and wanted the attention turned back toward the chief.

The next few minutes was all police talk: leads, evidence, interrogation, plans of attack, which direction they should take, and legal jargon with the Crown Attorney about subpoenas and probable cause. These were all subjects that never get discussed with a paramedic. We wait for calls. We aren't proactive and search out calls. Deployment plans are created based on past calls. The locations of those calls originated from around the city and where the demographics lead, but they're all reactive, not proactive. Vehicles get strategically placed based on past call patterns, hoping the trend continues. Throughout the day, ambulances are moved from one location to another in hopes the rigs will be placed in the right location if and when a call comes in. I never really viewed it as a science, but rather a best-guess scenario. This proactive police work was all foreign to me.

When Chief Stabenow concluded his speech, the officers pushed their chairs back into the tables and left the room. Galen stayed behind, chatted with the chief for a moment, then motioned for me to join them.

"The chief has something to ask you." Galen stepped aside.

The chief pulled out a chair and offered it to me. I sat, and he followed suit. Galen remained standing.

"I heard you got in quite a bit of shit for the stunt you pulled yesterday. Anything I can do to help?"

"Actually, I'm doing okay. Hurt my leg a bit. They couldn't exactly give me a suspension, but I got a few days off until my scratch heals." I rubbed my leg. The dressing over the wound made wearing long pants tolerable.

"I hate to ask you, but I need a favour."

The chief of police asking me for a favour? This is going to be serious.

"He asked for you personally."

CHAPTER 25

The man whom I had crashed into sat before me, silent, stoic, staring straight at me, almost through me, eyes unblinking. His hands were unshackled, fingers interlaced loosely. His feet were also unchained. I had agreed to his request providing there were police officers outside the door.

I sat, nervous, not really knowing what to do. He had summoned me, stating he would speak with me and me alone.

Several minutes passed without so much as a word or a movement. It was a challenge, a game, to see who would blink first. The steel door opened. An officer carried in a tray, balancing a small plastic pot of tea, two plastic mugs, milk and sugar, and placed it on the table between us.

"Ah! Finally, now we can begin. I was beginning to think they had forgotten. May I pour you one?" His mood changed in the presence of the tray of tea. He had a smile, a smile so wide I thought he had won his freedom and this was a celebratory drink.

"Please. One milk, one sugar."

He lifted the lid off the pot, peered in to ensure that the tea had steeped properly. When he was satisfied with the colour of the tea, he poured two cups, added milk and sugar into mine, left his black. Steam wafted from the cups.

"I find milk and sugar alter the taste of the tea. You want to experience the true natural flavour that only comes from drinking it black. Of course, steeping tea in a plastic pot and drinking from a plastic mug is not exactly refined."

He blew across the top of the cup to cool the tea and sipped. The grimace on his face indicated the tea was either too hot, or he disliked the flavour.

"Police tea is as dreadful as police coffee. Still, a bad pot of tea is better than a good cup of coffee." He held the mug with both hands as if he were cold after a long day playing in the snow. "Ask away. Anything you want to know. If I don't feel like telling you, I won't."

"Name? We still don't have your name." I knew the answer already.

Galen had sent his mug shot and prints to CSIS, the RCMP, the FBI, CIA, and Interpol. None of the agencies came back with a positive hit. The guy was an enigma: no name, no country, no record anywhere. The car was stolen, the phone was a disposable throwaway; the man simply didn't exist.

"You'll know soon enough."

"Why the attack on the hospital?"

He stared forward, sipping his tea. He wouldn't answer. My left foot bounced up and down. Unless he was looking under the table, he couldn't see how nervous I was. My heart was pounding; the feeling was overwhelming and confusing. I had to restrain myself. The anger grew each time I watched him take a sip of his tea as if we were out having lunch discussing political views or sports scores. I wanted to reach across the table, grab the back of his head, and slam his face on the table. I got right to the point.

"Okay, tell me about Purity!"

His eyes went from looking at the cup of tea to me. I'd caught his attention. "You know about Purity or are you guessing?" No expression.

"Everything!" I stared directly at him, unwavering, solid in my determination to extract more information from him if I could.

"You overheard the word and just threw your one and only trump card on the table. You know nothing." He seemed nervous. His tone hinted aggressiveness but his mannerisms did not. Another sip.

"Ask me."

"Who started Purity?"

"Hitler!" I raised my eyebrows to emphasize my point.

"Hitler had the right idea. Bad methodology, bad press. Fifty or sixty years ahead of his time, I suppose. What are your thoughts on Purity, Ethan?"

He sipped more tea. Chess. He was caught; he needed to change the subject. I doubted he wanted to remain silent. He asked for me. My strength was in hiding what I knew. He had to make another move. His position was not a tenable one, but where would he go? What bit of information would be sacrificed? I wasn't sure if he was assessing his position or playing a mind game. I decided to act.

"The attack at the hospital was desperate. Not the actions of an eagle. An eagle would be more direct, cause more mayhem. You must be a sparrow! You are a sparrow, aren't you? Timid, shy, making attacks from a distance. A weasel, a rat...you're nothing, a coward."

The cup slipped from his one hand, caught only by his index finger through the handle. A little tea spilled from the cup onto the laminate table. He righted the cup and reached for a napkin.

"I got it." I pulled a napkin from the tray and wiped up the few drops on the table. I placed the damp napkin back on the tray. "Well, are you?" I continued.

"A sparrow? Yes. A coward, however, would never attempt to do the things we are attempting to do. The world is changing, cultures blending. Immigration and multiculturalism doesn't work. You can't have a culture, a way of life, allowing immigrants to pollute your country and expect everyone to get along and smile.

Eventually, there has to be a breaking point where society says 'enough is enough' and makes everyone conform or kills the polluters.

"Our system makes everyone exactly the same from the inside out. And the funny thing is; other countries want what we are trying to develop because they don't like us any more than we like them.

"Would you mind if I refreshed my cup?" He reached for the pot and topped up his tea.

"Well?" I wanted him to continue.

"You're interfering with powers beyond your comprehension. Death is a nasty business and I'm not sure you want to sully yourself with this matter."

"In case you didn't realize, death is my business. I deal with it every day. I've become jaded, hardened; and death is what it is. I don't cry, shed a tear, or feel a pang of, well, anything, when I do a call. What does piss me off--and pisses me off greatly--is when someone fucks with my friends. You hurt my friends today for no other reason than to get my attention."

I stood, planted my fists on the table and leaned forward, putting myself inches from his face. He didn't flinch. He sipped his tea.

"I have no problem making a call to a few friends who are on the other side of your group to tell them exactly where you are." I sat back down. My point was made. Leaning back, I crossed my arms and watched him drink his tea.

Again, he refilled his cup, placed the plastic pot on the tray, shook it, and lifted the lid. "If this conversation is going to go on for a while, could I get a new pot, please? New tea bag and fresh water is a must."

As if on cue, a uniformed officer entered the room, picked up the pot, leaving the tray, sugar, milk, and mugs, and left.

I held the tea cup with two hands. I was used to drinking coffee, and, as my father used to say, tea is an anemic beverage with a bland flavour. Maybe he was right; I should try it black. Looking across the cup, I saw a man...a man I would pass on the street and not notice. Outside of the police interrogation room, the man sitting across from me could be anybody--a father, a husband, a community leader, a priest in some other life unknown to us. His brown hair was combed back from his face, and his features revealed no specific ethnicity. The colour of his skin was white, not tanned or brown, but white! I found myself wondering if he was one of the genetic results of the testing. Now I was feeding into the whole Purity paranoia.

The officer returned with a fresh pot of tea. The man inspected the contents to make sure his demands had been met. He poured another cup. He must have the bladder of an elephant. I would have taken two or three trips to the bathroom by now!

"You haven't touched your drink. Would you like a fresh cup?"

"Thank you, no!" I placed the cup on the table.

Time to play in the big leagues! I was getting impatient.

"Did you ever get your hands on the cipher or did you screw that up? Was that your one and only job? How does your organization work? Can they suspend you, fire you? Or is failure dealt with a little more harshly? Everyone else who screws up usually ends up dead."

Shit! Too many questions at a time; I should have asked one at a time.

"I hope your source has all the information, because no one in our organization knows everything. It is what keeps us safe. No one person has all the keys to the lock, so to speak. It is true that some have to be sacrificed for the greater good, but we know that going in. Is that something you would do for the greater good?" He sipped his tea.

"Ethan," he blew across the cup again. "I like you. Really I do. You have a youthful presence, fresh and unspoiled, like most of the policemen I meet. But you hide something deeper, something that made you angrier than your character usually allows. You really should see someone to sort through your issues. Perhaps we can schedule another session one day."

I lost the edge. He was now attempting to confuse me, mix emotions into the conversation. I was well beyond that.

"Your organization, Purity, Eagles, Sparrows, creating the Fourth Reich, sounds like the creation of a bunch of guys with performance issues. You're a con man. You sell snake oil and have fantasies of world domination.

"Do you remember that cartoon from the nineties, what was it called again ...oh, yeah, Pinky and the Brain. At the end of every episode, when the Brain screwed up his quest for world domination, Pinky would ask what they were going to do the next night and the Brain would reply, 'The same thing we do every night, Pinky; try to take over the world!'

"Well, what are you going to do now that you failed again? Try to take over the world tomorrow?"

I'd had enough for one day. I pushed away from the table as Galen entered the room.

"Can I see you for a second?" I knew Galen wanted to give me a break. I needed to get away for a few moments.

As the door opened, the man behind the table said loudly, "Your wife, Madeleine, you called her Maddy, right? Are you sure you know how she died?"

I snapped. Adrenaline fuelled my rage and pumped through me. In two steps I'd crossed the room, smashing my injured leg on the table corner, not knowing how, I'd managed to pick him up, but the next lucid moment I had, my right forearm was under his neck, pushing him up the wall. The sound of the tea cup bouncing off the floor cleared my head.

His face was red, eyes bulged, jaw clenched tight. My arm was pushing tightly against his neck. It felt good. I looked down to see his feet dangling. He was completely suspended by his neck.

He tried to speak, but the words did not come easily. "I own...you! We know ..." he tried to breathe, "the truth...of what happened."

"Ethan." A hand was placed gently on my shoulder. "Ethan, let it go." It was the calming voice of a friend.

I pulled away. The man fell to the floor holding his neck, his face still red. He was on his hands and knees at my feet. The urge to kick him while he was down was curbed by Galen pulling my arm. The man stood up, standing tall, breathing heavily; he tugged at his shirt, tucked it into his pants, composed himself, sat down, and grabbed my tea cup. He poured the contents of my cup on the floor and poured a fresh cup of tea for himself.

"Is this supposed to be the good cop, bad medic routine?" He sipped his tea.

CHAPTER 26

Galen sat at his desk. I was breathing heavily, my chest heaving with each breath. It felt as if my heart would explode with each beat. Sweat beaded my forehead and cheeks. My leg hurt. I rubbed it gently to ease the pain.

"What the hell were you thinking, pinning him up against the wall like that?"

I caught my breath and looked at Galen like I had been betrayed by one of my best friends. Galen should be supporting me. He'd cared for Maddy, too. They were like brother and sister. We had all been heartbroken by her death. To have some scumbag desecrate her name, even bring it up at all, made, to me, my attack justifiable.

"What did he mean about Maddy's death?"

I chose instead to answer his first question. "I'm not a cop. I'm not bound by the same rules of interrogation!" My breathing slowed.

"No, but I could charge you for assault. Good thing I had my back turned and didn't see a thing. That and the video recorder broke down just at that moment."

I knew I'd dodged a bullet; it seemed like this had become my new norm. Having friends in high places saving my ass does have its advantages.

I ran my hand across my forehead to wipe off the perspiration and Galen gave me a look of horror.

"Bud, umm, yeah, I think you better look at your hand!"

I turned my right hand over. My palm and fingers were coated in bright red blood and must have transferred to my face when I'd wiped the sweat.

Looking down, I noticed that blood had soaked through my khakis, creating a large, dark red stain. The area of blood on my pants grew larger with each passing second. Galen hurried for the first aid kit in the kitchen.

I grabbed a pair of scissors off of his desk and cut a hole in my pants. Pulling, I tore the pants horizontally, making one leg into shorts. Blood flowed freely down my leg. Lifting the pants a little higher, I found several stitches had given way when I ran into the table when I attacked the man. The stitches had ripped through the skin and had opened the wound. Four to five inches of the laceration was now a fresh wound again and the impact had caused the injury to bleed.

Galen always kept a stash of napkins in his desk drawer for sudden donut or chocolate bar emergencies. I opened each drawer until I found what I needed and retrieved a handful. The napkins, saturated with blood, shredded and left tiny bits of paper on my leg. I continued to clean my leg as Galen returned with the first aid kit.

He laid the open kit on his desk and stood frozen.

"What?" I asked as I continued to clean up.

"I think this thing has been picked clean. Not exactly sure who is supposed to make sure the kits are stocked."

"What have you got in there that I can use?"

Galen lifted a single Band-Aid, an empty plastic core from a roll of tape, a gum wrapper, and a few cotton-tipped applicators.

"What about a kit in your car?" Galen asked.

"Be serious! When have you ever known me to keep a first-aid kit in the car? Have you got any duct tape?"

Galen stood tall and yelled loudly, "Hey, everybody! Shut the fuck up! Duct tape."

The detectives opened their desks; the sounds of rummaging in metal drawers could be heard in the expanse of the room. After a few moments, one of the detectives found a prize and tossed it over the heads of other cops. Galen caught it mid-flight.

While Galen's friends were looking for the tape, I'd cut the stitches free that had let go and pulled them through my skin and tossed them in the garbage. Galen handed me the tape and I tore off several, one-eighth of an inch by four inch strips, and stuck them to the edge of the Galen's desk. I tore another longer piece, two inches by twenty four inches, and stuck it to the desk in line with the rest of the tape.

I tore a small swatch from the discarded pant leg and completely cleaned the area of blood before I could use the tiny strips of duct tape as Steri Strips. These are used as fabric sutures in the ER in areas of the body where it might be difficult to use proper sutures. Placing the first tape strip on the right side of the gash, making sure it adhered well, I pulled on it until the two sides of the skin met, then pressed the tape in place. I started the next piece of tape on the left side, just below the last piece of tape, pulled it tight to the right, and pressed down. I repeated this right to left, left to right process until the entire laceration was closed.

I removed one of my socks, cut off the section above the ankle with Galen's scissors, and placed it carefully over the wound. I wiped the blood from my forehead with the upper section of the sock. I anchored the long piece of tape to the side of the wound and wrapped it around my leg. The sock would act as a pressure dressing and absorb any small amount of blood that might leak out.

Standing up to flex my leg and test out my DIY repair job, I noticed my left pant leg now looked sorely out of place. Scissors in hand, I cut the left leg off my pants and removed my left sock.

I did keep a well-stocked first-aid kit at home and would clean the wound and apply sterile strips later. The kit had been Maddy's idea.

"Sure you don't want to go to the hospital?"

I shook my head while I cleaned my work area and placed the bloody pant leg in a plastic bag for proper disposal. "Thanks, but no."

"Finished?" The voice behind me was familiar and not one I wanted to face. Chief Stabenow stood above me with a stone face that did not appear too happy. He pulled a chair from another work area and sat beside Galen.

"Mind telling me why you never bothered to share that information with us before talking to that man?"

Frankly, it never occurred to me, and the interrogation room seemed like the perfect place to troll for more information. Besides, everything had been happening so fast, I'd barely had the time to catch my breath.

"It never came up. There always seemed to be more important things going on."

"In the future," he turned to Galen, "you pass everything--and I mean everything--through Galen if it refers to a case you two are working on. This is the way things work in the police department. Besides, I can imagine you will be asked the same thing the next time you see Liz. Tell Liz I told you to keep the information quiet. Got it?" There was no mistaking his displeasure. "Brief Galen now and I want that report by the end of the day!" With that, he stood, gave me a father's look of disapproval, and left.

"Am I in shit?"

"If you think this is shit, wait until Liz gets hold of you and reams your ass for withholding information. You're gonna fucking wish you were back in that interrogation room. You up to giving me that statement now?"

It was already past one in the afternoon, I hadn't snagged one of the donuts I'd brought for Galen and the guys earlier, and my stomach was rumbling.

Galen heard the growling, pulled a granola bar from his hidden stash of illegal foods he kept from his wife and tossed it to me.

"Thanks. Pen at the ready, bud?"

He waved it in the air to indicate he was ready for my statement. For the next hour, I spoke, Galen wrote and asked questions. I would forget facts and Galen knew when the story didn't flow and he would pull the details from me. A true detective in every sense of the word.

Later, after Galen had extracted every last detail of my meeting with the Purity guy, he offered to buy me lunch, providing I went home and applied a real dressing on my leg and changed pants. I think he was more than a little embarrassed by the way I was dressed.

As I stood, a uniformed officer burst through the doors leading to the stairway and came running up to Galen's desk. He was out of breath and couldn't get the words out fast enough, "Guy...your guy...dead in the cell!"

"Why didn't you call?"

He panted again, "Extension...was...busy." Galen always shut off his extension when he was taking notes. He was not a multi-tasker.

The officer was still panting when Galen moved faster than I had ever seen him move. His chair fell backwards as he pushed away from it and bolted for the stairs. The force of his weight sent the metal door crashing into the cinder block wall. I wasn't following like I normally would. Galen turned and the look gave away his question.

"Go. I'll get there."

I took a few steps. Pain seared down my leg, tape pulled at the hairs and I recoiled. Lifting my injured leg, I hopped better on one leg than if I tried to keep the weight off my bad leg. It was farther to the elevator than the stairwell, and it would take longer to get there. I opted for pain.

I hit the stairs, placed my hands on both hand rails, balanced myself and swung out taking four or five steps and landing on my left foot. Reaching forward I repeated and made the landing. Eventually, I made my way to the holding area.

A uniformed officer was pumping on the suspect's bare chest, hard and fast. No one was performing artificial respiration, and that was fine with me. Several officers stood around watching, Galen among them. The unconscious man's skin colour was pale, as if he had been dead for a few minutes before anyone had found him. I broke through the crowd and knelt down beside the patient's head.

"Airway?" I asked.

"Open," the officer on the floor replied.

"Witnessed arrest?"

"No."

"How long was he down before you found him?"

He shrugged his shoulders while performing CPR.

"Defib?"

"On its way," someone from the crowd offered.

"Nine-one-one?" I looked up.

"Already called," the same voice replied.

Doing chest compressions at a rate of at least one hundred per minute is not an easy task. Anyone out of shape will get tired pretty fast. It doesn't take long to become exhausted when performing CPR. You can notice your rate and depth of compressions becoming less effective over time.

He didn't decline my offer to take over CPR as I moved into position, knelt down on the opposite side of the patient and felt for a pulse.

"Stop compressions." I continued to feel for a carotid pulse, just to the side of the trachea, not by the ear like they show on TV. Once the compressions stopped, so did the pulse. I started doing compressions, hard and fast. No one offered to perform artificial respiration and I wasn't about to argue.

An hour ago, I wanted him dead. Was this prophetic? I felt no emotion, no sadness as I looked down upon his face. He was now simply another stranger on another call. This was nothing more than doing my job. Emotions never play a part in it.

Moments later, another officer arrived with a medical kit. He tossed it to the floor beside the patient's head and unzipped the main compartment. He pulled out a black and yellow PAD--public access defibrillator--and looked at it, flipping it over and over before placing it beside me.

I stopped doing compressions, and the officer who'd brought the defib took over doing compressions.

Pulling the pads from the back of the defib, I applied one pad on the patient's right breast below the midline of the clavicle. I placed the left pad under his left breast toward the back. The pads were already plugged into the defibrillator. There were only two buttons on this model, a round green "On/Off" button and an inverted red triangular "Shock" button. I pressed the green power button. The machine came to life telling me to apply the pads to the patient's chest. Already done! Next, the machine told me to press the flashing shock button.

The machine's automatic prompt advised everyone, "Analyzing heart rhythm. Do not touch the patient." We followed orders.

From past experience, I knew the machine would recognize a "No Shock" rhythm. When I first felt for the pulse in the patient's neck after the officer stopped doing compressions, there was absolutely nothing. Quite often, ventricular fibrillation or other heart rhythms will generate a weak, almost indistinguishable or faint pulse in the carotid artery in the neck if the blood pressure if high enough. In this case, nothing could be felt. The heart was not beating and a non-beating heart won't be shocked. If the heart is still attempting to work and there is fibrillation or a fast pulse, tachycardia, a rhythm where the heart is pumping so fast that the pump becomes totally ineffective, the defibrillator will send out a shock, knocking out the bad rhythm and hopefully allowing the survivable rhythm to take over.

As I feared, the defib declared, "No shock advised," meaning that the defib would be ineffective with this patient. The defib started a two-minute timer and I instructed the officer to perform hard and fast compressions on the dead man. I already knew the outcome was bleak.

The second officer rummaged through the first response bag and found a BVM--bag valve mask device. Doing artificial respiration on a stranger can be dangerous and something no medic would ever do. The BVM allows the rescuer to provide AR safely at a distance by squeezing a bag of air into the patient's lungs and covering the patient's mouth and nose with a mask. Using a BVM effectively is a difficult skill to master. I placed the mask over the man's nose and mouth, gently tilted his head back and squeezed the bag slowly twice every thirty compressions. As I kneeled down on the concrete floor, my injured leg started throbbing.

While the officer was doing compressions, I rummaged through the first-aid kit and found an oral airway, a short plastic tube that goes into the mouth and provides a decent patent airway under most circumstances. I placed the airway and continued to bag the patient. After two minutes of CPR, the defib analyzed again and gave a "No Shock Advised." The officer continued to do a great job of compressions and I ventilated twice by BVM every thirty compressions.

After the third consecutive "No Shock Advised," the sound of arriving medics asking questions prior to getting to the patient came from behind the crowd of officers watching the events unfold.

The crowd gave way, and the medics lowered their cot and removed some of their bags and defib. The lead medic recognized me, stood behind me and asked for details on the call. The other medic took over doing ventilations. Another police officer took over from the exhausted officer doing CPR.

Once the patient information had been given to the ACP medic, I went over to Galen and let the guys being paid do their job. I knew the EMS crew would be calling in to cease resuscitation on this guy. It had not been a witnessed arrest and no one knew how long he had been in cardiac arrest before he was discovered.

He had been dead before I got to him. As Galen and I walked away, I felt no remorse, no compassion, nothing. Dead, gone and forgotten, but I was puzzled: What killed him? While I'd been trying to save the prisoner, Galen had spoken to the officer in charge of the cells who had said the prisoner had been alone before and after the interrogation. No visitors, no one had spoken to him or had any contact other than Galen and me and a select few.

"Any idea what happened?" I asked Galen as we waited for the elevator. I was too tired and sore to take the stairs.

"He was alone in the cell. No one got to him except you, me, and a few uniforms. Probably heart, if the fucker had one. Hope it hurt." Galen stepped forward, repeatedly pushed the "UP" button, then pulled back and stood beside me. I was looking at him questioningly.

"Shut the fuck up! It makes me feel in charge, okay? Besides, I hate waiting."

"For a meal!"

The doors opened and we stepped inside.

I was starting to spend more time with the police than with EMS. I wasn't sure if Galen, Chief Stabenow, or anyone else here seemed to notice, but I certainly did.

133

CHAPTER 27

Back at Galen's desk, he had me write down a statement of events for the failed resuscitation of the man in the jail cell. Under "name," I put "Man in the jail cell." Shit, we still didn't know his name. Come to think of it, I still didn't know the name of the man who had come to see me with the story of Purity, the man who had attacked me, or the man who'd stolen the jump drive. They were all anonymous men, working for a previously unknown group, trying to change the natural course of mankind by genetics.

I kept writing, and fatigue crept up fast. My eyes became heavy and closed several times before I decided to rest for a few moments. I leaned forward, resting my head on my arms, and a memory formed behind my closed eyes...

*****

The Civic ER was busy. Tom and I had a young male patient in moderate respiratory distress. We placed our cot by the side wall and went to the triage nurse to transfer care of our patient. The poor kid had been stung by a swarm of wasps while cutting grass in his backyard. The ground wasps had only been protecting their hive and had attacked the one they saw as being the aggressor. The eleven-year-old boy had been stung more than a dozen times on his lower legs, arms, neck, and face. He'd swelled up and his breathing had become compromised.

Having a previous allergy to bees and wasps, his parents had been prepared and had injected him with his EpiPen. It helped, but his anaphylaxis continued to spiral out of control. They knew EMS would be a few minutes getting to the house, so before their son's throat swelled completely shut, they gave him several antihistamine tablets. With some difficulty, he'd gotten the pills down, but they would take more time to take effect than the boy had.

By the time Tom and I had arrived, his eyes had swollen shut, his breathing had become laboured and wheezy, and his parents were scared to death. Tom had started the IV, and I'd quickly injected him with 0.5ml of epinephrine IM (intra-muscular). It hadn't taken long for the epi to start taking effect. With the IV running, Tom had administered 50mg of diphenhydramine into the bag and set the IV rate flow.

En route, the boy's condition had improved, and with a Ventolin treatment to control his wheezing, he had stabilized well enough that we knew we would be on off load delay for quite some time.

That was when I saw her. A nurse walked past us, paying no attention to Tom and myself or to any of the other medics. I had always imagined what the perfect woman would be and, for the first time in my life, I realized dreams do come true. Physically, she was the culmination of every conceivable fantasy I had ever had: perfect in every way.

"She probably has the personality of my last girlfriend and the voice of a banshee. Be careful, Nash. You might get what you wish for."

Tom was right about one thing: I did get what I had wished for! Maddy turned out to be as beautiful on the inside as she was on the outside, and she had the voice of an angel.

Maddy ignored me for weeks. Intentional or not, she'd captured my attention. It was all business at first, then casual chatting, a phone number exchanged, first date, second date, a short relationship, then our marriage cut short by her death...a death I am still not over; a woman I will never forget. My life had changed for the better when we met, and since her death, I have been a bitter, pissed-off man with a grudge against the world and little respect for anyone or anything.

*****

"Time to go home, buddy." A voice, muffled, my shoulder was shaken gently.

Galen had seen me with my head resting on my crossed arms on the desk, eyes closed, fast asleep. He knew most of all that I was probably more emotionally drained than physically tired. My leg hurt, yes, but any mention of Maddy could still kill me inside. Having her name mentioned had brought her back to life in my dream.

I feel stupid for admitting it: I almost cried when I woke up. I was completely unaware that the loss of one person could affect another so immensely, that one person could consume the being of another. It had been a symbiotic relationship; we'd fed off one another. We were each more complete, more whole than apart, and when she died, I lost more of myself than I thought possible.

I looked up, images blurry, blaming the sleep for the dampness in the corner of my eyes.

"Go home." Galen is a good friend. Losing anyone else right now would devastate me. Losing anyone else? Does that include Becky?

"Yeah, you're right. I feel like a bag of shit."

"While you were sleeping, I had one of the secretaries run down to the pharmacy and get you a little gift."

I opened the bag he handed me and saw a box of Butterfly Strips inside. Almost the same as Steri Strips, they would close my leg wound properly and do a much better job than tape.

I sat in my car with torn pants, my leg bound in duct tape, and a splitting headache. I tilted my head back against the seat while I massaged my temples, trying in vain to clear my head. I should have asked for some Advil before leaving. My headache was only the beginning.

Summer was fading fast. It was still warm, not hot, but comfortable during the day and starting to get cool at night. The worst part was that it was dark by eight.

Each day would get a little shorter and a little cooler, the leaves would change colour and fall to the ground, snow would replace rain, and the beautiful greens and bright days of summer would be exchanged for dull, dreary, short days of winter. I have yet to find one truly redeeming feature of winter. As a Canadian, I am supposed to enjoy the cold, relish the snow, and thrive in the winter. Instead, I hibernate in my house, looking forward to the first day of spring.

I'd left Galen to settle the matter with Stabenow regarding the dead guy in the cell. The case was getting stranger and more convoluted by the minute, and all I wanted to do was leave and get back to the life I'd had before this all started.

During my nap on Galen's desk, Becky had texted saying that she was heading back to my place after her meeting with Ottawa EMS. She'd left no indication if her meeting had been successful in finding her a new position.

I guessed I would have to wait until I got home. It was an odd feeling coming home and having someone other than Maddy being there. I wondered what Maddy would think about being replaced. Well, not replaced. She could never be replaced, but something else.

I pulled onto the Queensway westbound lanes. I merged with traffic and followed the speed of the car in front of me. The air conditioning in my car hadn't worked since I purchased it, like most of the other options in the car; I was just lucky that it started each time.

Traffic was constant on the Queensway. Anyone who lives in Ottawa or has ever visited Ottawa knows just how bad traffic can be on the arteries that weave in and out of the city's downtown core. Traffic going into the city from either the east or the west in the mornings and reverse in mid-afternoon creates a bumper-to-bumper, snail's-paced commute. I loathe drivers who feel it's necessary to weave from one lane into the next, attempting to get into the fast lane and making the lives of everyone one else a little more difficult as we are forced to allow these idiots into our lane time and time again. Yeah! I was tired and pissed and in no mood for bad drivers. I felt blessed this time because I hit traffic just before rush hour began.

Coming up my street, I could see that Becky's car was already in the driveway. Pulling in beside her car, I opened my door and an aroma overwhelmed my senses. Someone had their BBQ fired up, and the smell of really expensive steaks grilling filled the air. Becky had the front door open by the time I was about to enter. She had a huge smile on her face, her eyes lit up, and I was sure she had good news.

This was not a good time to bring up the events of the afternoon.

"So, I assume things went well today?" I was already smiling too.

Becky was almost jumping up and down as she stood in the doorway. I purposely stood outside and waited for her to divulge the news. I knew there was something to be told.

She reached forward, grabbing my wrist, and pulled me into the house. She kept pulling me along, through the front hall, past the living room, into the kitchen to the backyard. My injured leg screamed at me to slow down, but I couldn't contain Becky's excitement. Out on the patio, Becky had set up a pop-up shelter and underneath was a table set for three: white linen tablecloth, candles, flowers, and wine chilling. Even Molly and Snickers were outside enjoying the late-afternoon warmth.

"Well, aren't you little Miss Suzy Homemaker?" I turned and smiled at her once again.

"I don't want you to get the wrong idea. I'm not moving too fast or proposing or anything like that, so don't be scared."

When she said she wasn't proposing, oddly, I felt a little disappointed. And relieved!

"Do you have to wash up or anything before dinner? Oh shit! You are hungry aren't you? I should have asked. Sorry! I'm just so excited."

"Yes. Yes, and I couldn't tell."

She looked at me oddly, "What?"

"Yes, I should wash up, yes, I am hungry, and I couldn't tell you were excited, but I do want to hear everything." I turned and looked at the table again. "And why are there three place settings?"

Eyebrows went up and down. "You'll see! And get your mind out of the gutter!"

I limped up the stairs, grasping the railing, taking one step at a time, putting all my weight on the uninjured leg.

Sitting on the edge of the bed, I pulled off my socks and threw them at the clothes hamper. Both socks missed their target and landed on the floor. Dejected, tired, and totally exhausted, I fell backward onto the bed. The world was lost, my head spun from fatigue, and I fell asleep as soon as my head hit the bed.

CHAPTER 28

I woke from my nap: covers pulled up high, a pillow placed under my head, feeling refreshed and hungry. The throbbing in my leg had subsided and it felt great. After the cobwebs cleared, I realized I'd probably missed Becky's dinner. I slipped on a pair of sweat shorts and a heavy T-shirt and headed downstairs.

Voices came from the patio out back. At the bottom of the stairs, I turned right and headed through the kitchen toward the backyard. To my surprise, the dinner plates were stacked on the kitchen counter, and Tom and Becky sat with their backs to me, each nursing a beer.

Becky heard the screen door slide open and stood to greet me. She had a grin that would have made the Cheshire cat jealous. She gave me a grizzly bear hug. Tom, still holding his beer, smiled and said nothing.

"Wakey, wakey, sleepyhead. When you didn't come right back down, I went to check on you and found you snoring away. I called Galen and he told me what happened at the station. How're you doing?" Becky sat back down and pulled a patio chair out for me.

As I passed Tom, I placed my hand on his shoulder. "Nice seeing you." He smiled again.

"What happened to that gut of yours? You look like you've lost quite a bit of weight."

Tom grabbed his gut and squeezed. "Ten pounds. I have to get back into shape for the road and I could feel that extra weight on my leg. I started to exercise and the weight just started falling off. Doubt I'll ever get my six-pack abs back, but I'm comfortable now."

I sat down, twisted the cap off the last bottle of beer on the table and drank a mouthful.

"Yuck! Warm!"

Tom got up from his chair. "I'll get you a cold one." He recapped the open bottle and went to the fridge for a fresh one.

"What the hell?" I watched Tom walking without the use of his cane, and now only with a slight limp.

"Lost the weight, easier on my leg."

Becky kicked my chair. "That was one of tonight's surprises, but you decided to sleep through it."

"The other?"

Tom returned with a cold beer and placed it before me. "You got your steady partner back. I went to Human Resources today, and once you come back, I will be riding third with you to get my groove on again, and after I am cleared for duty, the A Team is back on the job."

"And . . ." Becky was almost hopping in her seat.

Tom and I kept talking about his returning to the streets, knowing full well Becky was chomping at the bit to tell me more news. Tom and I were back in the groove already. This was one of our ways of messing with Maddy and it worked just as well on Becky.

"Excuse me!"

We both turned and smiled at her.

"If you have something to say, cutie, just say it."

"That's where I met Tom today, at HR--and I start in two weeks. Yeah! I'll be a--" she air quoted, "--'Training Coordinator Assistant.' Whatever the hell that is! They told me I will be assisting with the Continuing Medical Education series, training new hires, dealing with injured workers getting back on the road. Shit like that. I still have to keep my certification up and ride out to get my hours in, but," Becky smiled and shrugged her shoulders, "I'm back."

She continued, "After Tom and I cleared things up there, we went for coffee, and I invited him over to share our good news over a barbeque. But you decided to sleep through dinner." Becky realized I still hadn't eaten. "Shit, I'm sorry, hon, can I put something together for you?"

"Anything, don't go to any trouble."

Becky stood and went into the kitchen.

Tom lifted his chair and pulled it in tight to mine. His arm wrapped around the back of my chair, and he leaned in close.

"You two are getting mighty chummy pretty freaking fast."

"I know. Completely the opposite of the way I usually am. I really am liking it, though. I feel like a person again."

"She was talking about finding an apartment to move back to while you were sleeping. I'm just saying, you may not want to let this one go again. I don't know how you managed to get two really great girls--Maddy and now this one--but you are one lucky son of a bitch. Too bad she can't cook. Her potato salad really sucks. But on the bright side, she knows how to pick the good beer." He held up his Corona.

For the next few hours, Tom, Becky, and I talked about how we met, worked together, and managed to stay sane in Ottawa EMS. Molly and Snickers went in when the mosquitoes came out and took control of the backyard; we followed suit. We headed into the living room and drank a few more beer, ate, and just spent time together. Well past midnight, Tom eyes started to get heavy and he fell asleep on the couch.

Becky found a spare pillow and blanket and covered Tom before we went upstairs.

I was in the bathroom, toothbrush in mouth. Becky was already in bed and I thought it was the right time to ask.

"Have you thought about where you are going to stay now that you have a job again?"

"I'm gonna start looking tomorrow. I have to find something fast, get settled in before my first day. Wanna help me apartment hunt? It'll be fun."

"If you want, not saying you have to or anything, but why don't you stay here until you get things squared away and see how things go from there? I know you don't have a lot of money and first and last months' rent is going to clean out your savings. Besides, all your clothes are here anyway, and you already have a key for the place."

I was bent over spitting into the sink when I felt two arms wrap around me and a head buried into my back.

"I'll take that as a yes."

CHAPTER 29

The next morning, Tom had made a baked French toast dish that was waiting for us when we woke. French toast in a casserole dish, baked in the oven, I think that's what he said. It looked kind of weird, but tasted great.

Becky made a large pot of coffee. Tom insisted on real maple syrup, saying that the artificial "crap," as he called it, only ruined his mother's recipe. Over coffee and baked French toast, the conversation from the night before continued without missing a beat, and I got more details of Becky's new job and Tom's workout schedule to get him back into shape and ready for work. While we chatted and ate, Becky played foot fight with me under the table. We were like ducks, calm on the surface, but under the table, a fierce foot fight to the finish raged on without Tom's knowledge. I felt like I was in eighth grade again.

The day started great; good food, spending time with my old partner, Becky's decision to stay with me for a while, no mention of murder or the demise of mankind, and I hadn't received any threats against my life yet. All in all, things were going well.

After a quick cleanup, Tom went home, and Becky and I headed downtown to the Byward Market. By noon on a Saturday, the market was teeming with vendors and customers. The Byward Market is one of Canada's largest and oldest public markets, being the focus of the city since 1826. During the day you can find franchise stores, merchants selling homemade crafts, and farmers selling produce. By night, people come down for the restaurants and clubs. Either way, it's a blend of cultural diversities that you won't find in any other section of the city.

As we walked east on York Street, we wove our way through crowds as they gathered in front of their favourite shop or vendor.

Even after Tom's homemade French toast, we decided to pick up Beaver Tails to eat while we walked around...more carbs and fat, just what I needed!

Becky picked up a few pieces of clothing she needed and bought me a new pair of pants to replace the ones I'd torn at the police station the day before. I enjoyed watching her, not saying anything, browsing through the stores, looking at the merchandise, going from vendor to vendor. There is nothing quite like the feeling of a new relationship when you still can't get enough of each other.

My phone rang once when Becky was with a salesperson. Looking down at the display, Galen's number and face were displayed on the screen. I let it go to voice mail and switched the ringer to silent. Nothing was so important that it would interfere with my time. I pushed the screen up and sent Galen a quick text: "Unless someone is dying, it can wait until tomorrow."

I slid the screen back down and pocketed the phone.

Becky ran into friends several times, and I was introduced over and over again. At some point, I realized I was being looked over and critiqued in private behind my back. I think I passed most of the reviews--after all, Becky continued to introduce me to her friends.

A few hours into the walk, my leg started to remind me that I still had a wound that I was supposed to be caring for. We found a small café with a vacant table out by the sidewalk. A server stopped by the table with glasses of water and menus. We ordered sushi and bento.

"How's the leg?"

I rubbed my pant leg to massage the muscle. "Not bleeding, so I guess your wound care this morning is holding strong." I smiled at Becky. "I was kinda hoping that hot nurse in emerg could fix me up next time." I was sprayed with flying droplets of water.

"Hey, bud! I couldn't help but notice you look like you're in a fuck of a lot of pain there." The voice came from behind me.

I turned to face a young man, college aged, dressed as if he'd just left class. He didn't stand out from anyone else at the market. A leather backpack hung over the back of his chair.

"Yeah, a bit." Rubbing my leg to indicate where it hurt. "Good reminder to wear my seat belt."

"I got some killa shit to take care of that pain. Does more than take the edge off, it kicks it in the fuckin' stratosphere. Interested?" He was leaning in closer.

"Thanks, bud. I don't need anything..." My words trailed off as I realized that I had an opportunity to pursue this further. "Okay. What have you got?" I continued.

As nonchalant as pulling a phone from his pocket, he produced several tiny, clear glass vials. I recognized them immediately. Morphine! They looked identical to the ones we use on the rigs and in every hospital in the country. The hospitals hadn't reported any thefts of morphine, but Ottawa EMS had.

"Let me see." I extended my hand. Like a patron slipping a twenty to the maître d', he palmed me a single vial.

Becky looked over, eyes squinting. I looked up and understood her query. Slowly, and hopefully without drawing the attention of my new found friend behind me, I shook my head side to side hoping Becky understood.

One-ml, ten-mg, morphine, same packaging, same labelling, exactly the same as the ones we use, exactly the same as the vial pulled from the dead OD patient.

"How much?"

"How many you want?"

"Just this one."

"Fifty bucks and I'll throw in a syringe."

"Fifty! Forget it." I extended my hand to give it back.

"How much do you have?" he asked.

My dad had taught me to always keep my money in two pockets for several reasons, bartering with vendors while on vacation and theft. This was the same as bartering with a vendor on the beach. I'd always kept an extra twenty dollars or so in my right pocket, but the rest was in my left. I reached into my right pocket and pulled out a twenty, a five and some loose change.

"That's all I got--unless you take Interac?"

"Not fucking likely! How much you got?"

I counted what I had, "Twenty-nine bucks and sixty-three cents."

"Ask the hottie you're with how much she's got."

"Twenty-nine, sixty-three, that's all I've got. The girl stays out of it."

"Fuck! Fine!" He reached out, took the money, and let me keep the vial.

"And I need your number in case I need any more."

"You a fuckin' cop?"

"Do I look like a cop?"

He scribbled a number on the napkin and handed it over to me. "For twenty-nine bucks, find your own syringe. Next time, remember to bring a fifty." He stuffed the cash into his backpack and walked away.

I turned back to see Becky looking at me inquisitively, still silent. Then I turned to see if my new friend was out of hearing range. The crowd flowed like water in a turbulent stream; he had already disappeared in the wave of pedestrians.

I opened my hand and looked down at the glass vial. I extended my hand across the table so Becky could see what I had.

"Isn't that just like the ones we use?" she asked.

"We've been having problems with theft and kids OD'ing on the street with this shit." I pocketed the vial. "I better text Galen."

Pulling out my phone I realized I should have taken his picture or asked Becky to do it. Rookie mistake, I reasoned.

I sent a quick text to Galen, giving him a short description of the guy and telling him that I had a vial of morphine and the lot number of the vial. I tried to take a photo, but the size of the lettering on the glass was too small to be legible in the picture.

Galen replied to my text asking why I wasn't tailing the guy. Not with my obvious limp, I wasn't.

Galen wanted to see the vial of morphine right away.

I offered to meet him at a coffee shop to hand over the drug and give him a report with a better description of the drug dealer.

An hour later, four of us sat at the farthest table in the corner at Starbucks, watching Galen roll the vial between his index and thumb. Galen had brought along and introduced Darren Steckel from the Guns and Gangs Unit. He looked more like the type of guy he should be arresting rather than a cop. Darren sat silently. He didn't order a drink and seemed very uncomfortable being with us. I'm pretty sure Starbucks was not his first taste in coffee choices.

"After you texted me, we ran the lot number against the information provided by Ottawa EMS and this is definitely, or at least quite possibly, fucking stolen. Jesus Fucking Christ! We have to deal with pot, meth, crack, coke, guns, and now this shit."

Galen's choice of adjectives attracted the attention of a few of the patrons who turned and looked our way.

Galen handed over the vial to Darren who slipped it into an evidence bag.

"I appreciate your work on this. We haven't had any luck tracking down how the stuff makes it out of EMS to the street. Galen told me you're cleared for upper-level intel." Darren looked back at Galen, who nodded in agreement. "We are looking at various angles, links to hospital distribution, EMS distribution, direct from the manufacturer, everything. Our unit put an undercover worker at EMS HQ, but no luck yet." His voice was steady, shoulders square; his obvious intelligence was well hidden by the four-day beard growth, black T-shirt, black jeans, leather jacket, and boots.

Darren thanked Galen, stood, and walked out without another word.

Galen sipped his coffee, swallowed hard and put it down. "What the fuck did I just drink?"

Becky smiled, "That is a Sumatra Dark Roast coffee. I thought you would like it."

"Next time, sweetie," that condescending comment would surely not go over well with Becky, "just get me a real coffee, okay?" He leaned over, kissed Becky on the cheek, tapped me on the shoulder, and left.

CHAPTER 30

An entire week went past without a word from Galen, our little group, or anyone, for that matter, except Tom. Nothing important happened at all.

I was still off work and enjoying my free time. My leg was healing nicely. The rest of the stitches had held, and the strips only had to be replaced once. I was planning on removing the stitches myself that evening. I would be heading back to work in two days regardless of whether the stitches were still in, and at this point they were more of an irritation than anything.

Tom had begun calling more often and stopping by again on a regular basis. His exercise program had accelerated his weight loss and he looked more like himself each time I saw him.

Galen had been silent; no updates on the morphine thefts from work, no updates on the identity of the man who'd died in police custody, nothing at all. Is this how normal people live?

My life was starting to have a routine again.

Becky and I spent a lot of time together. Our relationship was moving along as expected, still new, still full of potential. Every day I discovered something new about her, building trust, sharing our likes and dislikes. It was the second-best part of a relationship.

The best part was living together, knowing the way your partner thinks and moves; anticipating their wants and desires before they do; being able to share every detail of your lives and create new experiences. At least for me it was. I'd found it once. I was hoping to find it again, but I guess I was always a romantic at heart. My mother told me I should always be in touch with my feminine side. I used to hate that about my mother!

Tom called the day before I went back to work and offered to car pool for work and make sure I shaved before leaving the house. He didn't trust my new used car, and he also didn't know I had grown up and started to shave everyday like a real man! Being in a relationship helped, I guess. Tom would have to drive out of his way to pick me up on the route to EMS HQ but he was excited to start work again. I had new-found excitement with Becky; Tom had rediscovered the joy of health and going back to work. He was very happy again.

Becky had left before I got home and had gone out with her friends. "Girls' night," she'd said. I had the house to myself. I had a quick dinner of white mac and cheese and toast, childhood comfort food, before a night of intense television watching. Snickers and Molly had staked out their spots on the couch, reading my mind, knowing what the night held for them. They each held a spot of honour on the couch: Snickers on the left arm, Molly on the back behind my head. They'd modified their behaviour after Maddy died. Both cats had been devoted to Maddy and would tussle to see who got priority seating with Mom. Eventually, both always ended up falling asleep, curled up on Maddy's lap while we watched a movie or a little TV. After Maddy died, their need for affection necessitated moving to my side of the sofa for human contact. They still sniff her seat cushion and back for a reminder of Mom and then look around the house wondering why she isn't coming back. It wasn't that long ago; I would still pull out a sweater and see if I could still smell her. Pathetic and a little weird, I know, but even something that small can fill a void so large in your soul...you grasp at anything to feel whole again.

Not once had Becky asked why the wedding photo of Maddy and me still hangs in the den. All the other photos had been taken down one by one, put away carefully, wrapped in tissue to prevent any damage to the frame or the print it held. This one particular picture represented the single happiest time in my life, captured for all eternity in a glossy eight-by-ten, mounted with a colour-coordinated mat and a solid cherry frame. It is and was a horrible picture of me. But it captured Maddy looking at me. Not so much a look but a stare, staring at me as if I was the most important thing in her life. I was definitely out of her league. I used to joke about it, and she hated it, but it was our ongoing joke until the end. I seriously doubted a day would ever come when that picture would be removed from the wall.

Magnum P.I. had already been selected as the night's entertainment. I was up to season six, another guilty pleasure dating back to my youth. I opened the DVD box and unfolded the swing tray. Between the swing tray and the second DVD was a tiny slip of folded paper. My brow furrowed, I looked around to see if anyone was watching. Who could possibly know that I would look here? Turning over the top half of the note, I recognized the handwriting.

"You realize Magnum was on TV before I was even born? Enjoy the night alone. Be home late. Love B." Becky!

"Love"--not "Luv," but "Love," as in the big thing. Had our relationship moved this fast? Maybe it had and I just hadn't noticed. The first time I get a "Love" is in a note! Maybe it was always implied. Or maybe I was reading too much into it. I folded the note, placed it back inside the DVD case, and closed it. A matter for another time.

Returning from the kitchen, I placed a can of Diet Coke on a coaster beside a can of Light Bar-B-Q Pringles. Before sitting, I checked the door, made sure it was locked, and confirmed that the new security system I'd had installed this week was armed and ready. I'd had so many intruders in my house in the past few months...I figured this wouldn't stop them, but might slow them down a bit. Only Becky and I had a code. The curtains were drawn, but I had to pull them back just a little to peer up and down the street to see if anything suspicious was lurking outside. I just didn't trust anyone anymore.

*****

Magnum drove his Ferrari along the coast as the familiar theme played in the background. Magnum harassed Higgins, the simple mystery got solved within the hour time slot, and I had enjoyed my time alone. As I watched Magnum, Molly had curled up to my right and Snickers had stretched along the back of the couch.

One episode done, I'd started the next as I worked on finishing my second can of Diet Coke. I liked this, a quiet night with the cats, some junk food, classic TV, and stress free. Well, my only stress was the wording of the note Becky had left for me. No worries, no headaches, no one trying to break into my house. My biggest worry had been whether Tom was going to be on time picking me up the next day.

After Magnum episode two was done, I'd had my fill of Pringles and Diet Coke and was ready for bed. The clock showed 9:30, still early, but I was tired. I turned off the television, returned the DVD to its case, Coke cans in the recycling bin, lid placed on the Pringles can and put in the pantry, wiped the table clean, and turned the lights off.

Midway up the stairs, the house phone rang. I took the steps two at a time, bolted for the bedroom, sat on the edge of the bed, and picked it up without looking at the caller ID.

"Beck?"

"Nope, but I am a fuck of a lot cuter in a bathing suit."

"Hey, bud. What's up?"

"Wanna go for a little ride? We got a lead on the case. Remember the dead guy?"

"Dead guy! Can you be more specific? I deal with dead guys every day. Besides, I was getting ready for bed. Another time, okay?"

"What are you, an old man? Christ, it's not even ten. Besides, there might be shooting, you know guns and stuff, and we need someone who knows that the sticky side on the Band Aid always goes against the skin." I could hear him chuckle.

"Why me? I hate guns and shit! Galen, I want to go to bed," I pleaded.

"You're part of my team. I'll be there in ten. Get dressed. I already picked up a coffee for you." With that the line went dead. There was no further debate.

I wrote a note for Becky in case she got home before I did. I paused before I was about to write my name. Do I put "Love," "Luv"? I decided on a cute, hand-drawn heart with "E" inside it. I placed the note in the key bowl so Becky would see it when she returned. This was getting complicated.

Galen yelled at the door when he showed up a few minutes later. I deactivated the alarm and swung the door open. A large hand holding a coffee greeted me.

"Ready?" he asked.

"Where are we going?" I was tired and really didn't want to go play cop.

"Do you remember the name James Percy Kautz?"

"The guy we picked up at Parliament Hill. Of course--he was the guy who started all this."

"Well, we finally found out where he lived. The tech guys just finished and said we could go in. Interested?"

"Let me get my jacket." Now I was awake.

As I stood in the front hall putting on my jacket, I heard the sound of the door knob being turned against the lock. The handle turned one way, then back and stopped.

I looked back at Galen and shrugged my shoulders. Slowly, silently, Galen pulled the Glock pistol from its holster and held the gun to his side. He reached forward and pulled me back behind him.

The door handle rattled again and turned all the way allowing the door to open. The door was unlocked. Deliberately, methodically, the door started to open. Galen grabbed the inside door handle, pulled the door open quickly, and pointed the gun straight ahead at the person standing in the doorway.

CHAPTER 31

"Jesus Christ! What the hell do you think you're doing?" Becky screamed.

Galen lowered his gun, re-holstered it, and stepped back, allowing her to enter. I moved around Galen and gave Becky a hug. She hugged back tightly. I could tell she was looking over my shoulder at Galen. She released her grip and walked over to Galen and round house punched him in the shoulder. Then she turned to me!

"Are things really that bad that it takes Galen to pull his gun when you get scared?"

"You said you were going to be late. You said in your note: late." I was babbling.

"I wasn't having a good time. All they wanted to do was flirt with the guys for free drinks and yell 'Whoo hoo!' a lot with their arms up." Becky raised her arms and waived them back and forth. "I was embarrassed and tired of the crap, so I told them I had a really bad headache." She noticed Galen staring at her.

"And you, Mr. Dirty Harry, what are you staring at?" Her tone had eased.

"Ah, well, ah, frankly, I was looking at you!" Galen was stuttering and staring.

"Beck, hon, you look freaking HOT! Totally wow!" I was eyeballing Becky myself. She stood in the hallway wearing knee high black leather boots with three inch heels, a very short, black sequin dress with her right arm covered and her left shoulder and arm bare.

"All the girls dress this way at the bars now," she argued defensively.

"I'm not arguing. I think you look great. I would be proud to be with you at the bar wearing that. I love it."

"I gotta start going back to bars if you girls really dress like that. Sorry for staring, but I can't get my wife to wear shit like that at home in private, let alone go out in public. Personally, I think you should dress like that every fucking time I come over." Galen continued to stare. "Would it help if I said please?"

"No, it wouldn't help." Becky leaned in close to me. "This may come across as needy, but I really didn't enjoy myself at the bar. I would rather be home with you watching Magnum and Higgy Baby."

"Higgy Baby? Have you been secretly watching my DVDs? You look this hot

149

and watch Magnum. Wow!"

"Don't be so impressed. Google." Becky noticed my jacket. "Were you guys heading out?"

Galen cut in. "We got a lead. We were just going to check it out."

I pulled back and looked at Becky, "If you want me to stay?"

"Not a chance. I had girls' night, which I blew, now it's guy time. Who knows, I may still be in this or something even better when you get home." Her eyebrows bounced up and down.

"I'll hurry back." I gave her a quick kiss on the cheek, reminded her to lock the door and set the alarm, and we left.

Sitting in the cruiser, Galen turned the key and brought the engine to life. "You're a fucking lunatic. If I had that, I would never leave."

"You heard her--it's guy time now. We have to go catch the bad guys. Besides, I love you too, big guy." I winked at Galen.

*****

We donned our nitrile gloves, cut the police tape, and walked into the apartment of James Percy Kautz. Not what I expected; nicely decorated, the sparse furnishings were tasteful and modern. There was very little food in the fridge; even less in the cupboards. It was small, one bedroom with a single bed, brightly coloured walls, modern chairs and couch, a large LED TV, but nothing to identify the person who lived here. There were no family pictures, no pictures of Kautz as a child...a man without a past or a future, it seemed.

I walked around the apartment, looking under seat cushions and flipping through magazines. On the TV stand, I ran my finger along a row of books. Mein Kampf, The Life and Death of Adolf Hitler, The Rise and Fall of the Third Reich, and other books caught my eye: book after book on Jewish lineage, Sobibor, Auschwitz.

"Hey!" I tapped the books so Galen knew where to look.

He looked closely, squinted, "Nah! Our techs went through each one."

"How did you find out this was his apartment?" I said.

"Fucking accident, really. We got lucky. None of the information the feds got on Kautz was legit. When the Feds did their background check, all addresses and personal references checked out. When we checked, the house he listed was sublet to someone else. Kautz only went back to collect his mail sent to his alias. It was listed to Tomlinson, the name he worked under at Parliament Hill.

"The landlord here said Kautz's mail was piling up in the box down in the lobby, so he came to check on the apartment and found it empty. He called police to find out if there was any information on him. The landlord said he and Kautz got along really well when he was here, and that wasn't too fucking often."

"What's the landlord's name?"

He opened his notebook, "Sengupta."

"And Kautz got along well with the landlord? An Aryan getting along with a guy by the name of Sengupta? Seems strange, don't you think?"

Again, Galen shrugged, not answering the question.

"Do you figure he had another apartment or house or stayed with a friend? 'Cause there isn't a lot to indicate the guy lived here much. There's nothing personal." I continued my amateur sleuth investigation.

"No way to tell. Our crime scene guys went over everything in this place, top to bottom, front to back, side to side, and up and down...toilets, drains, pipes. Nothing, not a fucking thing. We figured he stayed with someone and used this apartment only now and then. With the lack of furniture and shit, we figured this was probably a place where he could bring someone or crash if he had to. The place the Feds checked out was a high-end rental, nice, expensive, and perfect for show."

I walked around looking, not with the eye of a cop, but with the eye of a medic. "How old was Kautz?"

Galen flipped his notebook open. A few pages flew up. He stopped and scanned, "Thirty-two."

"Did you find out if he had a medical condition?"

"He had really bad allergies. He had a Medic Alert bracelet saying he was allergic to bees."

I mumbled, "He had allergies, bees, possibly cats, dogs. If I was Kautz, I would keep an EpiPen, antihistamines around just in case."

"What the fuck are you doing?"

"Thinking out loud. Did you find any meds here?"

Galen checked his notebook. After referring to his notes, he shook his head side to side.

I walked around the apartment, looking in drawers, cabinets, anywhere I would keep medication. "Galen, where do you keep your meds? Kitchen, right?"

"Yeah! How did you know?"

"Cabinet beside the coffee cups, or in the same cabinet as the cups, right?"

"You looked when you were at my house."

"I know you. First thing in the morning, you get a coffee, read the newspapers, and take all the meds for your high blood pressure, Ramipril or Atenelol or both? What about high cholesterol?"

"Atenelol. And yes."

I kept looking around the apartment for places to hide an EpiPen and meds. Where would I hide some medication? He would've been hiding all the items in the apartment that could give his previous life away.

I looked at everything eye level; nothing. I looked low; nothing. As I walked around the apartment looking up toward the ceiling, I noticed a small semicircular scratch in the bathroom door frame where the door fits inside the jamb. Reaching up, rubbing my index back and forth over the scratch, I felt the tiny indent in the wood. Then I ran my hand over the top of the door to find out what was causing the cut in the wood. My hand found something metallic.

Looking around, I found a small chair and positioned it under the door frame.

"Can you hold the door still so it doesn't move, please?" Galen walked over and held the door tight. I was now tall enough to look down upon the top of the door.

"Would you mind telling me what the fuck you're looking for?"

I didn't respond.

Instead, I found a small metal cap, maybe an inch or so in diameter, resting slightly above the surface of the wood. It was set just high enough to scrape the door frame, leaving its telltale sign. The diameter of the cap prevented the item it held from falling down inside the door. Squeezing the cap of a small metal bottle, I pulled it free from the top rail of the door. Once the aluminum tube was fully removed from the door, Galen could see what I was doing.

I handed the eight-inch-long tube to Galen and he handled it like it was a grenade, cradling it with two hands. He sat down on a chair and stared at the tube. The dull silver cylinder looked like a cigar tube on steroids: instead of a rounded bottom, it had a flat bottom and a flat cap that screwed on one end. The thickness of the wall made the tube seem fairly strong. There were no exterior markings anywhere on the cylinder. The tube weighed only a few ounces at best.

"How the fuck did you know to look there?"

"My brother would hollow out the top of his bedroom door and hide his stash of dope there. My parents never found it. My brother is very smart. He knew people typically look at eye level and down. I figured if Kautz was as smart as my brother, he would hide his stash up high, too."

Galen shook the tube and looked up at me, "Should we?"

"This is your turf. I don't know the first thing about what we should or shouldn't do. But, if it was up to me, I'd open the freakin' thing." I stood beside Galen waiting for him to open the aluminum tube.

Galen held onto the cylinder and slowly turned the cap. The cap twisted freely. He placed it on the table and peered inside the container. He looked back up at me with a blank stare.

"I can't see a thing." He pointed the cylinder toward the table and tilted it slowly causing the contents to spill. The tumbling contents made the sound of plastic sliding against metal, sounds of small items falling out and hitting the table: pills, tiny shards of paper and a Gizmo jump drive. We both turned and gave each other a wide open gaze.

"What the fuck?" Galen reached for the drive, flicking the other objects out of the way, and held it high.

"A copy of the information we lost, or what?" Galen never took his eyes off the drive.

"Who knows? All I know is that I am not gonna use my laptop to look at it and you should take it to your IT girl and have her dissect it. And call Liz now! No, forget that. Call her after you have your tech look at the drive to see what is on this thing."

Galen retrieved an evidence zip-lock bag from his jacket, dropped the drive inside, and sealed the flap. He secured the envelope inside his jacket pocket.

While Galen was busy with the drive, I snooped through the other contents on the table: antihistamine tablets for his allergies; pieces of paper torn from larger sheets with notes scrawled on them; a single tiny key, possibly for a small lock, post office box, or something similar. That was it. I lifted the tube from the table and looked inside the cylinder. The edge appeared to be off, as if something was curled up inside. I tried to reach it with my index finger but whatever it was, it was too far down. I smacked the inverted tube against my palm several times causing the trapped air inside to emit a deep resonating pop each time. I looked in again and saw what appeared to be a curled photo around the perimeter of the tube. It was almost at the end of the cylinder. I reached in with my index finger and applied pressure against the wall and slid it out.

I unrolled the print and was looking at the black and white photo of a beautiful woman. The paper was thick and still glossy, and old, very old. It was a portrait photo, small, two by three inches, and the scalloped edges were tattered from years of handling. The emulsion on the photo had cracked and was missing in some areas, but it did little to hide the beauty of the woman who had posed for the photographer. I tuned the photo over and read what was written in faded ink: Yocheved Badenstein.

"Isn't that name Jewish?" I asked Galen.

He grabbed my hand and tilted the photo for a better look. "I would lay odds it was Jewish. But what is a sworn Aryan doing with a photo of a Jewish lady?"

"How old do you figure? The lady in the picture, I mean."

Galen thought for a moment, "The picture looks like something from the forties, maybe the fifties; might even be earlier. She looks like she might be late twenties or early thirties. That would make her," he paused, counted in his head, "between ninety and one hundred years old. If she's still alive!"

I stood and walked about the room. "This is more confusing than ever. We have a supposed dead Aryan, who brought himself back to life using the name of a man he most probably killed. Then he gets himself killed again, but this time there is no doubt he's dead. He has books about Jewish lineage and the Third Reich in his home, a hidden picture of a Jewish lady, and secretly works for a group who got their start under Hitler. Not to mention, this group will kill their own members to get information on a drive that we can't decipher, have no idea what it does, or what it is intended to do to whomever. Have I got that straight?"

"Yup, pretty much. Except you forgot one thing: what's all the other shit on the table?"

I hate head games--hate this whole good guy, bad guy stuff. I like black and white with no shades of grey...simple, nothing complex.

We sat down on the couch and rummaged through the artifacts on the table: bits of torn paper, pills, and the key. Each piece of paper was examined, one side, then the other, and placed written side up. Each piece of paper had only a single letter or number on it. I arranged the letters in alphabetical order: A – B – F – H – H – N – O – 1 – 1 – 1 – 3, vowels, consonants, and numbers.

"A,E,I,O,U." I put my finger on the pieces of paper with "A" and "O" and dragged them on top of the row. That left B – F – H – H and N. I dragged away the numbers and put them aside for now.

Like a puzzle, I kept dragging letters and placing them in various arrangements in an attempt to create words. Nothing we did made sense or created any words we could think of.

Galen rubbed his face, stared forward, stood and walked over to the row of books. He picked up Mein Kampf and displayed the book to me. "What says the letters form an English word?"

"How the hell are we supposed to know what German or Jewish word this is supposed to make? It's late. Who can we find at this hour to help?"

"You know what, it's really fucking late! I can't wrap my head around this shit anymore, you know that? I can't keep track of who's on what side, or even how many sides there are. This shit is just too much."

"Let's call it a night and go home."

While Galen was collecting the evidence and placing it all back in the tube, I pulled out my cell phone, hit memo, and keyed in ABFHHNO1113.

I snapped off my gloves and placed them along with the aluminum tube in the plastic zip-lock evidence bag Galen always carries.

*****

I opened my door, punched in the code to silence the alarm, closed the door, and reset the security system.

I was tired; my eyes were heavy and itchy, my thigh muscles ached. I tossed my watch, keys, and wallet into the key bowl. I kicked off my shoes and flung them to the back of the closet. It was almost two a.m., and I had to get up in a few hours to work my day shift with Tom. I needed sleep badly. I crawled upstairs, forgetting to brush my teeth, and climbed into bed.

I felt the familiar presence of someone sharing my bed. She rolled over and spooned me as I grunted from the ache that still haunted my thigh injury. I fell asleep before I could do anything more.

CHAPTER 32

I walked through the lab, stumbling, losing my balance as the room swayed from side to side like an ocean liner in rough waves. Grasping for the counter, I held tight to right myself. I spotted the vial of purple fluid I was searching for and reached for it. Before I could grab it, the vial hopped from the counter and ran to the sink. The vial teetered, balancing on the edge, threatening to dump itself down the drain unless I backed off.

With both arms out wide to the side, I let the vial know I didn't pose a threat. With each sway of the lab, I inched closer to the sink hoping to catch the vial off guard. After a few moments, I was close enough to make an attempt to take possession of the glass vial.

I waited for the next swell to hit the lab, bracing myself for the upcoming sway. When it hit, I reached forward, but the vial leaped, ran to the edge of the counter, and jumped off. The glass vial shattered, and purple fluid flowed freely on the floor. The tile began to bubble, and smoke billowed up, burning my nostrils.

The tiles began to morph, changing from a flat ceramic plate to a pliable membrane altering itself into human form. It twisted, screeched, and began to form a face. Slowly, cheeks, forehead, nose, and lips appeared. They began to take human form, and the face before me scared me.

Maddy began to speak, but I couldn't hear her. There wasn't any noise. Maddy began to scream, but I still couldn't hear her.

I yelled at her, asking her to stay. Her eyes rolled back. Solid, black eyes filled the cavity. Her cheeks began to sink inward, her head tilted to the left and her skin melted away from her gentle features into smoke.

The smoke twisted into long strands of hair and wrapped around a face that took shape. Chin, lips, nose, they all began to take a form more current. Becky's face appeared in black and white wisps of smoke. She looked sad; was it something I did or was about to do, or something she did? As I reached for her, my hand penetrated the smoke and caused the image to disappear.

I begged her to come back. The smoke began to change again. Male features began to take shape, matted hair, covered in blood with the forehead blown open.

A gaping hole showing bone and skin and soft tissue beneath formed in front of me. Brain matter clung to the jagged edges of the bone. James Percy Kautz yelled out in pain, but again, there was no sound. I strained to hear what he was saying and when I looked at him, I could see through the hole where the bullet entered the back of his head and exited through his forehead.

James's eyes began to vibrate side to side; his head pulsated in rhythm as the vibrations increased. The faint sound of bells could be heard in sync with his eyes going from one side to the next. I reached over to grab his head and hit the button to silence the alarm clock.

I bolted upright, wet with sweat, panting, breathless, the sheets kicked loose and lying on the floor beside the bed. Becky's side of the bed was empty.

I swung my feet over the edge of the bed and sank my head into my hands. Smoothing my hair back, I could feel the cool wetness of the sweat on my hands.

"Are you up yet?" Becky yelled from downstairs.

I took the steps two at a time, pants in hand, one arm through a shirt sleeve, one blue sock, one black sock. Thank God I had remembered to put on underwear before darting downstairs.

Tom was standing at the base of the stairs, sipping a coffee. Becky was shouting at me from the kitchen to hurry. I heard Tom snickering that regardless of which girl was in my house, I still couldn't get up on time.

"Sorry I didn't get a chance to shave. I was up late last night," I apologized.

Tom grabbed my cheeks and squeezed, spoke as if he was talking to a baby, "You're still as cute as a button. But put on your freakin' pants. We gotta move."

Becky came out, handed me my cooler filled with whatever she could throw together on short notice. She leaned in close and whispered, "Too bad you came home so late last night. I had some stuff planned."

"I heard that." Tom handed his coffee cup to Becky. "You guys are already acting like an old married couple."

Becky gave Tom a dirty look that left nothing to the imagination.

Tom picked up speed to merge with traffic on the Queensway and kept the speed up so we could book on with time to spare. Tom looked great. He was excited to get back to work. He had been off far too long and needed this right now. Being injured and living alone with nothing to do can play havoc with your mind.

I sipped my coffee as Tom drove, resting my head on the side window. I was still remembering fragments of the dream that had woken me that morning. My mind was still in overdrive from whatever had made me dream. I had never had nightmares like that before. I put it down to stress and helping Galen. Taking another gulp of coffee, I sat upright and enjoyed the commute.

Tom pulled into Ottawa EMS headquarters. As we entered the building, medics surprised to see Tom after such a long absence were congratulating him on his return to work. Tom stopped to chat, catch up with old friends, while I walked on. "Catch up when you're done."

Tom just smiled back. He was enjoying the attention.

I booked on, was assigned a rig and a new partner, Jared Racicot, tall, slim, short jet-black hair, long sideburns, young. Jared had been with Ottawa EMS for just under a year. His new-hire eagerness had worn off and he seemed comfortable working alongside us. He usually worked the dreaded afternoon shift that started at 15:00 and finished in the middle of the night or morning, depending on your point of view, at 03:00. With my penchant for going through partners in the past year, it had been getting harder to get people to work with me. Jared was different. When the shift was offered on the rotation, Jared jumped at the chance to break from the mundane day-to-day routine. Before booking on, he seemed genuinely excited to be part of my team, but not too excited.

Jared and I walked through the garage, chatting, getting to know each other before the shift started.

"Hey, Nash, was that Tom I saw back there?"

Jared and I both turned to see Terry Hobbs, one of the equipment technicians responsible for restocking and cleaning the vehicles each shift.

"First day back as a third person ride-along. He gets to do all my dirty work until I clear him. Now that Tom is back, are you guys gonna start to use "Nash" again, so I can file a harassment complaint against you?"

"Hey, Terry," Jared smiled at him.

"Nash just seems to fit when Tom's around."

"You go say hi to Tom while we get the truck. Nice seeing you again. It's been a long time."

"Too long." Terry turned to go meet up with Tom. As he spun, his backpack slid off his shoulder, fell, and hit the concrete floor. The unsecured open side pocket of his pack spilled its contents, and a yellow bullet box bounced off the hard surface and came to rest, letting a few vials of morphine roll out.

Terry looked down, saw the morphine vials, looked back up at me, and bolted. He left the backpack on the floor and ran toward the front hall where Tom was standing with a group of other medics.

"Tom!" I yelled. He turned to see Terry running toward him. Tom had a broad smile on his face. He opened his arms, caught Terry as he tried to make his way past him and Tom spun him around.

"Buddy!" Tom was still smiling and giving Terry a huge hug. Terry fought to pull away, but Tom was too strong and held him tight. Tom stopped spinning and put him down and before he could say anything, Terry made a dash for the hallway. Tom's hug had given me the time to catch up to Terry and, as he ran, I pushed hard against his back, sending him sprawling into the wall. He hit the wall face first, bounced back off and fell into my arms. I pushed him again into the wall. Terry turned, out of breath. Blood flowed freely from his nose. He leaned forward and placed his hands on his knees to catch his breath. He wiped the blood from his nose with the back of his hand and cleaned it on his pants.

Tom and the other medics ran up and met us in the hall.

"Would you mind telling me what the hell is going on? Have you totally lost it?" Tom's usual smiling face was now showing concern for my sudden odd behaviour.

"I think this might have something to do with it!" Jared held up a few vials of morphine. Terry looked up at Jared, put his back up against the wall, and slid down to sit on the floor. The blood continued to flow from his nose.

The other medics knew of the thefts. Tom looked around for some answers.

"I'll explain later," I told him.

Seeing the commotion, a supervisor walked over and saw Terry sitting on the floor and Jared holding the vials of morphine.

The supervisor spun his index finger in a circle, his voice stern with anger. "All of you, with me. Now!"

Jared and I had finished giving our statements to the police and were having a coffee in the lobby outside the conference rooms while Tom and the medics still had to give their statement of events. The deputy chief of Ottawa EMS was sitting in with the police as each medic described what they saw and did.

One by one, each medic who witnessed the skirmish walked out of the segregated interviews like they had been the one stealing narcotics.

The deputy chief exited one of the rooms, coffee in hand. His clip-on tie had been removed, his top shirt button was undone, and he looked exhausted, almost zombie-like.

"I want to thank you guys for what you did. Terry Hobbs is being arrested for theft and distribution of a controlled substance." He just walked past us and continued down the hall.

Jared and I decided it would be best if we went to the garage to wait. It was not long before Tom caught up, gave an enthusiastic "Hi" to Jared, and told him he was riding third so he could get his skills refined and return to full duty. For Tom, this would just be another day at work, and the events wouldn't faze him one way or the other.

"We were told not to talk about this to anyone. Did you guys get the same rhetoric from the cops?" We shook our heads in unison.

"Well, I am here to get back into the game, so you guys lead the way." Tom couldn't have been happier.

CHAPTER 33

Tom had been cleared by the Ottawa EMS medical director, the physician who licenses medics to perform their skills in the street. The medical director delegates our paramedic advanced skills to be performed as an extension of his or her licence.

In Ontario, depending on where you work, the service medical director might permit the medics to perform more or fewer skills as required by the Ontario Ministry of Health. A primary care paramedic, or PCP, may have a higher skill set in one part of the province than another, depending on the aggressiveness of the service medical director. The same goes for advanced care paramedics, or ACPs.

Tom needed to get the rust out of his IV lines, so to speak, and until he did, I would have to supervise his work until we both felt he was ready to work independently.

Unfortunately, my new partner, who had been assigned to me that day, would be the Sherpa carrying the gear and watching.

Tom rode in the back out of respect for our PCP partner. He realized that he had been out of commission for quite some time, and it wasn't Jared's fault, so while I sat in the passenger seat, Tom sat in the back, leaning forward through the small window to chat. The conversation went from Tom's weight loss, to Jared's thoughts about returning to school for a career change, to Becky's moving in with me.

Just before ten, dispatch sent us on a Code 3 call to a residence for a patient complaining of side effects from a new medication.

Tom looked up through the window. "Jared, buddy, pal, new friend, feel like taking this one?"

"So, shovel the crap calls onto the PCP, eh? Nice move, old-timer!" Jared knew that the comment wasn't made to make fun of his skills, but we get medication interaction calls almost daily.

Jared booked in-service and drove to Gladstone Avenue from Parkdale Avenue. Gladstone Avenue begins at Parkdale Avenue and continues east for several kilometres to Carter Street. The street goes through several styles of homes and classes along its length. The west is not known for its affluent homes, but rather its pre-war houses or two-storey apartment buildings that line both sides of the street. These were small, one-and-a-half-storey brick homes that had been built on lots barely large enough to warrant owning a lawn mower. You could simply mow the lawn with a hand-held weed trimmer! Each house mirrors the other in design and size. The only variations between houses were the renovations done over the past decades to personalize each home. Each house had a narrow, single-lane driveway that led to the backyard; and a small, covered veranda. Many of these were adorned with cheap plastic chairs and tables, as though fearful that anything more expensive would be stolen while the owners were asleep or away for the day.

A young man stood in front of the house where we were dispatched, casually waving us down as we drove along the street. He didn't seem too concerned that we had arrived without lights flashing and sirens blaring in the morning sun. Jared booked 10–7 scene and parked parallel to the street, the back of the rig in line with the start of the driveway.

As I exited the passenger side, the young man walked directly toward me, speaking as he approached. "My dad took some new multiple sclerosis medications this morning before breakfast and hasn't been feeling well since."

"How long ago was that?" I asked. Jared was still on the other side of the truck, Tom in the back.

"Let's see; he took them early, around seven, ate just after that, and right after breakfast said he started feeling, like, you know, not good."

Jared had opened the back door to the rig, Tom had hopped down and they were pulling the cot out with all the bags lying across the mattress. I updated Jared, who would run the call. We closed the back doors, locked the rig, and lowered the cot at the steps of the front veranda. The patient's son stood at the top of the steps and waited for us to follow.

"Go ahead, sir," Jared instructed the young man as we all followed him into the house. "What's your dad's name?"

"William. He goes by 'Billy.'"

Just inside the front door and to the right was a narrow staircase with a white-painted banister and railings, the paint no doubt hiding the beautiful wood beneath. Directly ahead, the hall led to the kitchen at the far end. To our left, Billy lay on the couch in the living room.

Jared approached the patient, acknowledging his wife standing off to the side, who was smiling politely at us. I've always wondered what goes through the minds of family members at times like this: strangers walking into their house, intruding on their privacy, seeing how they live, the décor and the smells of their ethnicity. They have enough to worry about; the health of a family member or friend...someone in their home has taken ill...9-1-1 had to be called, and complete strangers invade their home.

"Hi, Billy. I'm Jared. This is Ethan and Tom." He made no gestures to differentiate us from one another. "Is it okay to call you Billy? What seems to be the problem?"

Tom pulled Billy's wife and son aside to get their version of the story. Often, family members will answer questions asked directed to the patient and skew the diagnosis. As medics, we want to get as much of the story as possible, but if one person controls the entire scene, we can receive a biased view of what transpired. I stayed with Jared and acted as the driver partner would normally in a crew of two.

"I took my meds this morning just before breakfast. It wasn't long after I just got this feeling that rushed over me. I got tired, feeling like crap, just weak and tired, you know." Billy squinted his eyes to reinforce his statement.

"How long after you took your meds did this feeling come over you?" Jared continued the investigation.

"Maybe ten...at the most ten minutes...no, under ten minutes."

"Okay, and what medical history do you have, Billy?"

As I was setting up the defib to monitor his vitals, I overheard Billy tell Jared his medical history: he had been recently diagnosed with multiple sclerosis, had diabetes, and was a non-smoker. He recited his meds.

I ran a set of baseline vitals and watched Jared perform a full body assessment to see if the new medication was causing anaphylaxis, an allergic reaction. The patient presented with no signs of urticaria (hives), or other common indicators of anaphylaxis.

As Jared continued, I turned on the oxygen tank, set the litres per minute at ten, and placed a non-rebreather mask for higher oxygen concentration over Billy's mouth and nose.

"Jared, vitals." Jared continued to look at Billy, completing a visual exam as I read the vitals: blood sugar level 9.8, pulse 118, SPO2 91 percent on room air, blood pressure 167/104, respiratory rate 22, temperature 36.7. I handed Jared the four main cables for the ECG as I started a right-hand, anti-cubital IV of normal saline, TKVO (to keep vein open). Jared attached a lead with a monitoring electrode to each shoulder and one to each ankle, at the same time checking for any swelling of the ankles. No swelling was noted. The monitor was set to take Billy's vitals every five minutes.

"Any new or recent coughs?" Billy shook his head no. "Recent out-of-country travel? Any pain at all?" Again he shook no. "Billy, can you be a little more precise in your description of the feeling you got? Can you take one finger and point where this feeling hurts the most?"

Billy used his left index finger, raised it, waved and touched the centre of his chest. Jared looked at me, "Twelve-lead please."

"Billy, do you have a history of any heart problems? Again, you have no pain?"

"Nope and nope." Billy smiled. "MS is bad enough, isn't it?"

"Billy, I have to open your shirt and we are going to run a test, sort of a three-dimensional view of your heart type of test. I'm going to place more of these sticky round things on your chest. This test will tell me if you are having any type of heart trouble. While we're doing this, can you tell me what the chest pain feels like?"

"It's not pain. It's just more like a gas bubble. Maybe I need a good belch, you know. I thought chest pain was like on TV, with pain down the arm and neck, clutching your chest and stuff. My doc said my heart is fine. He tested me when I was diagnosed with MS."

"Everyone is different and chest pain can present differently. One being no pain, and ten being the worst pain you ever felt, how would you rate your chest pain right now?"

"Four on ten. No real pain at all. Is my MS the reason why I don't feel like I'm having a heart attack?"

Jared and I didn't respond, but continued to attach the electrodes to Billy's chest. I entered Billy's age and gender into the monitor and asked him to breathe normally and remain still while we performed the test. In less than a minute, the monitor printed out the twelve-lead diagnoses. I didn't even have to read it: plain as day, Billy's ECG showed a marked increase in his ST elevation on multiple leads. I tilted the strip of paper to give Jared a better look. He saw it, too.

"What's wrong?" I really need to work on my poker face. Billy must have seen the concern on my face as I reviewed the ECG strip. Billy's voice brought his wife, son, and Tom back to the living room.

Jared turned to me for guidance.

"Billy, your heart runs on electricity. These cables we put on you capture the electrical current running through your heart. If any of the heart muscle is damaged from a recent or even past problem, the current will show us what that problem is, and, more important, where it is. One or more of your arteries that supply your heart with blood may be blocked and damaging your heart muscle. We have to treat it now and get you to the hospital." I tried to keep it simple.

The wife spoke up behind me, "What kind of heart problem?" Her voice screamed concern and was a little panicked.

"We aren't stupid. Can't you be a little more specific?" the son demanded. Every patient or family member reacts differently when we treat a patient in their home. They typically act one way in the privacy of their own home and another in the hospital with the nurses and doctors.

"It's called a STEMI, ST for the part of the ECG reading that we are looking at, E for elevation, and MI for Myocardial Infarction. Basically, it's a blocked artery on your heart."

Billy's wife put her hand over her mouth, instant fear came across her face.

"I feel fine. Really, just a little tired," Billy said through the mask, trying to sit up.

The son went over and knelt beside his father, "Dad, just lie down and let these guys do their job, okay? I'll take care of Mom."

"Ethan!" Tom called out quietly. "No allergies. I have his medication list, nothing out of the ordinary. Takes his meds as prescribed and I've got his health card."

I thanked Tom, found the bottle of ASA in our drug kit, and handed it to Jared.

"Billy, it's really important you understand. You don't take a daily aspirin... you don't have any allergies to aspirin, do you?" Jared wanted to make sure. Billy shook his head side to side. "You haven't had a stroke or hit your head or had any bleeding from your head in the last few days, have you?" Again, Billy shook no, but Billy's face started to show panic. Jared altered his voice. He wanted to show that we were not panicking and neither should he. "I need you to chew these aspirin. Use your tongue and spread them around your mouth, over the gums and cheeks, don't swallow them, okay?"

Jared handed Billy the pills and lifted the mask so the patient could place them in his mouth.

"Now, chew them up, and while you do, my partners are gonna get our equipment ready. You just lay right there, don't move."

"I can walk out," he offered.

"We'll carry you out. That's what you're paying us for."

Tom stayed with the patient. Jared and I carried out the large trauma bag. I set up the cot at the base of the stairs. Jared retrieved the stair chair from the side door. As we entered the house, I quietly said, "Nice catch. Really good job diagnosing that one."

Jared said nothing, but smiled a little.

When we entered the house, Billy and his wife were talking quietly in private. Tom hung back. When the wife heard us bang our equipment, she quickly removed herself from the room and stood beside her son.

"This is a special chair. When it opens up, it becomes a chair and has these tank tracks that we can use to roll you down the stairs. It's important that while we move you, you don't reach out or throw us off balance. Got it?" Billy nodded.

Tom and I set up the stair chair and positioned it alongside the couch. Jared lifted Billy from the supine position to sitting and then we helped Billy shuffle into the chair. Jared lifted the oxygen line while the straps were being tightened, "It's a good thing you called us when you did. The sooner we get you to the Heart Institute, the better. You done good, sir!" Jared knew it was better to give positive reinforcement to the patient and family than to offer false hope.

Tom and I brought Billy down the stairs, and Jared carried the oxygen case and defib. Working in a crew of three has a lot of advantages. After a quick transfer from the chair to the cot, we loaded Billy into the back of the rig, booked 10–8, Code 4, lights and siren, and headed for the Heart Institute. I turned the truck west on Gladstone then south on Parkdale Avenue.

I let Jared continue his care of the patient with Tom in the back to assist. There wasn't much more we could do.

I heard Jared tell Billy what would happen when we arrived at the hospital. Things would happen very fast. A team of specialists would meet him inside and prep him for treatment. If he met the criteria, Billy would either receive a special clot-busting drug that would dissolve the clot that was occluding his coronary artery or they would insert a balloon in the blocked artery and expand it, allowing the blood flow to return to that section of the heart.

Traffic was light. The patient lived only a few kilometres from the hospital. With lights flashing and siren blaring, I steered the rig around cars on the Queensway for nine blocks, turned left on Ruskin Street, then right on Melrose Avenue. The emergency entrance is a quick right after the turn onto Melrose.

I booked 10–7. We pulled the cot from the truck restraints and rolled it through the double glass doors down the hall to the cath lab. As soon as the automatic doors opened, we were greeted by a team of waiting nurses and doctors who guided us to an empty room where more medical personnel waited to perform their magic.

Once the patient was transferred to their table, I removed our cot and equipment from the room and left Jared and Tom with the team leader to give the scene report.

Smooth as silk. Calls don't often go this well: whether it was the patient, the presenting problem, our team, or the distance to the hospital from the scene, everything just seemed to flow. Wiping down the equipment and the cot, I had a renewed sense of gratification for the job. "This is why I do this!" I thought to myself.

*****

Calls went as expected all morning, nothing too taxing. Any skills that Tom needed to work on weren't required. Shortly after one, dispatch gave us time to eat before reassigning us to the next call.

We made our way to Bronson and parked across the street from Carleton University. Brewer Park is situated on the east side of Bronson Avenue, with two ball diamonds, green space, and a lime-green, slime-covered pond. It's a perfect place to park, grab a few minutes to eat and relax before the next call comes in. If you happen to fall asleep, the rig is secluded enough from passing traffic that they wouldn't know the difference! As long as one of us kept our eyes open in case a supervisor or someone drove by, we could catch a few minutes of shuteye.

Tom offered to sit up front so I could relax in the privacy of the patient compartment. Considering what time I got home last night, it didn't take me long to fall asleep. But then my cell phone vibrated in my breast pocket and startled me back to reality. I looked at the call display. The photo of a large, red-haired man was pictured above his office number.

"Galen?"

"Have you had a chance to play Scrabble with the letters yet?"

"I went to bed late last night, went to work for seven this morning, and it's what," I looked at my watch, "just after noon and this is our first break. Yeah! The first thing I want to do is go over the stuff we found from last night. I want sleep, bud. I feel like a pile of reconstituted cow crap."

"Too bad. I passed it along to a few guys who spoke German and Hebrew. The letters aren't part of the Hebrew alphabet, but German and English are pretty much the same. It took about ten minutes or so, and guess what we came up with?" Galen paused expecting me to guess.

Silence.

"Fine. You're not gonna guess, are you?"

"I'm tired, beat, whipped, and all I want to do is sleep. My mind is day-old oatmeal. No, I'm not going to guess."

"Bahnhof."

"And that means what?"

"'Train station' in German. And I'm willing to bet that key in the tube is for locker 1113, or some variation of those numbers."

"Galen, try again. There are no lockers at the VIA train station."

"Are you sure?"

"Pretty."

"Can you meet me there?"

"Hang tight. Tom, can you ask dispatch if we can go to the train station? Police request we attend."

A few moments later, we had been cleared to change our location to the east end of Ottawa.

*****

The car was parked at Carleton University, quite a distance from where the ambulance was parked. Military-grade binoculars were used to monitor their movements, and a parabolic microphone captured their conversation. He held the binoculars in one hand, and a cell phone in the other.

"Did you get that? He's heading for the train station."

Silence.

"Would you like me to follow?"

Silence.

"Of course I will."

Silence.

"What about the response team? Should they be prepped?"

Silence. He nodded his head as if the person on the other end could see him.

"Yes, I realized how important it is to recover the documents."

The line went dead.

*****

The Ottawa train station is situated on Tremblay Road, just south of Highway 417 or the Queensway. The building was extensively renovated in 2009, opening up the main section of the station and giving it a more spacious, modern feel, with exposed girders, glass, and skylights adorning the ceiling; a large, circular kiosk acts as the main hub for ticket sales and customer service.

Two Ottawa Police cruisers were parked under the open girder canopy when we arrived. Taxis from various companies, obviously upset with the police cruisers blocking the path of their fares, leaned on their horns and yelled obscenities at them. The officers were oblivious to the cabbies' plight. Under the canopy, a bank of doors greeted customers to the train station. A bilingual sign, commonplace in Ottawa, greeted everyone to "Ottawa Station" and "Gare d'Ottawa." Jared pulled around to the front of the cruisers, killed the engine, and exited with Tom and me.

Galen walked over to meet us. "Who's the new guy?"

Jared extended his hand, "Pleased to meet--" His voice trailed off as Galen turned to Tom and me. Jared pulled his hand back, straightened up, and turned to listen to Galen.

"Tom, you're looking good. Nice to have you back in the field."

Tom simply nodded.

"Ethan, that picture we found of the lady hidden in the tube was traced back to Auschwitz. Her name was on the list of prisoners, but after that, no record of her anywhere. So why would Kautz have a picture of her?"

"No idea. What about the second jump drive?"

"More numbers. A lot of them, different from the first jump drive, different sequence, different numbers. Another part of the code? IT is looking at it, but I'm not holding my breath on this one, either."

I was disappointed. I really had hoped that the second jump drive would hold the key to unlocking the first jump drive. "Did you look into the lockers?"

"You were right, Ethan. There haven't been lockers in the station for decades. They have a bag service. For a fee, VIA's customer service will keep luggage locked up for customers with valid train tickets. I checked and there was a train ticket issued to Tomlinson, but nothing for Kautz. The train ticket was open, which means the concierge will keep the bag in security for as long as the customer pays for storage. The bag was dropped off just days before Tomlinson or Kautz was killed, but he paid for a six-month hold."

Galen didn't wait for a response. He turned and walked inside. We followed. The two uniformed officers followed suit. Our train of Ottawa Police and Ottawa EMS snaked its way through the crowd to the central circular kiosk. Black poles with webbing extended between each, directed customers to various kiosk windows. Behind the central kiosk, a circular ramp led to the lower level.

A middle-aged lady, very well dressed in a dark blue pant suit, hair pulled back, and flat pumps, greeted Galen. Her VIA name badge simply said "Sandra." She must have been the one Galen had spoken to earlier. She extended her hand. This time Galen shook it.

"Thank you, Detective Hoese, for having the search warrant prepared when you arrived earlier. It didn't take long to find the package you described in the warrant. I have it in my office. If you will follow me, please?" She turned on her heel and began a brisk walk on the polished white floors. Again, the line of police and EMS officers made its way to the far side of the terminal.

Sandra swiped her pass card at the sensor. The door clicked, and she pulled the main door open to the business offices. We all followed her down the hall past several doors. People sat at their desks and looked up as we passed. Near the end of the hall, Sandra stopped and swiped her card again. She turned the door handle, and Galen followed her into the office. The office was small, only large enough to accommodate Sandra, Galen, and me. On her desk lay a brown leather attaché case.

I stared at it, unable to take my eyes off of it. The tan-coloured leather showed its age and vintage. Scuffs and scratches only enhanced the appearance of the case. The leather appeared thicker than anything we could find today or would be able to afford. The thick leather appeared to be as supple as fine cloth after decades of use. Its simple flap was held in place by two straps with holes punched in them every half inch and small belt-style buckles. The centre handle was rounded, thick, and worn to the original user's grip. In the centre of the flap was a bird with wings open at its side; and held firm in its talons was a German swastika.

The mike pinned to my epaulette squawked a message, bringing me back to the present.

Galen was already seated, looking up at me, motioning for me to take the seat next to him.

I pulled the chair back, sat down, and looked at Sandra and Galen.

"Is this the case you are looking for?"

Galen looked up from the case momentarily and, almost inaudibly, replied, "Yes!" and went back to examining the case. Without lifting his eyes, he continued, "Did you scan it? X-Ray it, anything?"

"We have a private security company that comes in sporadically with dogs to sniff the building out for drugs, but we don't have the resources for X-Ray scanners." Sandra sounded almost apologetic.

"Did you have a chance to go over your video surveillance and see if you could spot who dropped off the briefcase?"

Again, Sandra sounded remorseful, "Our feed is on a fourteen-day loop. The date the briefcase was dropped off was well beyond our fourteen-day security recordings. I'm sorry."

Galen reached for the circa World War II leather briefcase and held it close for examination.

"Do you have someplace private where we could open this?" he asked.

Sandra stood and pushed her chair in, "I have plenty to do. Take your time. Find me before you leave, please." With that, she left us alone.

Tom stuck his head in the doorway, "Can I join?"

I remained silent and looked at Galen. He motioned Tom in with a nod. Tom turned the volume down on his portable radio to reduce feedback between our two radios.

"So, we know what Bahnhof means now. But what about 1113?" I asked.

Galen held the case up for inspection. With a hand on either side of the case, he rotated it one way, then the other, twisted the case in the air, flipped it, shook it--all the while, examining the case for any signs of potential danger.

"It didn't explode when I shook it. No metallic sounds. I think it's okay!"

"Really?" I said. "This is police forensics? You shook it hard enough to cause it to explode even if there wasn't anything explosive in it!"

"We really should take it to the lab first, you know. But, I can't safely transport this thing until I know it's safe." He looked at me. "Public safety and all."

Galen put the case back on the desk, pulled on one strap, releasing its buckle, then the other and gently lifted the main flap. Half way up, the flap caught and held fast. Galen leaned forward and peered under the flap.

"Look at this."

I bent over. Our heads touched. Under the flap, a small combination lock with four digits visible had been installed, connecting the main body of the attaché to the flap.

"Well, we know what the numbers are for now, don't we?" Galen looked up at me. Four digits, how many combinations are there? So four numbers, it looks like ten digits so that makes how many possible combinations?" Math and Galen don't go together very well. "I would guess, a lot!"

"We have a head start, remember, 1,1,1,3?"

"Yeah, of course." He handed me the briefcase. "You try."

I held my breath, stared at the case and my mind went blank.

"You could just slice the side of the briefcase open, you know. It's just leather." Tom's voice broke the tension.

"No fucking way! If this thing isn't claimed, I want it." Galen tapped the case.

"It's gorgeous."

"Enough!" I placed the briefcase on the desk and Galen held the flap up so I could see the lock unobstructed.

"1,1,1,3. Okay, let's start."

I rolled the wheels to show 1113 and tugged on the flap. Nothing! 3111, tug, nothing. 1311, tug, without any resistance, the flap released itself from the lock and fell backwards onto the desk.

"No fucking way!" Tom exclaimed.

Galen and I looked back at Tom standing behind us.

"Beginner's luck," I smiled.

CHAPTER 34

Galen pulled the leather flap of the briefcase back gently, handling it as if it were an antique work of art whose paint might crack if handled roughly. With two hands, he slowly rotated the case so the opening was facing us. He pulled open the top part of the case, revealing a cavernous space filled with papers. Galen looked in, failed to see anything hazardous, and began pulling out the papers.

I cleared as much off of Sandra's desk as I could. Galen slowly spread the papers across the surface of the desk. Without even noticing, Jared had entered the room and now the four of us were standing around the desk, looking down at yellowed sheets of paper arranged on the desk like magazines on a coffee table. They were all written in German, with a stylized eagle, its wings spread and holding a laurel wreath surrounding a swastika, printed at the top left corner of each sheet. The pages were all handwritten in thick, black ink. Various dates appeared, all from the latter years of the forties.

As Galen carefully moved the pages to the side, a white page stuck out among the sea of aged sheets. Galen tugged the page from the bottom of the pile. Several white sheets were bound with a single staple.

Galen turned these pages upright and found the bundle actually held about a dozen pages. The cover page displayed a colourful blue, red, white, and gold oval logo from the National Research Council of Canada. The working title on the page read "Genes, Genomes, Modifications, and Ramifications of DNA Manipulation. Caroline Wald, 2012, CISTI Public Catalogue."

Galen held the papers before me, shaking them wildly. "What the hell is an NRC report doing in a bundle of Nazi documents belonging to a group that wants to change everyone's DNA?" He was upset. "What the fuck does this title mean? What the fuck is CISTI?"

Tom pulled the sheets from Galen's hands and began flipping through them. Only the cover page had any text and in the top corner of the page "Purity" written in ink and circled over and over again forming a dark blue ring that left impressions on the subsequent pages. Tom flipped to the first page, and then quickly turned each page over, revealed page after page of numbers similar to what we found on the jump drives.

"Eleven pages! Did you see this? Eleven pages of numbers! Holy crap!" He held the pages up high, waving them in the air.

"And did you notice the date? The report from the NRC is dated just a few days before the call you responded to at Parliament Hill, Ethan," said Tom.

Jared looked up from his phone: "CISTI is the Canadian Institute for Scientific and Technical Information." Jared looked directly at Galen. "Thought you wanted to know?" He paused. "Oh, and another thing, you said the author of the report was Caroline Wald?" Galen nodded. "She's dead! According to the Ottawa Sun, she died from an apparent suicide in her home." Jared turned his iPhone so that we could see the article.

"Kautz must have wanted to encrypt the report to hide it from the rest of the group when he found out the results of the study. After seeing what these guys are capable of, I can understand why he did it." I added.

Tom tossed the encrypted report on Sandra's desk face down, noticed something and quickly reached for the pages again. There were more handwritten notes on the back of the last sheet.

Tom went silent, and his eyes kept scanning the words. His head cocked back and forth; under his breath he said, "Blah, blah, blah" a few times, but continued to skim over the document. He finally finished reading it to himself then looked up at us.

"You guys ready for this? I have no clue what this is about, Galen, since Ethan has told me nothing, but I know what the final conclusion says. Ready?" He scanned the room. We all stood frozen with vacant stares.

He cleared his throat, "The final analysis of the client-supplied concept of a computer-modified DNA sequence conclusively proves that any endeavours brought forth by the study herein would ultimately result in a non-viable test subject."

My thoughts went back to baby Clara. Brought into this life, nothing more than a laboratory test, knowing full well she was probably never going to survive.

Tom looked up at us. I looked back at Tom. Galen remained silent, not moving, digesting what he just heard.

Tom waited for Galen to say something, anything. Galen's mind had to process the conclusion of the report. It didn't register, and he waited for Tom to translate it into English. "Whatever this guy had," Tom waved the pages in the air, "he wanted the NRC to test their theory to see if it would work. And apparently, it didn't!"

Galen turned to me. I shook my head. "None of what they said they could do, they can't. That must have been the reason Kautz went to work for the government, so he would have a legitimate reason to speak with the NRC. They wouldn't question an aide of a member of Parliament asking for a study."

"It doesn't work. Regardless of whatever fucking reason, it doesn't work!" Galen looked back and forth between me and Tom. Jared, completely lost, stood there wondering what we were so excited about. "It doesn't work!" Galen kept shouting.

Galen pulled Sandra's chair from behind the desk and fell into it, almost falling backwards. "It didn't work, and all those people died for this," he placed his hand on the briefcase, "for something that didn't work to begin with!" Galen spoke quietly, with a heavy heart. At first he was elated; then saddened.

Suddenly, I realized everything that I had gone through was for nothing. "So the encoded information on the jump drives was probably test results or studies all leading to this conclusion--information not meant to fall into the other group's hands." I sat down, too, feeling nauseated.

"Do you think there are copies of this report anywhere else?" Galen asked.

"I dunno. What did you say about CISTI being a public organization? Maybe the report is listed on their site?" I turned to Jared. "Can you look it up?"

Jared thumbed his phone. Electronic beeps echoed in the room with each key stroke. He swiped his thumb up.

"No longer available. 'Removed at the request of the author.'" Jared never looked up from his phone. "Sorry, I'll keep looking."

I looked up to see the two uniformed officers who had accompanied us into the station standing quietly outside the door looking in. Like Tom and Jared, most of what they heard they couldn't possibly have understood, but they knew what had happened in the past few weeks. And what had happened wasn't good.

Silence. No one spoke. No one wanted to speak.

Galen stood, collected all the papers, and placed them back in the leather briefcase. We remained silent. He closed the case flap, not connecting the combination lock, and fed the leather straps through the buckles, cinching them tightly.

"Until further notice, no one--" Galen pointed at each one of us individually, "--no one will speak of this, talk about it, discuss it or even think about it." He looked at each of us again. "Have I made myself one hundred percent, totally fucking, do-not-mess-with-me, clear?"

A noise from the main lobby interrupted our conversation. We went silent. There it was again. This time the sound repeated itself rapidly.

"Fuck! That was a gunshot!" Jared yelled.

"Not just a gunshot--those are automatic weapons!"

CHAPTER 35

The two police officers who had entered the train station with Galen turned toward the lobby. The hallway filled with train station employees who had been in their offices. They huddled together waiting for someone to take charge. They talked over each other. Cell phones came out and frantic calls were made.

One of the officers spoke directly to Galen, ignoring Tom, Jared, and me. "We heard it, too. I already called in a 'Shots fired!' We're going out to investigate. You?"

Galen looked around. "Go find out if it actually was gunshots. Radio back and let me know. I'll get all these office people outside. There has to be a back door. Find that manager we were just speaking to, if she's still here, and tell her to implement their emergency plan, if they have one."

They turned and ran down the hall toward the security door. The radio attached to Galen's belt started to chatter with cruisers responding to the train station and police officers talking back and forth over the air.

"Tom?" I asked.

"I'm on it. Great first day back. You're a shit magnet, you know!"

I smiled. "Just like the old days...10–2000 if it is shots."

"Got it." Tom knew to press the red button on our portable radio in case of emergency. Pressing the button was an instant call for help from dispatch, no questions asked.

Tom followed the same path the two officers had just taken.

"Jared?"

"I know. Follow Tom. If anyone's hurt, all our gear is still in the truck. How do we treat patients until we get our gear?"

"MacGyver it!"

"Mac what?"

"Kids...Improvise! You do know how to improvise, don't you?"

Jared shrugged his shoulders, turned and left.

I remained in the office with Galen. He held the briefcase close to his chest. Looking around the office, it was apparent he was searching for a place to hide the briefcase to prevent it from being taken while we went out to investigate.

"The shots may be a diversion to get us out there and leave the case behind, or they could be shooting their way in here. Either way, we have to hide it--and someplace good."

"High, in the ceiling tiles," I offered.

"Behind a desk?" Galen rebuffed.

"Pull out all the paper, leave any file folders in the briefcase. Leave everything in plain sight."

"What the fuck?"

"Grab any file off the desk, put the NRC papers and reports in it. Remember the name on the file. Stuff some random papers from the files in the Nazi briefcase and then hide it somewhere."

"Good idea." Galen grabbed a file folder from the pile on Sandra's basket. He pulled a dozen or so loose papers from the VIA files and put them in the briefcase, locked it and inserted the important NRC documents into the VIA file and placed it under some of the other files in the basket. He slid the briefcase behind the wall unit.

"Done! Now let's get these people out of here."

Galen shouted over the small crowd that still remained in the hall. The talking came to a sudden stop and everyone turned to face Galen and me.

"Is there a back way out of here?" Galen asked.

"Down the end of the hall, turn left. There's a security door that leads to the staff parking," one woman offered.

Galen pointed down the hall behind him. "That way and left?"

The woman nodded in agreement.

Galen turned to me and ordered me to take up the rear. He turned the volume down on his radio, drew his gun, held it before him, and took the lead. He walked slowly, checking each office for workers hiding inside as we passed. He closed each office door after checking they were clear. At the end of the hall, he motioned for everyone to remain behind the corner as he opened the security door. I walked to the front of the line and peeked around the corner, watching my friend do his job. This is something I had never seen him do in all the years I have known him.

Moving with stealth that defies logic for such a large man, Galen silently and patiently pushed the panic bar on the door, releasing the latch bolt. Looking through the tiny slit, seeing nothing, he slid from standing behind the door to behind the wall. Gun in right hand, he squatted down and, inch by inch, pushed the door open with his left hand, careful not to make any noise. The door was more than halfway open. Galen seemed to look relieved when suddenly, through the door, gunfire erupted, piercing the metal door and leaving tiny holes with shards of metal protruding from them. I pulled back behind the wall only for a moment and then looked again.

Galen fell to his back, kicked the door open with both legs, forcing the door to slam against the person standing behind it. The shooter exhaled and moaned loudly, then jumped from behind the door, pointed his assault rifle where Galen should have been standing behind the door, squeezed the trigger and bullets flew, striking the empty wall at the end of the hallway.

Galen rolled out on the floor and pointed his gun up at the assailant, pulling the trigger over and over and over again. Galen didn't stop shooting until the man fell backwards and his gun was empty of bullets. The firefight was over.

I turned to the VIA train staff behind me, "Stay here!"

I scurried over to help my friend. Galen was already on his feet. He raised his pistol, the magazine fell to the ground, and he reloaded another. He heard me. Without turning to face me, he signaled me to stop. I slowed my pace, hugged the wall, and continued to approach.

Galen stepped through the doorway and stood over the body. The man lay motionless, bleeding; there was no movement. He was wearing a bullet-resistant vest over a grey shirt. The holes in the dead man's shirt showed evidence of where Galen's shots had hit the mark in several locations. Other shots had hit the vest and left depressions in the Kevlar but the kill shot was the single shot to the left side of the skull. The mask he wore was undamaged.

Galen reached down, pulled the rifle from the man lying at his feet, and slung it over his shoulder. He walked farther out from the building, pointed the handgun up to the top of the building, scanning the entire roofline of the one-story building, swung it around and pointed it along the side of the building and behind, then forward. Galen continued to walk to the end of the building, looking straight along the sight of the pistol. He paused, turned, and walked back to the door, motioning for me to join him.

We met at the open door. Galen stood beside the body and scanned the surroundings for other threats. The assailant was wearing a white Guy Fawkes mask complete with rosy cheeks, grey tactical pants, a grey tactical shirt, and a military vest with pockets covering the front. He had no other body armour and no helmet. Galen pulled the mask off to reveal a complete stranger staring back at us with a deathly gaze. I felt sorry for him. He almost looked scared. Maybe he had been!

"Don't ever do that again, you fucking idiot! When I say stay down, you stay the fuck down. Got it?" I nod. "Is he dead?" Galen asks me.

"Pretty sure. Unless that big section of his skull was already missing before you shot him!" My physical assessment involved kicking the man's arm lying on the ground to see if he moved. "He has a tactical vest with tons of magazines, but that's it. How come he doesn't have a helmet or any other protection?"

"Budget cuts! How the fuck do I know?" Galen snapped.

"What the hell kind of assault rifle is that, anyway? It looks like something from the Transformer movies."

Galen holstered his handgun and swung the assault rifle from around his side to the front.

"I've never seen one of these before. I believe it's an F2000 from Russia or some commie state or something--rare as shit. Lightweight, you can operate it with one hand, leaving the other hand free for whatever else. I love it. Think he'll mind if I kept it for a while? Not sure why they didn't come in full assault gear." Galen bent over to retrieve some magazines from the dead man's vest and let out a muffled groan. He stood up in pain and grabbed the side of his stomach.

"Pull your jacket back," I ordered.

Blood stained his dress shirt. I moved to the side and examined the wound site.

"You are one lucky son of a bitch. With your fat ass and gut, how the bullet only managed to graze your side is beyond me."

"Actually, it's a scratch. I cut myself on one of the bullet holes in the door when I pressed up against it as I walked past. It's my groin that hurts. I think I gave myself a hernia when I kicked the door open." He looked down the hall and yelled, "Let's move!" He reached down and pulled several more magazines from the tactical vest and stuffed them in his jacket pockets.

Single file, the men and women ran down the hall. They had to step over the body as they exited the building. Some of the more curious had to look at the body as they stepped over him; others tried to avoid looking. Galen led again, and I took up the rear.

When we got to the edge of the building, Galen scanned our surroundings, making sure the area was clear.

"Run! And when I say run, I mean you fucking run! Don't look back. Don't stop until you are so fucking tired you puke. Got it?" Galen made sure the office staff knew exactly what he meant. "Now go!"

With that, they ran west across the lot. Some of them had their car keys in hand and headed for the parking section. Others took Galen's advice and ran. Some ran past the parking lot. Others ran south across the tracks.

Galen turned the volume back up on his portable radio. The two officers inside were yelling back and forth on the air, asking for reinforcements. Gunshots blared over the air.

Galen pulled his gun and two spare magazines from his belt holster and handed them to me. "Good job back there, Ethan. You remember when I taught you and Maddy how to shoot this thing at the police range years ago?" I nodded. "I'll go around front, see if I can get behind them. You wanna go back and cover Tom, don't you?"

"Sure, why the hell not? I heard Tom radio in a 10–2000, so more police and EMS tactical will be coming shortly." I held the gun at my side. I felt uneasy carrying it. Galen noticed my apprehension.

"If anybody asks where you got my gun, tell them you stole it from me."

"I hate guns, you know."

"I know, and I hate blood. We're even."

CHAPTER 36

I ran back, hugging the side of the building toward the back door, gun at my side, spare magazines weighing me down. I emulated Galen's tactical manoeuvres, looking for anyone wearing assault gear or carrying weapons.

I made my way back to the security door. The man was still lying in the same position we'd left him. His body had kept the door from closing shut. I had to close the door to prevent anyone from following me in. I patted the body down, looking for anything I could use. Galen had taken a few magazines of bullets for that futuristic assault rifle, but left others. All the other pockets appeared to carry the same thing.

Reaching down, I grabbed one of the dead man's arms and tried to pull him away from the doorway. He was too heavy to pull with one hand. I stood up, looked at the gun in my hand. I fumbled for the pistol's safety switch, located it, set it and stuck the gun in the small of my back.

Pulling the dead man by his wrists with both hands, I was able to drag him a few feet. Just then, I heard a voice over a radio. It wasn't mine. Looking up, across the parking lot, I saw nothing. No movement, but there it was again. I rolled him to one side and found a two-way portable radio. When I'd picked the body to drag him, I must have dislodged the headpiece and now I could hear the radio communication with the other members of his team. Releasing the Velcro flap, I pulled the radio from the back of his vest and secured it in my pant thigh pocket. One small advantage, I figured.

I pulled the body a little farther, allowing the door to swing closed behind me. Pushing on the door to make sure it was locked, the door swung open with little resistance. I noticed one of the bullets had hit the striker assembly and blown off the latch that keeps the door locked. There was nothing to keep the exit secured.

I looked around for something, anything to latch the door. Nothing! I ducked into one office, then another. Damn it! I had to find something to lock the door.

More gunfire! The door would have to wait.

I drew the gun from my pants, released the safety and held it close, walking slowly down the hall, periodically checking behind me, above me, then forward again. The sounds got louder as I approached the main door leading out to the concourse. Shouting could be heard between bursts of gunfire. The automatic assault weapons would send off a barrage of bullets, followed by one or two single shots from handguns.

Reaching the door, I crouched low against it. Remembering how easily the bullets from the assault rifle had pierced the metal door, I took cover beside the door, behind a cinder block wall. The panic bar, the same as the one on the back door was keeping them out and me in. I reached up to push the bar. My hand trembled so bad, it sent waves of panic down my arm to my stomach. I tasted a little vomit in the back of my throat. I fell back and curled up behind the wall, frozen.

"What if I have to get back in?" I didn't have the pass card for the security system, but the back door was open. No one but Galen and I knew that.

I reached into my pocket, found some loose change, picked out a dime, and held it to the latch. Standing, I pushed the panic bar, causing the latch and safety pin to retract into the housing, but I needed to open the door further in order to jam the dime in place. An inch, maybe two would do it. Again, I holstered the gun in the small of my back, coin in one hand; the other held the panic bar in place. Patience, I told myself. Slowly, I opened door just enough to fit the dime under the security pin under the latch. I released the panic bar and watched the latch for any movement...none! It had worked.

I keyed the EMS radio mike. "Tom!" No answer. Again, louder, "Tom!" No answer. If anything had happened to Tom, I would feel responsible. It would be my fault. I couldn't let that happen. The nausea, panic, and fear abruptly disappeared. I took in a deep breath, retrieved the gun, holding it against my chest, hit the panic bar with my hip, and rolled out the door.

I stood, zombie-like, staring out at the scene before me. The two police officers had taken positions behind concrete pillars. Jared was behind a train display. The glass display had been shattered by bullets. The train model once proudly displayed was now nothing but bits of plastic debris strewn about the floor. Jared saw me, held his index finger over his lips motioning me to be quiet, then kept lowering his hand like a command ordering a dog to lie down.

Scanning the lobby, I still couldn't locate Tom or Galen. Only one person lay motionless on the floor in the middle of the concourse. One! Better than what I had expected when I opened the door. Several more people had taken cover behind pillars, chairs and displays. I know I would have run like hell for the nearest exit if someone had entered the station and started shooting. I hoped most of the VIA passengers had done the same.

One man in grey military gear and a white mask was firing sporadically at various sections of the station to keep everyone at bay. Another intruder was running from one section of the station to another, obviously looking for something. I heard gunfire from behind the central kiosk. From the scene before me, I estimated three assailants.

I realized Jared was right. I was standing in full view of the assault team. I ducked low and took cover behind a similar display to the one Jared was using. The two police officers were preventing the assailants from getting any closer to the staff offices that I had just come from.

"Where's Tom?" I yelled at Jared.

Jared shrunk in fear upon hearing me shout. He held up two fingers then pointed to the back of the station.

One of the armed assailants heard me yelling, pointed his rifle in our direction, and fired. The bullets hit the wall behind me, shattered the glass over my head and chipped the concrete beside me. The sound was nothing like the sound effects in the movies. Weird how that came to mind as bullets flew around me, and all that protected me was a small concrete display. The bullets continued to glide past me, hitting the far wall and sending chunks of concrete flying off in all directions. Then I heard a different sound. The handgun made a popping sound; the assault rifle made a constant chirping sound like a loud bird.

I must have distracted the assailant long enough to give one of the police officers an opportunity to get in a few shots. The distance between the officer and the assailant was forty or more feet. There was little chance the police bullets would find their mark.

Bullets kept zipping over my head, striking my concrete cover, sending glass cascading down onto my head. I held the gun tightly in my hands, as I felt the glass cut me leaving tiny lacerations as it rained down over me.

"Jesus Christ!" I yelled. Spit flew from my mouth, sweat burned my eyes. My body was in overdrive. I could feel my heart pounding in my chest, hitting my sternum. The pulse in my temples pounded.

The automatic firing stopped for a few seconds, replaced with the metallic scraping sound of the assault rifle's magazine being changed. The distinctive pop, pop, pop of the police handguns could be heard while the gunman reloaded.

The barrage aimed in my direction ceased, and the assailant took aim at the officer who was firing at him. The police officer took cover before the assailant had a chance to send any shots his way. I peeked over the top of my protective cover and saw the assailant walking toward the officer who had been firing at him. The second police officer, taking cover behind another pillar, took aim at the man in grey and fired a few times to distract him. Both officers would be running out of bullets soon. I knew the cops carried several spare magazines, but never enough to level the playing field between a handgun and an assault rifle.

The assailant turned around and fired in the direction of the second officer. He couldn't make up his mind as to which direction to shoot. He kept firing at both officers to keep them at bay. Maybe that was his intention, not to kill them, just to keep them busy.

Peering over my cover, I realized the distance between the intruder and I was far greater than I thought. I could never hit him from this distance with my limited skill but I had to try. I stood, pointed the gun at the assailant, stared down its barrel, and noticed that my hands were shaking. Not a minor tremor--both my hands were trembling. I could never shoot a person--I can't even kill a mouse!

I looked over the assailant's head. He was walking under several glass roof panels. I squeezed the trigger and fired, once, twice. Like Galen had done earlier, I fired until the magazine was empty. Several shots hit the metal framework. Others found their mark, shattering the panes and sending glass raining down from thirty feet above, directly over the man.

The heavy-duty glass broke away in both large pieces and small shards, and fell hard on the man as he walked. He fell to the floor, covering his head with his hands. His rifle slid forward away from him as he went down. More glass came down upon him as he lay curled up in the fetal position. Even as the glass continued to fall, the man started screaming in pain. Blood had started flowing freely from his wounds. He was rocking back and forth on the floor. His hands held a jagged piece of glass that was protruding from the side of his thigh. His clothing was cut in several locations with red stains weeping through.

The police officer ran from his cover position, kicked the assault rifle away, grabbed the man by the collar and, with no regard for the man's injuries, dragged him behind a pillar. The cop didn't want to be left out in the open while there were still more gunmen unaccounted for. The officer pulled the man's arms behind his back and cuffed him.

"Jared. Feel like getting over there and helping out the cop?"

No reply. Jared looked, saw the area was clear, and ran with his head low to join the officer.

Outside, the sounds of sirens filled the air. Tires squealed to a stop, doors slammed, and voices were raised. The cavalry had arrived. It would be some time before they entered the building. They had protocol to follow, regardless of what was happening inside.

Galen was still missing, as was Tom.

The main concourse was silent, deathly silent. All the noise had come to an abrupt halt. Goosebumps formed on my arms. I waited behind my cover for someone to say something...anything.

The two uniformed officers came out of hiding and started to secure the area. One stood guard, scanning the area for any further signs of the remaining intruders, while the other ran to the front entrance and ordered more backup inside.

Police officers in full tactical gear entered the building with military precision. Crouched low, rifles up high, pointed directly forward, they fanned out to gain control of the lobby. Once in position, the tactical officers would secure a location. One officer held the post and the rest of the team would move on to the next location. That procedure was repeated over and over again until the entire north side of the concourse was secure. If there were any gunmen left, they were well concealed or had left the building.

I changed magazines, set the safety, stuck the gun into the small of my back, and made my way onto the floor to start treating the injured passenger still lying motionless on the floor.

Jared had stabilized the gunman's wounds as best he could with what he had available. He came over to help me. I was still scanning the area in case I saw anyone wearing grey tactical gear in the vicinity. Fear had kept me alive so far.

I felt for a carotid pulse in the patient's neck. Nothing! There was no chest movement to indicate an attempt to breathe. I pulled my flashlight out and checked his pupils--they were fixed and dilated already. He had taken several shots to the torso. Several tiny holes could be seen in his clothing. He was on his back and there was almost no blood. I expected that there would be exit wounds once we rolled him over.

"I'm going to get all of our gear from the bus while you treat this guy. How is he? If the police have secured the area, will our guys start showing up anytime soon?" Jared asked.

"Don't rush for this guy!" I stood up. "Dispatch should be sending the tactical medics in first. They should be outside or here already. If not, check with the police incident commander and if he says the scene is safe, get his name and tell dispatch he okayed the scene and to send as many rigs as possible. We need to have the police check the entire building to make sure it's safe and there are no more casualties. How's your guy?"

"Cut up like paper through a shredder! Sore, in pain, but he'll live. Good shooting, Tex! I left him with a cop until I get my gear."

"Has Tom shown up? Where did he go?" I asked again. Jared shrugged his shoulders and turned to leave. "Find a free cop and have him escort you until this place is locked down tight. I don't want any more medics going missing."

The police tactical squad was posted at several points throughout the lobby. The tension appeared to have broken, and more regular uniformed officers entered the building. I walked over to the lone gunman in custody. He was sitting; his arms were behind his back, handcuffed and in obvious pain. Jared had wrapped a discarded jacket around the glass to prevent movement and control bleeding.

I knelt down to his level. "How're you doing?"

"Fucking peachy!" Another Irish accent.

"Let me take a look at some of those cuts." The piece of glass protruding from his thigh was properly stabilized. Jared had done an excellent job, considering he used a jacket and the gunman's bootlaces. The bleeding had stopped, but his leg would have to be immobilized before moving him. "You're lucky that didn't hit your femoral artery. You could've bled out pretty fast. Believe me, I know. Keep that leg still until we get you to the hospital."

While I was checking the other lacerations, I noticed the gunman looking past me. I spun around and in the corner of my eye I saw a man in grey tactical and mask, open the security door and enter the offices where Galen had hidden the NRC files.

"Hey!" I turned looking for the police. "Hey!" I shouted. With all the police talking in the concourse, my voice echoed and was drowned out in the concrete and steel structure. No one paid attention to my calls. My own EMS radio squawked loudly in my ear with dispatch calling crews to the point that I could barely hear what others were saying.

As I stood there yelling trying to get the cops attention, Ottawa EMS tactical medics entered the main foyer. Dressed in special-issue uniforms, helmets, and ballistic vests, and carrying black medical bags, they followed their police escorts into the building. I waved them down and caught the attention of one of the medics. "Get a cop!" I yelled. My voice was drowned out by radio chatter and all the police talk. "Get a cop!" I pointed to the door. When I turned to look at the door, the figure had already disappeared inside, the door slowly closing behind him.

I jumped to my feet and ran as fast as my fatigued legs could propel me. Exhausted and mentally drained, I knew that what I was doing was wrong but I couldn't give up now. The hydraulic door moved slowly and I watched it fluidly close and lock before I arrived.

"Fuck!" Unable to stop my momentum, my body slammed into the steel door. Grabbing the handle, I held my breath and pulled. My dime was still in place and was holding the latch open!

Too late to turn back. I retrieved the gun from my belt, released the safety, and held it high. I stood beside the door, pulled it wide, and slid quietly inside. I was back to where I was only a few minutes earlier.

I was becoming familiar with these hallways. I knew which doors were supposed to be closed and which ones had been left open. With the handgun held high, I inched forward, looking ahead, above, and behind me. The gun started to feel comfortable...a feeling I was not entirely happy about.

At each office door, I paused, listening for any sound emanating from within. A few offices down the hall, I heard some furniture being overturned and desk drawers being opened and slammed shut. Cautiously, I made my way farther down the hall. The sound grew louder. Each calculated step brought me closer to whoever was in there making the noise.

"Four-five-six-three, call Ottawa," my radio blared. Panicked, I looked down, fumbled for the volume knob to silence the radio. Done! I looked back up. He stood before me, pointing that futuristic-looking assault rifle at me. My handgun was pointed down by my side. I didn't stand a chance. Looking past his gun, I saw the eyes of a child. He appeared to be no more than twenty, scared, unsure of what to do.

"I'm putting the gun down." At a snail's pace, I lowered myself down to lay the handgun at my feet. When I looked up, the gunman looked even more afraid than he had moments earlier. His hands were shaking, sweat glistened off his face, and I could almost see him trembling.

"Scared?"

"No! You're the one who should be scared."

"How old are you?"

"Age is a state of mind. That's what they keep telling me, anyway."

"They're right. Maturity comes with experience, though. And you look way out of your comfort zone. I'm not gonna do anything to make you pull that trigger." I stood back up.

For what seemed like an eternity, the young man stared down the barrel of his gun at me, unsure of his next move. I knew that the longer the standoff, the more courage he might develop, and the lower my chances of survival. I had to play the trump card.

"I know what you're looking for."

He started to shake. "Don't fuck with me!" he yelled back.

"Back up to the next office and let me in and I'll get the briefcase for you. That's what you came for, right? The briefcase?"

His eyes widened. He realized I truly did know what he wanted.

Without uttering a word, he methodically retreated; his sight never strayed from me. When he got past Sandra's office, I told him, "Stop. If you want me to get it, I have to walk past you into that office on your right."

"No. You might have another gun hidden in there." His youthful voice cracked. "Tell me where it is."

"Behind the wall unit. Leather case, old."

"Come with me." He backed up into the office, turning to see what was behind him then turning back to me. "Where?"

I pointed to where Galen had hidden the briefcase. "There, behind the wall unit."

Backing up farther, still facing me, he lowered himself, blindly fumbling to locate the briefcase. He pressed his hand against the wall, the floor, and the back of the wall unit until he found his prize. He stood with the briefcase in hand and tossed it at me.

"Open it," he yelled, unsure of what to do.

I tugged on each strap, knowing that Galen had locked the combination before hiding it. I pulled back the flap and it held fast.

"There's another lock. I don't have the combination. Do you?" I shook the bag to prove there were contents in the satchel. "There's something in there. It has to be what you're looking for." I placed the bag on the desk.

"Back out of the office. NOW!" He grabbed the briefcase and shook it to confirm there was something locked inside. He never checked to see if the briefcase was locked or not.

As ordered, I backed out slowly. He seemed more scared now than ever. And that got me really worried.

"Do you even know what you're supposed to get?"

"This!"

"Then you got it. No one else has to get hurt." I continued to back out into the hall the way we had come in, leaving the hallway toward the exit open for him to leave. He continued to face me as he left the office. With his back to the hall leading to the exit door, I realized that he wouldn't notice the dead body lying just outside until he was almost at the door. Already nervous, if he panicked when he saw his dead friend, he might shoot me. I backed up farther, giving him plenty of room to make good his escape.

The young gunman looked behind him, saw the red and silver illuminated exit sign and continued backing up down the hall.

"Don't follow me." His hands were still shaking. The assault rifle was pointing directly at me. I was scared he might squeeze the trigger accidentally.

"I'm no hero. You got what you came for. Leave." My voice was calm, monotone, non-threatening.

His paced quickened. Having made his way to the corner, a male voice suddenly yelled out, "Is anyone down here?" A uniformed police officer appeared behind me. The gunman pointed his rifle past me at the cop and pulled the trigger. I dropped hard to the floor and curled up in the fetal position, with my hands over my head. The sound of automatic fire continued in sporadic short bursts as bullets flew above my head.

When the noise stopped, I looked up and the gunman was gone. Still curled up, I rolled over to see the officer, now also prone on the hallway floor. I jumped up and ran to his side. No blood, no holes, all good.

"You okay?"

He turned to face me. "Holy shit! I think I pissed my pants! Yeah, yeah, I'm okay!" I helped the officer sit up. He dry-heaved once and then vomited down the front of his shirt and pants.

I looked down the hall toward the exit. It was clear; no sign of the gunman. The officer would live, only his pride slightly tarnished from the sudden expulsion of his lunch.

I ran down the hall, stopped, hunched low, looked around the corner. All clear! I ran to the exit. The dead body was still in the same position I left him in. Stepping over the body, I glanced up, surveyed the edge of the building, and then looked back inside. Clear! I ran along the south wall, stopping at the corner of the building, and looked west to the parking lot. I had expected to see the gunman jumping into a waiting van and being driven away like they do on TV. Instead, the parking lot was blocked by police cruisers and the road that leads to the front of the VIA station had Fire, police cruisers, and ambulances parked in a chaotic mess. If I were the gunman, I would never attempt to escape through that. Instead I would go south. Looking along the train tracks, "There!"

Several hundred yards to the west, a man in grey, carrying an assault rifle and a briefcase was running along the gravel shoulder of the tracks. A VIA passenger train roared west on the first set of tracks beside him, preventing him from running south until the train passed. He kept turning; looking behind him, afraid someone might be giving chase. Again, I amazed myself and continued to make foolish decisions: I would go after him.

The papers the briefcase held were useless. If he got away, they would realize that we still had what they came for and would return for them. Maybe not today, but someday! I wanted to put an end to this today.

I pushed against the wall behind me, forcing my tired legs to run as fast as I could on the unstable gravel along the tracks. With multiple tracks permitting trains to travel east and west south of the train station, trains could pass by at any time without stopping. Each set of tracks had a covered walkway to shield passengers from the sun, snow, and rain when they disembarked.

Had someone called VIA to cancel all stops at the Ottawa terminal until the police secured the scene? Had the engineers been ordered to divert to other destinations or simply stop along the route? I had no way of knowing if those options were even possible.

I kept an eye on my target up ahead. He would occasionally stumble on loose gravel, correct himself, and keep running. I did the same. He held onto that gun and briefcase tightly, not wanting to lose possession of either. The gap between us was growing. He was younger, running on adrenaline; I was older, running on vengeance! I had lost track of Galen and Tom and feared the worst.

The train eventually passed us. Gun and satchel in hand, he darted across the first set of tracks. Horns blared. Another freight train approached from the west. It would be close. Would he chance it? I was far enough behind him that he wouldn't have to worry about me catching up by the time the train passed. I followed my target and crossed the first set of tracks so we would be parallel in case another train was scheduled to travel on the first set of tracks. I was in luck. He'd decided not to attempt to cross in front of the oncoming train. I had my chance and pushed hard against the gravel to pick up my pace.

My lungs burned; my heart pounded. The lactic acid in my thighs screamed for me to stop. I couldn't. The distance between us shortened. He never looked back. Instead, he was focused on running as fast as he could to get away.

I kept pushing myself harder. The sound of my boots crunching on the loose gravel reminded me of the noise and the difficulty of running in freshly fallen deep snow. I was determined to catch up with him, regardless of the pain searing through my legs and my lungs begging me to stop. The scar tissue of my thigh laceration pulled with each step and I feared it would rip open.

The second train caught up to us and continued to speed past. The wake it created made the chase more trying. Once the train passed, the gunman could run south, cross over one more set of tracks, and then he would have an open field to Terminal Avenue, where he might have a vehicle waiting.

We were less than twenty feet apart, and he suddenly stopped, turned, dropped the briefcase, raised his assault rifle, and aimed it at me. The rifle bounded up and down with each deep breath the gunman took. I reached for the handgun I'd stuck in the small of my back. It was gone. I ran my hand along my belt and found nothing. I'd left it on the hallway floor.

"Leave me alone!" he screamed. "I have to bring this back. Please, just leave me alone!"

It was almost impossible to hear anything over the thunderous clanking of the train. "Tell me who you work for and I'll stop!" I shouted.

"No! Stay there or I'll shoot. Don't make me! Please!" He was breathing heavily, his words spoken between breaths. With the gun held high, he blindly reached down, fumbled for the handle of the case, took hold, turned, and ran.

I was too exhausted to follow. I was spent; I had given the chase all I had; now all I could do was watch him disappear. He ran alongside the train. His legs tired from the run, his feet stumbled in the gravel and he fell forward losing his hold on the briefcase. The briefcase flew up and fell forward under the path of the train. The draft caused by the speeding train caught the case and brought it under its metal wheels and ate the leather briefcase. The fragile leather gave, ripping the seams and crushing the combination lock. The papers it held caught in the wind, lifted upwards and went for a ride along with the train as it continued to speed along the track.

The young man lifted himself to his knees as he watched the papers get torn and shredded and float away in the draft of the train. I walked to him; he paid no attention to me. His head hung low, realizing that he failed in his task to retrieve the information it held. The train rolled along the tracks.

"It was worthless, you know," I said calmly, standing behind him.

"What?"

"I read the report before you guys got here. It doesn't work. Go tell your boss that."

Still on his knees, he turned to face me. "Really?"

"Really! It doesn't work. Decades of research and it still doesn't work. Probably never will. Playing God is best left to whatever God you believe in."

He stood. "Why are you telling me this?"

"So you can tell them. You an Eagle or a Sparrow?"

"Eagle. You know about us?"

"Almost everything there is to know. Leave. Get outta here before the police get here. There's been enough killing for one day."

He stood, started walking, dragging his gun in the gravel, crossed the tracks, and headed for Terminal Avenue. I recovered the tattered leather case from the tracks. Papers lay strewn on the tracks, I picked a few up and glanced over them. One was a memo about staff parking; another about staff breaks. Galen had stuffed the briefcase with useless internal memos. On instinct, without thinking, I chased the guy down to retrieve a briefcase with memos about staff parking and breaks. I dropped the papers, and they fluttered for a few feet and landed in the gravel. I tossed the rest of the papers in the wind and headed back to the VIA station.

CHAPTER 37

By the time I made my way to the back door, the entire building and ground perimeter had been secured by the police. Cruisers were parked along the road, officers patrolled the grounds. Yellow barrier tape had been strung from the back door, around the body lying on the ground, to a pole a dozen feet away. Two uniformed officers stood by the body, still on alert, stopped me as I approached.

"Do you know where Detective Hoese is?" I asked.

"Let me check." The officer keyed his lapel mike and asked for the location of Detective Galen Hoese. The conversation on the police portable went back and forth, each person thinking they knew where Galen was, or where he was supposed to be. Finally, they realized he was unaccounted for.

"It seems we may have misplaced the detective. No one can locate him right now." The officer looked concerned that one of their own had gone missing. He then looked past me and pointed with his head. "Him?"

"Who're you looking for?" I knew the voice coming from behind.

I spun around to see Galen and Tom. Galen had lost his suit jacket, his tie was pulled loose, the top two buttons were undone, his shirt tails were pulled from his pants and sweat glistened on his brow. Tom, on the other hand, looked like he came straight from a photo shoot for GQ magazine.

"Where the hell have you two been?"

Tom smiled at Galen, "You wanna tell him?"

"I'm not gonna tell him. No fucking way!"

Tom turned back to me with a toothy grin, "Sorry, apparently, we're not gonna tell, at least not now, anyway."

"Detective, they want you up front." One of the uniformed officers broke in.

"Gotta go do real work, boys. You guys stay here and count Band-Aids." Galen walked past me, placed a hand on my shoulder, and smiled a broad, warm smile. He whispered, "Glad you're okay!"

"Hey, fat boy!" Galen turned and I handed him the tattered briefcase. He took it from me, turned it over, inspecting its torn condition. "Story for another time, I guess. Oh, that thing you let me borrow," I formed a gun with my hand and held it close to my chest, "is on the floor, just inside." Galen gave a slight nod indicating that he understood.

"I guess I better go back and help the troops." Tom stepped around me and headed into the building.

I stood silently for a moment with a dead body at my feet, and two uniformed Ottawa cops wondering what had just happened. Alone, I turned, thanked the police officers, and went inside.

In the main lobby of the VIA station, police were everywhere. There were more cops inside the station than we probably had medics covering the entire region of Ottawa–Carleton. The police had begun gathering in small groups, each with their own responsibilities; some were taking notes, others crouched down examining evidence, while others were assisting other teams of the Ottawa police.

One lone Ottawa EMS crew remained with several officers standing around the cot where the patient injured by falling glass was boarded and collared, an IV running, the monitor tracing his ECG and taking his vitals. Jared was one of the crew members helping. Tom walked over to the EMS crew. There was a brief exchange of words, heads nodded in agreement, and the crew lifted the cot and exited the building.

A year ago, I would have joined them instead of standing back. Patients had always come first. Now, I'm still trying to do my job, but other forces have been pulling me away from what I loved doing. In some strange way, I felt out of place, embarrassed almost, that I wasn't there for the patient. Maddy would have said it was fate. I say, "shit happens" and learn to live with it. Or, as Galen would say, "Fuck it!" He always did have a way with words . . .

I joined Tom and Jared, who were collecting equipment for the crew. We gathered the bags left behind and carried them out to the truck. The crew was just loading the patient in the back of the rig. The patient couldn't see me. He was handcuffed to the cot rail, his head held in place with tape; a bulk dressing kept the glass from moving and causing more soft tissue damage.

Outside, ambulances were lined up in the staging area like customers in queue. If there were more patients to triage, each rig would accept the next patient and dispatch would assign them a destination based on their injuries and available beds in the ER. As it was, the ambulances and crews would wait to ensure that there were no more patients and would leave the scene only after the incident commander released them.

We tossed the gear in the side door. Tom quickly spoke to the driver of the crew, and they booked in service to the Ottawa General. Our rig was blocked in by an EMS supervisor's white SUV with black and yellow striping. The light bar was flashing, and the supervisor was leaning on the hood of the vehicle, writing in his notebook while speaking on his cell phone. With a telepathic conversation, Tom and I looked at each other knowing full well it was inevitable that we would be reprimanded for our part in the incident at the VIA station. Jared headed directly for our rig.

We stood before the supervisor. He refused to even acknowledge our presence; he simply continued the conversation on his cell and wrote in his notebook. Tom and I shifted our weight from one foot to the other and waited for the supervisor to finish what he was doing.

Without saying anything more, he simply pocketed the cell phone, folded his notebook, curled his index finger back and forth at us, beckoning us to follow him to our rig. We followed him to the back door. Jared was inside, preparing the gear for our next call. With a single word, the supervisor made his intentions known to Jared: "OUT!"

Jared didn't dare say a word; he shot us a surprised look and simply followed the order to vacate the rig. We climbed in, and the supervisor slammed the back doors shut. He sat in the captain's chair at the head of the stretcher. Tom and I took our place on the bench seat and remained quiet. There was nothing but silence...deafening silence. I couldn't even hear the commotion going on outside, my mind was so exhausted.

The supervisor pulled out his notebook, read to himself. Again, more silence. If this was done for effect, he was adept at it. The longer the wait, the greater my feeling of dread. His movements were planned and executed to maximize our discomfort. Tom and I dared not speak or move, and even our breathing was shallow to avoid increasing the tension in the back of the rig.

The supervisor finally closed his notepad, placed his hands on his knees, leaned back into the seat, and was just preparing his diatribe of discipline as the back doors flew open. Before the supervisor could utter a word, Jared stood before us, "It's Galen."

"This has been fun. Another time, maybe?" Leave it to Tom to increase the tension! Tom and I flew out the back doors, pulled the cot from the locking bar, dropped the carriage, and followed Jared to where Galen was sitting on the curb.

I faced Galen, placed my hand on his shoulder for payback, "What's up, bud?"

Galen looked pale. He always sweated, but he was really diaphoretic now. "I don't feel so good," he answered.

CHAPTER 38

Tom and I have always worked well together. We have a symbiotic relationship: We feed off one another, read and anticipate the other's thoughts, and coordinate the treatment and patient care.

Jared pulled the oxygen bag and monitor from the cot and placed them beside Galen. He turned on the oxygen, set it at ten litres per minute, and applied a non-rebreather over Galen's mouth and nose.

Tom pulled out the oxygen saturation sensor and handed it to me. I placed it on Galen's left index finger. Tom handed me the blood pressure cuff, and I wrapped it around Galen's right upper arm. Jared lowered the cot while Tom readied the monitoring electrodes and applied the first four leads to Galen's wrists and ankles.

I continued my examination while Jared and Tom did what we do every day.

"Can you describe what you're feeling right now?"

"Don't be so fucking condescending to me. I've seen you do this a hundred times."

"Okay, you take the lead." I smiled. I should have known better with Galen.

"Pain, here." He pointed at his chest, right over the sternum. "Hurts, heavy-like, not a lot, three on ten, maybe. Just came on suddenly, scary as shit. I'm a little short of breath, more from being scared. No heart history, although my doctor keeps telling me he wants me to change a lot of things. Come to think of it, you tell me the same things all the time. High blood pressure, I'm gonna be a diabetic in a week and a half if I don't watch what I eat. Cholesterol is in the stratosphere. Enough?"

"Enough." I smiled at my old friend. I couldn't let him know how worried I was.

Jared stuck a tympanic thermometer in Galen's ear and he tried to shoo it away like a mosquito. Tom tapped me on the shoulder. I looked down at the monitor. His vitals were, for the most part, stable. Blood pressure 210/133--I would have been more surprised if it hadn't been high--pulse 118, respirations 28, temperature 36.8, ECG looked good--NSR (normal sinus rhythm).

Tom was preparing the twelve-lead for a more detailed view of Galen's heart to see if there was cardiac damage we hadn't picked up on the initial trace. Tom usually places the leads, but instead he handed them to Jared; he was part of the team today.

Tom knelt before Galen, "I'm gonna start an IV. Any objections?"

Galen knew better than to argue at this point and gave his consent with a nod. Tom started an IV of normal saline in the dorsal vein on the back of Galen's left hand.

Jared walked around. I stepped aside as he opened Galen's shirt, counted the ribs for proper lead placement, and placed the monitoring electrodes as required.

Galen looked completely uncomfortable with his fellow cops standing around him watching as we performed our tests. I turned and looked at the cops, giving them a silent order to leave, and they heeded my visual request.

Jared asked Galen his age. Galen seemed more embarrassed about having chest pain at his age and gave it hesitantly. Tom entered Galen's age and gender into the monitor and started the twelve-lead test. A few seconds later, the paper spewed forth with detailed cardiac information: "NSR, No abnormal rhythm detected."

Tom handed Galen two 81mg ASA tablets and told him to melt the tablets in his mouth and not swallow them.

"Good news: We can go through this on the way to the hospital," I smiled at my friend.

Jared pulled the cot closer, placed it beside Galen, and laid out the sheet.

Galen knew we wanted to lift him onto the cot and wanted to avoid the embarrassment of having several men carry him to the stretcher. "I can stand!"

Under normal circumstances, Tom and I would never let anyone having chest pain walk to the cot--to avoid excess strain on the heart--but Galen was around his fellow cops and knowing Galen, he would die of embarrassment if his co-workers saw him being carried out by medics.

Tom was on one side of Galen, Jared on the other, and I in front. One of the police officers moved the equipment to avoid having his detective trip over them. Galen stood, pivoted, and sat on the cot.

We secured the monitor and oxygen, raised the cot, and headed for our rig. The supervisor was at the back door waiting for us.

"This isn't over."

"Very diplomatic of you," Tom said loudly to ensure the cops following us heard every word.

We booked in-service and, within five minutes, we were parked at Ottawa General's Emergency. Several police cruisers were already there waiting for us, and we were led immediately to a treatment room. Tom and I gave our report to the triage nurse and told Galen we wouldn't leave until we were allowed in to see him; then we left the room.

Later that evening, Galen had been moved to a room down the hall, away from the main section of the ER. Galen was nervous, and his wife was frantic at the thought of what might have happened. To help him get some rest, he had been sedated. Galen slept peacefully...actually, loudly! His snoring was enough to wake the dead or at least keep the people awake in the adjacent rooms. All tests for any cardiac problems came back negative; his troponin levels were normal, an enzyme in the blood that is only present after a cardiac event and the ECG trace showed a healthy and steady normal sinus rhythm. The IV was still running, but no meds flowed. He had no extra supply of oxygen, his blood oxygen saturation levels were almost 100 percent and he no longer complained of chest heaviness. I suspected they would discharge him shortly.

As it turned out, the chest pain might have been stress related. It was still a strong indicator for a relatively young man who carried around an extra 150 pounds to start taking better care of himself.

Galen's wife had gone home to get some rest. Several members of the police department, as well as Becky and Tom, had all come and gone. Only I remained, waiting for the doctor in charge to sign Galen's release papers. I sat back in chairs designed by relatives of those who invented torture equipment during the crusades. These chairs were never meant to cradle and comfort relatives visiting their sick or injured family members and friends, but rather hasten their decision to leave.

A man in a lab coat came in, cliché stethoscope around his neck, metal clipboard, and small tablet in his lab coat pocket, looked at the monitor and jotted down some notes. I closed my eyes, put my head back and smirked. I remember the days when doctors and interns had their pockets full of small reference manuals. They didn't carry tablets with the latest reference apps, updated regularly, and at least a few games loaded as well for stress relievers.

"Galen should be going home today, Ethan." It was a familiar voice.

I bolted from a seated position to standing and faced the man who had sat across from me in my living room. He looked the part of a doctor, refined, elderly, and with a simple stolen lab coat and ID badge, he could walk around unnoticed. The shortened sleeves of the lab coat didn't cover his gold cufflinks.

"In your opinion?" I really wanted to come back with something witty and sarcastic and felt let down with such a lame response.

"I had someone more adept in the medical field than I read his file before I came in and told me your friend is fine. After the sedatives wear off, they plan on releasing him. He's a lucky man to have such caring friends and co-workers."

"I met some of your co-workers today." I sat back down in my uncomfortable institutional chair.

Like a real doctor speaking to family in such a setting, he placed the clipboard on the table and sat on the corner of the bed. He seemed very relaxed, unconcerned about security or someone coming in to discover he wasn't who he was pretending to be.

"I know. Well, actually, the other guys. My former co-workers. They will do anything to achieve an end to the means. From what I understand, it was a complete failure."

"Complete and utter disaster."

He adjusted himself on the bed.

"Just so you know, we planted enough evidence, gave the police a few willing lambs to take responsibility for today's events. Years ago, we never would have attempted such an overt and intrusive action. Times have changed and, as the saying goes, out with the old, in with the new. Video games and television being what it is, these younger guys can't wait for things to come about on their own and accept little responsibility. The real people responsible will never be brought to justice. They aren't even in the country, and you would never be able to convict them of this. The axiom is true, there is one law for the rich, another for the poor."

He pulled the stethoscope from around his neck and played with it.

"If you have enough money, you can pay off whomever you need, buy the silence of someone, pay someone to say the right thing," he cocked his head to one side, "or the wrong thing."

He stood, walked over to the window and looked out. Below, Smyth Road traffic flowed east and west, headlights marking their paths. Spotlights from the roof illuminated the parking structure below. It was not a very attractive view.

"We did discover that it was the NRC who completed the report on our study. It won't take long to get a copy of the results."

"Yeah, I wouldn't be too sure about that. First thing I did after Galen was seen in Emerg was to call my friend at CSIS. I told her about the report. I gave her the one and only copy from the train station, and she rushed over to the NRC a few hours ago with a clean-up team to remove any trace that the report was ever seen, evaluated, discussed, or written about, and I can imagine whoever worked on the report has been sent to some remote centre in Iqaluit to study frozen polar bear shit and ice flows. They will probably ship them their clothes later."

He smiled an honest smile, not one of anger or condescension but he looked truly happy. He walked over to me, held out his hand. I shook it. He had a firm grasp, strong and steady. He smiled.

"You're a fast learner. I feel better knowing the report is in your hands rather than the Eagles. In the end, the results don't matter, do they? Your friend is safe and sound. Tom is back on the job. Becky is happy with her new lot in life, and I paid for an upgrade to your home security system. Really, those cheap home security systems only keep out amateurs and honest people. After all, who knows when I may need to stop by again? Unannounced, of course."

"You know a lot about me."

"Always know and study your adversary before confronting him."

He walked to the door, grabbed the handle, and turned to face me. "Ethan, I truly enjoyed meeting you. I'm getting old and maybe my ways are the ways of the past and I should step aside for the younger generation to take over, the way they did for me. I look forward to our next visit. Take care of your friend." He patted Galen's foot as he walked past.

The hydraulic system slowly closed the door behind him. He'd left the clipboard and stethoscope behind. Some doctor would be irate to have had his badge, scope, and lab coat stolen. Pretty minor stuff after today.

I opened the door and looked down the hall. The stranger stood tall as he walked, still looking the part, turned a corner, and disappeared.

I heard a noise behind me and turned to see Galen waking from his sedative-induced nap. He pushed himself up to a seated position, readjusted the sheets, lifted the sheets up high over his lap and peered beneath them.

"If open-back gowns are such a great idea, how come no one uses them at home? Jesus, I look like a fucking dork. Can you hand me my clothes, please?"

His clothes had been hung up in the closet by the hospital staff. Tugging on them, the suit and shirt sprang from the hangers, and I tossed them on the bed.

"Take your time. Let the meds wear off. You'll be getting out of here later today." I sat back down in the chair.

"Did I thank you?" Galen asked as he donned his shirt and pants. He couldn't even look at me. Embarrassment or something else, it didn't matter to me. The sentiment was genuine.

"Don't worry about it. Besides, it was a team effort."

"I wanted to ask you why you flipped out the other day when the guy in the interrogation room told you he knew how Maddy died. Why did you freak out on him? Everyone already knows how she died," he added as he tried to stand. He sat back down on the edge of the bed.

"Not the time or place to discuss it. You should get yourself ready to go home. I'll go and see if they are ready to discharge you or if they plan on keeping you for another day."

"What was it? Did he hit a raw nerve or what?"

"It was the 'what' part, okay?" I felt my cell phone vibrate in my pocket. Pulling the phone out, hoping that it was Becky asking me to come home right away for some emergency.

"If I didn't pull you off, we probably would be booking you for manslaughter right now."

"Enough!" I barked.

I answered the phone without checking call display. "This is Ethan."

"Hi, Ethan. Sorry I haven't called before now but I've been really busy. I have to tell you that really was some wicked driving on the highway when you crashed your Porsche. The look on your face was priceless. It really was. Remember?"

I felt a surge of adrenaline send a burning sensation up to my lungs. A feeling of uneasiness fell over me. My palms became sweaty. I could feel moisture forming on my forehead. I thought I was about to die when the man who crashed into me had a gun pointed at my head. He was shot and killed by the police just as he was about to shoot me.

"You died! You were shot! I saw you die!" I screamed. Galen bolted from his bed, rushed over and stood beside me to listen in. I tilted the phone so Galen could listen in.

"I wasn't the one who died. That guy was more of an employee. And you! What am I going to do with you...you're sorta like unfinished business. And Mom always told me to finish what I start."

Then the line went dead.